Angels Among Us

Angels Among Us

Volume 2 in the Millennial Quest Series

A novel by John M. Pontius

BONNEVILLE BOOKS ™
Springville, Utah

ISBN: 1-55517-675-5
v.1

Published by Bonneville Books
an imprint of Cedar Fort, Inc.
www.cedarfort.com

Distributed by:

Typeset by Marny K. Parkin
Cover design by Barry Hansen
Cover design © 2002 by Lyle Mortimer

Printed in the United States of America
10 9 8 7 6 5 4 3 2 1
Printed on acid-free paper

Library of Congress Cataloging-in-Publication Data

Pontius, John M.
  Angels among us / by John M. Pontius.
    p. cm. -- (Millennial quest series ; bk. 2)
  ISBN 1-55517-675-5 (pbk. : alk. paper)
  1. Men--Fiction. I. Title.
  PS3566.O616 A82 2002
  813'.6--dc21
                                        2002010064

To my beloved wife, the music in my soul.
I love you

In gratitude to:

The Author of all truth, for all things, forever.

*My parents for their love, example, encouragement,
and editorial labors.*

*My children whom I know love me because
they pretend to actually read what I write.*

My dear friend Shayne for always believing.

*Lyle Mortimer and the editors and staff at CFI
for making three a charm.
Terri Jeanne, editor extraordinaire.*

Family and friends too numerous to name.

Readers whose joys and tears I never see but truly share.

Thank You

Introduction

Angels among Us constitutes the second installment of the Millennial Quest series. It has been my intent with these books to follow one man's journey in righteousness from beginning to end. By beginning, I am referring to that life which preceded mortal life, and by end, I mean beyond the grave, beyond the millennium, and into eternity. Certainly the cost of the journey is the process of honing and purifying, and we often see that process include trials, occasionally great trials. But overarching all this is the fundamental truth that righteousness brings joy into the lives of those who seek and find it. I speak not only of joy at journey's end, but joy along the way—the whole way. I hope you will see this truth in the lives of the characters of this book.

This book and the next take Sam to the dramatic and glorious events sought by all righteous souls since the beginning of time. It has been thrilling to write.

The stories and characters in this book are fictional. The many spiritual experiences described within are based upon the author's hopes and imagination.

No matter how flowing the language, or graphic the mental images invoked, or sweet the emotions, all the spiritual occurrences, visions, visitations, conversations and glorious events in this novel are purely fiction, and should not be considered anything more than faith-filled fantasy.

No attempt is being made to define doctrine or to describe events as they should, or even might occur in someone's life. What you are about to read is a novel, written with love, faith, testimony, and the hope of blessing your life. Still, it is only a novel, and as such is not intended to do more than entertain and uplift with stories of righteousness, and grand spiritual blessings.

This is not a biography of my life. All the events in Samuel's life are the offspring of my imagination.

Having so said, may I also note that most of the events of spiritual impact in this book are fictionalized happenings based upon scriptural accounts of similar events in the lives of the ancient faithful.

I have great faith in the idea that Father did not cause these great epiphanies to be recorded in scripture simply for our entertainment. I believe these magnificent events were included in holy writ to show us that we too can walk the path of holiness and receive equally glorious blessings. I believe these blessings are at our fingertips, as achievable today as in any period of antiquity. It is this sweet believing that has given these stories vivid life and believable form.

I invite you to read *Angels among Us* with a light and cheerful heart, and to ponder, as I have, the incredible power of what lies just beyond the veil.

Prologue

Spirit of Fire, volume one of the *Millennial Quest* series, chronicled the uniquely challenging and formative years of Sam's life from his childhood through his mission to South Africa for the Church of Jesus Christ of Latter-day Saints. Those amazing years made possible all you are about to read.

This book opens with Sam on a plane returning from his mission to South Africa. The young lady with him is Dawn, a recent convert of his.

Sam and his companion found Dawn living in a modern-day castle complete with moat, turreted walls and battlements. With her father's permission they taught her the Gospel, and explored the secret passages of the castle. However, when her father's business partners declared their intent to terminate their business affairs if Dawn joined the "Mormon cult," he ordered her to quit taking the lessons. She refused. Faced with the loss of great wealth, her father disowned his only child.

Dawn was allowed to take nothing with her, not even permitted a ride from her home. She walked away with nothing more than the clothing she wore. To punish her rebellion her father disinherited her and illegally took her personal assets. Even so, her resolve was firm, and she pressed forward in her joy of the Gospel. Being of legal age, Dawn chose to be baptized in spite of this great opposition.

As she and Sam were standing in the waters of baptism her father rushed into the room and begged her forgiveness. Even so, he never forgave Sam for "taking her away." In spite of pressing invitations to return to her castle-home, she felt compelled to find a new life elsewhere. Her inheritance now restored by her father, she came with Sam to America to find a new life and to fulfill the measure of her existence.

Somewhat prior to this, Sam had saved the lives of Melody and Marcia MacUlvaney, two young ladies he met on a train upon leaving his missionary service in the tiny African nation of Rhodesia. While standing in the airport about to board the plane to return home, he was handed a package from these girls' father. Upon opening it, Sam was startled to see a very large 22-carat diamond as a token of their father's deep appreciation for Samuel's role in saving his daughters.

Dawn's father's wealth had been gained in the flourishing, and somewhat colorful, African diamond trade. Her father immediately recognized the incredible value of the stone. Sam unwisely dismissed his urging to leave the stone with him to be shipped later to America. What Samuel did not realize was that powerful men stood poised to rob anyone foolish enough to transport just such a stone.

Chapter One

The Price

Sam fell asleep holding Dawn's hand. Just as his mind slipped into unconsciousness he had a small thrill of wonder. He had been released from his mission while still in Africa. Now for the first time in two years it was perfectly legal for him to sleep during the day. A part of him wondered in that same instant why he was more fascinated with a nap than with holding a beautiful woman's hand for the first time in his life. That question remained unanswered as he drifted off to sleep.

It took over twenty-four hours and two refueling stops to reach Heathrow International Airport in England. As the plane descended toward the runway Dawn became increasingly more nervous. Finally, she leaned over to him and spoke softly in his ear.

"Sam, as you know, my father and I have transported many diamonds out of South Africa and into England. It is perfectly legal, but still a tricky and sometimes dangerous business. I need you to trust me and do as I ask."

Sam nodded for her to go on, a look of concern on his face.

"I need to tell you what I suspect will happen after we land. I'm positive someone from customs will try to steal the diamond here at Heathrow. I don't expect to be mugged or robbed, but they'll try to trick us into just handing them the diamond. The way they usually do that is by telling you that you must declare all gems and jewelry in your possession. If you're dumb enough to just hand them the gems, they impound them for customs, and you never see them again."

Sam stared at her with wide eyes. "We don't have to declare the gems?"

"No," Dawn assured him. "The truth is, this airport terminal is international soil, and as long as we don't leave the terminal, we are not legally in England. You don't have to declare anything unless we take it out of this terminal. So, don't let them trick you. Besides, when we step foot off this plane we won't even have the stone in our possession, because I'm going to leave it on the airplane."

"But . . . how?" Sam stammered. Dawn ignored him, continuing with urgency. The plane was in a steep descent.

"It doesn't matter how. What matters is that the people we are dealing with are powerful and ruthless. They will use every means both legal and illegal to take the stone from us. They think we have a stone that is worth upwards of a million dollars, and they will be very nasty about getting it. They will probably search us, threaten us with jail, and everything else they can think of. They can do little more than attempt to intimidate us into handing them the stone. Our best defense is that we don't even know what they are talking about."

Sam shook his head as if trying to clear it. "That isn't entirely the truth. I can buy everything else, but I do know what they're talking about."

"Sam, I know, I know. But it is a very small white lie," she said, holding up her thumb and finger almost touching. "It is only to keep us out of the grasp of some very bad people. If we play dumb, and they can't find the stone, they won't have any reason to keep us from boarding our plane out of here." Dawn paused and lowered her head. "But, there will undoubtedly be several hours of unpleasantness before they will let is back on the plane."

Sam nodded. "I'll just have to repent later, I guess," he said with mock gravity.

Dawn smiled gravely. "This is serious. Don't underestimate them."

Sam's smile faded to a reflection of the dismay he felt boiling within his soul. "I hate this," he said with quiet fervor.

Dawn nodded sadly. "The only thing that really matters is that we get back on the plane. Do you understand? No matter what, get back on the plane. OK?"

"I understand," Sam said above the roar of the plane.

"I'm sure Daddy has been working to get our people in

place to avoid that. However, they really haven't had much time. I don't know what's going to happen. I'll do my best, but unless Daddy has succeeded, we have little hope of keeping the diamond."

Sam thought about this for just a few seconds. They had just touched down on the runway, the big engines straining to bring the jet to a stop. The whole cabin was shaking as if it would come apart. Somehow, it felt appropriate for the circumstances they found themselves in.

"Dawn, listen. That diamond isn't important to me. It was a gift, and I don't really care if it's lost. What I do care about is that you don't get yourself into trouble, or get arrested. I would feel terrible if you got in trouble trying to keep my diamond safe. I just don't care that much."

"I understand," she said, placing a hand on his arm. She smiled warmly. "Just promise me one thing. Go with the flow. Act perfectly innocent and naïve. Play the dumb American. And, no matter what happens, just get back onto the plane. This is important. No matter what you see, get back onto the plane. Promise me you'll do that."

"Why? I mean, if you are in trouble, I couldn't just walk away . . ."

"Listen to me, we are almost at the terminal. No matter what you see, just get back onto the plane. This is more important than I can explain right now. Promise me," she said in a voice burdened with anxiety.

"All right, you promise me that you know what you're doing, and I'll promise to do as you say on faith alone. You have to know I don't like it, though."

"I know what I'm doing. So?"

"All right, I promise."

At his words, she relaxed visibly.

• • •

It didn't take long for it to happen. They deplaned through the rear door, and walked down a short hall. Dawn stopped in the ladies room for a few minutes.

An arrow directed them to the left, and they came to a

large room. Through the middle of the room was a row of glassed booths. An armed guard sat in each booth, with an armed guard standing on the far side of the booth. Low metal railings formed paths up to the booths.

"This is where we split up," she whispered cryptically, and veered to the left. Sam had no time to do anything but walk toward a booth to his right. The line was long, and it took a while to reach the booth. He listened carefully to the conversation of the passenger before him. The guard in the booth was a woman. She looked the passenger in the face as she took his passport and thumbed to the picture on the first page. She turned to her left and tapped into a computer terminal. After a moment she nodded.

"You are required to declare anything you intend to import or sell in England, items of value in excess of one thousand pounds, regardless of whether or not you intend to sell them, and items which you bought in a country other than your country of origin. Do you have anything to declare?"

"No," the man said.

"It is illegal to import drugs, any live plants or animals, or weapons of any type. Do you wish to declare any of these?"

"I have a prescription drug for my illness is all," he said.

"Prescription drugs are exempt," she said. "Do you intend to stay in England, or are you just passing through?"

"I will be staying about two weeks."

"The purpose of your visit?"

"I'm visiting family outside London."

Again, she tapped into her terminal, then stamped a page in his passport.

"Thank you, sir. Have a nice stay in England." She gave him a cold smile and shoved the passport through the small window.

Sam slid his passport through the slot. She studied his face for a moment as she took the passport. She thumbed to the picture, and looked up at him again for a split second. She typed rapidly on her keyboard and waited for a moment. A frown crossed her face, and she typed again. After a moment, she picked up a phone and dialed. He could not hear her conversation, but she glanced at him several times.

Finally she motioned for Sam to go through the gate "Mr. Mahoy, would you come with me please?" The gate buzzed as he pushed it open. She motioned for him to follow her. The other guard fell into step behind him. His heart began to pound. He wondered what they wanted, and strongly suspected it was the diamond.

Sam was perplexed and frightened as he followed her a short distance to a door which she opened with a key. The room was about ten feet square, grimy and poorly lit by a small fixture high overhead. Its only furnishings were two grimy metal chairs and a small table.

Sam stopped uncertainly just outside the room. It was as if his feet had suddenly become very heavy. The female guard impatiently motioned him inside, and directed him to take a seat. She left him and locked the door.

He waited for over an hour, spending the whole time worrying about Dawn. He was startled from his worries when a key suddenly rattled in the door. It opened, and a man in coveralls carried Sam's only suitcase into the room and laid it on the table. He left without a word.

After a few minutes, a young woman in uniform entered. She was short and slight of build. Her hair was dark brown, cut quite short. While not attractive, she was what some might consider cute. Sam felt his nervousness relax a little. She smiled at him, and walked forward to shake his hand.

"Sorry to keep you waiting, Mr. Mahoy. I'm Rita," she informed him. Her accent was heavily British, though somewhat musical. Sam wanted to pepper her with questions, but restrained himself by merely nodding in reply. "I've been asked to conduct a routine customs inspection. We do this randomly to insure compliance with our customs laws. There is no particular reason you were selected, so please relax."

Sam nodded, but could not bring himself to relax.

After asking him the same questions the lady in the glass booth had, she asked: "Do I have permission to search your baggage? You have the right to refuse, in which case I will seek a court order, which may cause delays to your travel plans."

"I don't care," Sam said.

"Thank you. Do I need a key?"

"No, it's not locked."

She turned the case toward her, and opened the latch. She took out each article of clothing, and felt along each seam. She carefully refolded each item and laid it on the table. It went slowly and finally Sam sat back down. She continued until she came to a gift-wrapped box. She carefully opened the paper with a penknife, then the box. It was a small beaded purse for Beth. She opened the purse, and felt inside. She closed it all up, opened a drawer in the table, and took out a roll of sticky tape. When she had finished, it was difficult to tell it had been opened. She did the same for each gift.

After a long while, every item was lying on the table. She carefully ran her hands around the inside of the case until she satisfied herself it was not concealing anything. Finally, she began putting his belongings back into the suitcase. When she was finished, his case was packed more neatly than when he had done it.

"Thank you, Mr. Mahoy," she said and smiled. She opened the door with a key and quickly left. This time, he waited for almost two hours before a key again slipped into the door.

This time, a man accompanied Rita, the girl who had searched his bag. He also seemed friendly, but was somewhat agitated, or perhaps impatient.

"Mr. Mahoy, I understand you are returning from a mission in South Africa for the Mormon Church?"

"That's right," Sam said.

"Were you given anything of value in South Africa which you brought aboard the plane?"

Sam's mind snapped into high gear, searching for an honest answer that did not include mention of the diamond. "Well, I received several gifts in the airport. Someone gave me a flute . . ." He paused as his mind spun. "Oh gosh, I think I left my flute on the plane," he said, his voice filled with despair.

"Don't worry, sir, we can get it for you. Please be patient," she said. They gave each other a congratulatory glance and both left. They returned a while later with his flute case. She set it down on the table and opened it. Again, she carefully inspected each piece and set it on the table. She took her knife, cut the lining around the edges and lifted the interior. This she carefully inspected until she was satisfied. She shook her head at the man, whose face fell. They both left without a word, leaving the flute case dismantled on the table. Sam stood, and put it back together as best he could. The case was ruined, but it would hold the flute until he got home. He placed it inside his suitcase.

His stomach was rumbling by the time they returned again. This time there were two men. He was sorry the girl was not there, and considered they had upped the stakes.

"Sorry to keep you waiting," the first man said perfunctorily. He was not in the least sorry. "We have reason to believe you are concealing a certain illegal item on your person. We need permission to search your body. You have the right to refuse, in which case we will seek a court order, which may cause substantial delays to your travel plans. If you consent, you will be out of here in a few minutes."

Sam thought about it for a moment. They were determined enough that he knew he would eventually have to submit. He frowned, and nodded.

"Please remove your outer clothing, sir."

He took off his suit jacket and tie. They searched these thoroughly, and placed them on the table. They continued to ask for certain items of clothing until he was standing before them in his garments. When they asked for them, he hesitated. They merely asked again. He reluctantly surrendered.

"Just one more thing, Mr. Mahoy . . ."

When Sam was finally escorted from the room, he truly felt violated yet oddly vindicated. His greatest concern was for Dawn. Maybe they had not connected her to him. He hoped not. If they were willing to do this to him, there was every likelihood they would do the same to her, or worse. But he was finally free to leave.

It was late in the day, and he only had a few hours before his plane left. He bought something to eat, and walked to the boarding area, hoping to find Dawn. She was not there. His heart sank as he took a seat next to Elder Palmer, who seemed in a trance of expectation.

As they waited, four other missionaries they had not seen

before joined them and they chatted about their missions. Two were returning from England, one from France, and another from Denmark. They were traveling together at least as far as the States.

By the time the final call came to board his plane to New York, Dawn was still missing. Sam paced back and forth, waiting, hoping, and debating what to do. Everything in him told him to get on the plane. He sat down and prayed earnestly, and felt a peace settle over him. He knew he should march onto the plane.

The peace departed abruptly as he watched the big plane roar into the sky. He knew it was an error to remain behind, yet he could not bring himself to abandon Dawn. He just could not. He hoped Heavenly Father would forgive him and still protect him. He hoped with all his heart that this disobedience would not in some way make things worse for Dawn.

He wasn't worried about the church objecting. He had been released from his mission in South Africa by President Clark. His plane tickets would still be good, so he wasn't stranded. He had some money for food, but not enough for a hotel. He would have to act quickly to find Dawn. His resources were very limited.

Sam found a pay phone, and placed a collect call to his parents. It was a difficult call to make. When he finally hung up they were still objecting and insisting he get on the next flight out. He told them he would, knowing he had no intention of doing so. So far today he had told more lies than in the previous two years. He felt ashamed and a feeling of defiance settled over him. They just didn't understand. Besides, he could take care of himself. All he had to do was find Dawn.

He immediately made his way to the airport security office. The door opened to a small room containing a single desk. He approached the bored-looking woman behind the desk. She slowly looked up from a pile of papers and regarded him expressionlessly.

"I need your help," he began. "I arrived here with a traveling companion. I think she was taken into custody by the customs people. I haven't heard anything about her and I want to know what's going on." He thought he had used the right mixture of pleading, and demanding. He didn't want to seem either helpless, or overbearing.

The woman asked him several questions. She asked to see his passport, and after thumbing through it, handed it back. She turned to the computer terminal beside her and typed. Sam tried to count her keystrokes to see if it was Dawn's name, or his. He couldn't tell. He could see by her eye movements that she was carefully reading the screen. She occasionally stole a glance at him, which served to further increase his apprehension. After what seemed like a long time, she turned back to him.

"I will arrange for you to speak to my supervisor." Sam thought he detected a hint of accusation in her voice. He wondered if she knew something damning which he did not. He wanted to scream at her to tell him, but he corralled his raging fears with difficulty. She flipped off her terminal and departed through a back door. He studied the yellowed ceiling tiles, and dented furniture. It seemed as if he was back in the interrogation room, and he felt his innards knot up. After a short while, she returned and led him down a hall, and to a larger room, and left him alone. He was relieved she hadn't locked him inside.

After a few minutes Rita walked in. He was relieved to see it was she. He stood as she entered.

"Mr. Mahoy," she said with a note of surprise in her voice. "I thought you were on your way to America. I'm surprised to see you still here. What can I do for you?" Her tone seemed genuine, and he decided to speak candidly.

"I wish I *was* on my way to America. However, I arrived here with a young woman I was escorting to America. I promised her father to see her safely to the States. She missed her flight, and I could not leave without her. Can you help me find her?"

"What was her name?" she asked as she produced a pad from her hip pocket.

"Dawn Pauley," he said, and was dismayed to note that she didn't write it down. Instead she shoved the pad back into her pocket.

"How well do you know Miss Pauley?" she asked guardedly.

"I met her in South Africa and was involved with her as a missionary. She joined my church and wanted to come to America. I was to accompany her there. After that, she had her own plans."

"I see. So you weren't lovers?"

The question shocked him. "I was a missionary," he replied indignantly. "We don't take lovers."

"Yes, of course," she replied, a bit chastened. "Were you business partners?"

"Once again, I was a missionary. I had no business dealings at all. I was her escort and her friend in the church. I'm concerned about her."

"Did you know she was wanted on an outstanding warrant for smuggling?"

"Smuggling? You mean from some prior trip to England?"

"Yes. You had no knowledge of this?"

"No, certainly not. Why would I? I taught her the gospel, and she said nothing of having gone to England, certainly nothing of smuggling." This was the truth; it was her father who had explained their business dealings, to which he had painted a legal hue. Sam knew he was walking a fine line, but it was nevertheless the truth. Besides that, he seriously doubted that the accusation was even legitimate.

"It is illegal to bring anything over a certain value into this country with the intent of selling it. This is especially true of gems or jewelry. Were you aware of her bringing anything of this type into this country to sell?"

Sam bridled. "Our travel plans didn't even include leaving the airport. Check our reservations if you doubt it."

She nodded as if this had already occurred to her. She smiled and indicated for him to sit. He took a folding chair. She pulled a worn wooden chair to where their knees were nearly touching. She leaned forward and studied his face.

"I took the Mormon missionary lessons last year. I didn't believe what they were telling me and didn't join."

"I'm sorry," Sam replied honestly. It felt like a great loss, and he wanted to probe into her rejection of the gospel, but did not.

"You're sorry? Why?" She seemed genuinely bothered by his answer.

Sam sat for a moment waiting for the familiar urgings of the Spirit to guide. He was surprised when nothing happened.

The only feeling which entered his mind was that he had removed himself from the Spirit, not the other way around. He felt grieved at his disobedience, yet knew what he wanted to say.

"You seem like a nice person. I can see goodness in your eyes. I can't believe you seriously investigated the church without coming to a knowledge of its truth. I said I was sorry because you would have been very happy with the Gospel in your life."

"I'm not unhappy now," she said, a little defensively.

"I'm glad," was all he answered. Without the Spirit, he hardly knew how to have a conversation on spiritual things. Sam wanted to bear his testimony, to teach her, to touch her heart with truth. But, sadly, he could not.

Rita sat and motioned Sam to do the same. She shook her head as if weary of this conversation, and abruptly changed the subject. "Well, I guess that has little to do with your friend, Dawn. I'm afraid she's in deep trouble, and there is little you can do about it."

"Actually, it has everything to do with it," Sam replied abruptly. The Spirit had moved him so suddenly that he had nearly blurted out his answer before she had finished speaking. He was so relieved to have guidance again that he felt giddy with relief.

"What has my taking the missionary lessons to do with Dawn's legal problems."

"It has to do with truth," Sam replied evenly.

"Truth?

"Truth, and the courage to obey it."

Rita cleared her throat as if annoyed. "I don't appreciate . . ."

"You know the church is true," he interrupted.

"What?" she demanded hotly.

"When the missionaries taught you, you gained a testimony."

"What gives you the right to assume you know what I felt back then?"

"Truth," he replied again.

"I don't know what you are talking about. I'm not going to . . ."

"You can't escape the truth by walking away. The truth is, you still know what the missionaries told you is true. You chose

not to be baptized because you didn't want to live by yourself."
His answer puzzled him, yet he knew it was true by the urgings
of the Spirit, and by the stunned expression on her face. There
was a long moment of silence.

"Even if what you say is true, it has no bearing on Dawn,"
she replied defiantly, but in a small voice.

"Actually, it has everything to do with it. Let me explain."

"Please do," she said loudly. She was both repelled by this
conversation, and inwardly stunned. It was as if her soul demanded
to hear his words, and another part of her wanted to throw him
in jail. The mixture of emotions was both puzzling and frightening.

"You chose not to join the church, not because it isn't
true, but for other considerations."

"Perhaps," she allowed.

"Those other considerations were very important, but they
have now evaporated, and you feel betrayed. My point is you
sacrificed truth, and the lasting happiness it brings, for what
turned out to be a lie, and you are now miserable."

"I wouldn't call myself miserable, I'm just . . ."

"Now, you are faced with the same dilemma. The truth is,
that neither Dawn nor I have broken any laws of this country.
You have searched our baggage, and our persons, and have found
nothing. The charges you are holding Dawn on are fictitious.
You know this, yet there are other considerations."

"Assuming you are correct," Rita replied in a small, but
defensive voice. "What other considerations might you be talking about?"

"You don't want to lose your job," he said. She fell back
in her seat as if hit across the face.

He wasn't finished, or better stated, the Spirit wasn't finished. "Truth, once again, and a course to lasting happiness in
doing what is right, is being confronted by your need for temporary gratification."

"You are making wild assumptions which . . ."

"Which we both know are true. If you wish, I will tell you
how to bring happiness back into your life."

There was a long pause. Her voice was small, almost plaintive. "How?" she asked finally.

"First, release Dawn."

"I can't. It is not within my power. You don't know what would happen. Not only would I lose my job, but I'd probably be charged with a crime myself. No, it isn't possible."

"Second," he said.

She looked at him with amazement, a "Don't you ever give up?" look on her face.

Sam continued. "Second, go back and re-study the Gospel. This time, when you feel the power of its truths, submit yourself to baptism. These two things will start you once again on the road to happiness."

"Even if I believed what you said was true, I . . ."

"You do believe," he interrupted softly.

Rita frowned. "Even if all that were true, this is also true: I have no power to release Dawn. She has been charged with a serious felony. I'm sorry."

Sam felt deflated. Once again the Spirit departed, and he was left to himself. He felt orphaned and sick at heart. His soul had been alive and energized while the Spirit was upon him. Now, he felt helpless and sick to his stomach with fear. He was about to abandon himself to it, when he remembered the calmness and courage he had briefly felt a few moments ago. He knew those sweet feelings to be real; these feelings of despair had to be a lie, even if they were very believable at this moment. He struggled to pump up his courage.

A look of compassion came on Rita's face, and she patted him on the knee. Her next question surprised him.

"Do you love her?"

"Yes," he replied without hesitation. It was true, but probably not in the context she meant. His love for her was real, large, and beautiful, but it was not romantic. He felt no urge to explain his answer.

"If you will tell me where the diamond is, I can get her released," she said candidly. "That's all they want. Tell me, and I can have you out of here in just a few minutes."

He was about to blurt out everything he knew about the stone, about handing it to Dawn, about her contact in England, everything. He opened his mouth to spill it all, but was suddenly constrained by the familiar feeling of the Spirit. When he spoke, something entirely unexpected came out.

"Is it against the law to transport jewelry through this country?"

"No, of course not," she replied.

"If Dawn had any jewelry on her, it was her intent to take it to America. The truth, if it matters to you at all, is that she has broken no law, and you know it." Sam lowered his head as tears came to his eyes. "Apparently, truth is no longer the issue."

Rita thought about this for a moment. "Actually, it still can be," she countered thoughtfully. "The truth is, someone wants that stone and is willing to do anything to get it. If you know where it is, you had best tell me. Otherwise, Dawn is going to languish a lot of years in prison."

"If I knew, if I even had a clue, if I knew anything that would release her, I would tell you. That is also the truth."

"I believe you," Rita replied almost reverently. She stood and left the room. She returned later with a sandwich and soft drink. She smiled sadly as she handed them to him, then departed without a word. He wondered why it would make her sad to give him a sandwich. Just the same, his stomach grumbled its appreciation as he hastily ate. He felt as if he had an ally at least, even though a useless one. After eating he rapidly grew sleepy. The world seemed to be spinning very slowly counterclockwise. Sleep swept him away just as he realized something was very wrong.

• • •

Sam had no idea where they took him. He tried to force himself to remain awake, but fell asleep again watching telephone poles whiz by in the darkness. Several times he awoke to loud voices. His body felt leaden and exhausted until sleep took him away again. He had a vague memory of stumbling to another vehicle, perhaps more than once. He slept very soundly for what seemed a long time, then was awakened as the car rolled to a stop on a gravel road. Someone opened the door from the outside. He stumbled out into the night; his mind felt fuzzy and refused to analyze his surroundings. All he could think about was going back to sleep.

Without a word the driver closed the door, climbed back

into the car and drove into the night. The night was cool, and even though it was not cold enough to harm him, Sam felt a chill seep into his bones. The darkness was complete, and impenetrable, and except for two red tail-lights rapidly diminishing in the distance, he could see in neither direction. He walked two steps, felt the ground disappear from under his foot, and found himself rolling down a grassy embankment. He came to a harmless halt on flat ground, face down in long grass. He pushed himself to a stand, and found the bank. It seemed pointless to climb back onto the road, and he laid down in frustration. In moments, a troubled sleep almost forcibly took him.

Sam awoke to sunshine on his face, and gnawing hunger pains. He realized as he awoke that he had not eaten since the night before. He was lying on a sloping bank of grass. Not far from the bank a dense stand of trees began. He stood and surveyed his surroundings before climbing the short hill to the road. All around him massive trees extended in every direction. Majestic, mist-shrouded mountain peaks seemed very near.

Sam turned in a complete circle. "This doesn't look like Kansas," he said aloud, then chuckled darkly. "It doesn't even look like England."

Deciding to take inventory of his assets, he fumbled in his pockets and was shocked to find his wallet and passport missing. He found a single piece of paper money. It was not American currency, and as near as he could tell, not English either. He shoved it back into his pocket. He assumed that the driver had taken his things while he had been asleep in the car.

The road was narrow, scarcely more than twin dirt trails in dense grass growing thickly upon a wide lane cut through the forest. The road was winding and narrow, hugging the mountainside above precipitous canyons below. It was obviously seldom traveled. It reminded him of a mountain maintenance road more than a highway. Resigning himself to the idea of a long walk, Sam picked up a stout stick about four feet long that reminded him of a baseball bat. A childhood memory stirred; he selected a small rock and hit it solidly with the stick. It whined loudly as it flew into the woods, striking something with a loud *thunk*. Sam almost smiled. It was so satisfying to bop something soundly that he did it several times more.

15

Finally he headed in the direction the car had departed into the night. He walked for most of the day, seeing nothing but dirt road and endless trees. He did not see a single car all day. Whenever he grew weary or bored, he clobbered a few more rocks. It gave him a childish sense of being in control, at least of the rock.

Night was beginning to settle when Sam came on a small stream. He climbed down a short grassy slope. The water looked clean, and tasted sweet. He drank until he was full. He slept cold and miserable by the stream.

The second day of walking was even harder. His body rebelled against the hunger and he felt nauseous. He continued to walk until hunger, thirst and fatigue overpowered him. He stopped by another stream, drank until he no longer felt hungry, and surrendered to bone-chilling sleep.

Day three found Sam too weak to do much more than stumble along the dirt road. Finally, he could move no more and sat on the grassy side of the road. It suddenly occurred to him that he was in desperate circumstances. Whoever had dumped him out here in the woods had picked a road few people traveled. He wondered if the road was even open to the public. In three days he had seen no cars. For the first time in his life he felt completely hopeless. Not only was there an incredible emptiness in his gut, but there was an absence in his soul which felt worse than any starvation. The emptiness was so profound that he had trouble identifying its cause.

When the truth finally caught up with his sluggish brain, Sam was shocked to realize that this emptiness was the absence of the Holy Spirit from his soul.

A word, a thought, a concept crystallized in his mind—"chastisement." At first the word meant nothing, yet the concept was crystal clear. He had offended the Lord through his disobedience. He had walked away from what he knew was right, and relied upon his arm of flesh. A blackness settled over his heart which seemed to grip it with an iron fist. It was so compelling that he felt as if he had to struggle to draw each breath.

As this thought jelled in his mind, Sam felt coldness creeping up his spine. A touch of something unholy brushed through him, and he shuddered. Darkness settled on his soul, and he contemplated his disobedience, his undeniable failure and his worthlessness.

Sam considered all these things with harsh self-loathing, and he laughed at the sudden plunge he had made to a Telestial reward. But his laughter was bitter, and the very sound of his voice called forth tears. Once the first drop was spilled, it was like a river overrunning its banks, and he wept, at first silently, then violently, until every tear within him dried up and his sobs rent his soul to its very fabric.

Suddenly an electric sensation slapped his consciousness, and Sam's head snapped up. A familiar warmth surged through him, and as quickly left. But, it was enough, and his soul fed on the warmth, sucked at the light like a drowning man sucks at air through clenched teeth, scarcely able to believe water no longer surrounds his face. In one blinding instant he saw this long dark reverie for what it was, and President Clark's words echoed in his mind as loudly as if he were there. "Beware, my boy. For God's sake . . . for your sake, beware all your life."

When the tears began this time, they were tears of humility, of repentance and sweet surrender. He fell on his knees in the cold, damp darkness, and poured out his soul to God. As desperate as his circumstances were, as empty and weak as his body was, these things were no part of his plea. His were the words of repentance, of humble acknowledgment of sin, and of sincere commitment to obedience. Again and again the wave of darkness assailed him, and lashed him with its cold fury. Yet so sweet was the peace of his surrender to the love he felt overflowing him that the darkness soon spent its last lie and departed.

All the night through Sam sought forgiveness. At times his prayer was a terrible struggle, held back by his own fear of unworthiness. At others, it was as sweet as the purest love, and as warm as an angel's embrace. When his mind finally returned from this grand communion it was early morning and the sun was just finding its way toward the tops of the trees.

Sam found himself lying on his side, his knees drawn up as if he were kneeling, his hands clasped before him. He was surprised to find he was shivering, for he felt nothing but deep internal warmth, and a glorious feeling of forgiveness. He closed his eyes again, and for a long while poured out his gratitude in worship more powerful than speech, more lyric than poetry, and more beautiful than choirs of angels. It seemed to him as if his voice for a time ascended unto God and joined the myriad of beings who sing His praises both day and night.

Suddenly, without warning, and much to his regret, it was over, and he stood with sudden purpose. He was almost too weak to walk, yet he felt no fear, no hesitation and no doubt. He turned toward the forest.

After a short struggle through dense undergrowth, the trees seemed to spread out, and opened into a pleasant, sunlit clearing. The same stream by which he had slept wandered through the glade. Had he not been so far from home, it would have been a glorious discovery, an almost magical find as if from a storybook of castles, and queens.

For the first time in many days it seemed obvious to Sam what he must do. Each thought came to him separately, without explanation. Without understanding why, he removed his suit coat and tie, and hung it carefully over a branch. Next he unlaced a shoelace from his shoe and tied it to a willow so that it bent into a small bow. Selecting several dried branches, he looped the bow over one, and carefully began drawing it back and forth. The dried stick twirled back and forth. One end of the stick he spun against a dry piece of bark, the other on a rock in his hand. In a surprisingly short time a spiral of smoke arose from the branch. He laid a small bundle of grass next to it, and in a moment a tiny yellow flame appeared. He nursed it carefully until he had a small fire burning warmly. He laid on a little more wood, and in not many minutes was warming himself by the fire. Sam shivered violently, and realized how close he had been to hypothermia. He fed the fire, and waited for the warmth to penetrate to his limbs. With the return of warmth came a return of his energy.

Sam was, of course, still hungry, but not devastated by it. He actually considered intentionally continuing his fast as one of gratitude for his deliverance, but felt an urging to the contrary. He simply obeyed. Memories of things he had done as a Boy Scout popped into his mind, and he returned to the small stream. He lay in the shadow of a tree and inched on his belly toward the stream. He had tried this many times as a scout, and had always been unsuccessful. It did not surprise him to see a small fish against the bank swimming slowly in the current.

Moving as slow as it is possible for a human to move, Sam inched his hand into the water, moved it under the fish, and slowly closed his fingers. The fish fought for freedom, but his hand closed tightly around it.

In minutes it was on a stick and turning slowly over his fire. The smell was divine, and wafted gently through the trees. Sam intentionally cooked it slowly, lengthening the cooking time from a few minutes to half an hour. His body screamed for the food; his logic urged him to eat the fish, stick, guts and all. Yet, within him, a quiet, simple urging kept him from consuming the food now available to him.

Following an urging from the Spirit, he slowly turned the fish near the fire for nearly an hour, just keeping it warm. Sam heard a branch snap in the distance. He smiled to himself, an almost giddy sense of happiness sweeping through him. The happiness he felt had nothing to do with the distant sound of brush and twigs being disturbed, but the quiet joy of obedience: difficult, illogical, unexplained yet successfully executed obedience.

Whatever was making the sound grew nearer until it stopped a short distance from his clearing, waiting warily in the bushes.

"I believe this is done cooking," he said loudly. "Come have some breakfast."

A ragged figure pushed through the bushes with a strangled sob. He stood as Dawn limped toward him at a run. He caught her in his arms, and held her until she released him. Tears had made muddy tracks down both cheeks. Her hair was tangled with dirt and debris, her dress was smudged and torn. Her eyes were lackluster and sunken. He stepped back a little and raised the fish between them. It was deliciously cooked by now. He pulled a piece of white meat from it with his fingers and held it to her lips. She took the small bite. Her eyes rolled back into her head in an ecstasy of taste. He continued to feed her and himself until the small fish was gone.

They sat near the fire, where Dawn curled up against him and fell asleep. He continued to feed the fire as he held her. Sam pondered the significance of the fact that she had said nothing from the moment she had found him until she had fallen asleep.

He knew it meant something, something both important and unique, yet his mind refused to understand it.

It was late in the afternoon when she awoke. He had also slept, and they both struggled to make their bodies move again. Even though his only meal had been tiny, it seemed to have rejuvenated him, and he felt strong once again. Dawn seemed less recovered, and swayed back and forth while standing.

A moment of awkward silence passed, then they both tried to speak at once. Dawn held up a hand, and Sam fell silent.

"I'm so sorry, Sam. . .!" she began, but tears cut her short.

Sam was stunned. It was he who had failed to obey! He reached out to her, but she pulled away. He simply could not understand her words, or her rebuff.

"Dawn, what's wrong? You haven't done anything to me! Why are you crying?"

She looked up at him with such pathos that he wanted to hold her, stroke her hair and tell her everything would be wonderful again. He could not.

"Oh, Sam, you have no idea what I've done to you. I thought I could beat them. I thought I knew what they would do, and how to get the stone past them. They threatened me with all kinds of horrible things, but I thought I knew what to do. I held out, and played innocent, and acted stupid. I did all that until they laid your passport on the table. It was then that I knew they had detained you. They said you were in custody, to be tried for smuggling, and would not be allowed to return home. I panicked and took them to the stone. I gave it to them."

Sam laughed. "Dawn, I don't care. It was never worth all you went through for it. I'm glad you gave it to them. I just don't care."

"You don't understand. I took them to the restroom on the airplane. What we do is flush the stone down the toilet in a special bag. One of our people retrieves it, and that's all there is to it. Well, they went through the sewage, and it was there. They took it out, and it was a fake."

"A fake?!" Sam demanded.

"Well, it was a real diamond, the right size, but it was almost valueless, deeply flawed and discolored. All that effort was to protect a stone of very small value. They were furious, and swore you would still be prosecuted. I think they drugged me, then brought me here three days ago. I have no idea why they dumped me in the forest. I thought they were going to kill me."

Dawn paused as the memory of her terror marched through her like an invading army. "I have been wandering through these woods, praying you would be alright. For a while I just wanted to give up and die. I felt so ashamed for causing you all this pain. I'm still so ashamed! I . . ."

"Dawn, they lied to you."

"What?"

"They lied. I wasn't detained. I intentionally missed the plane. I didn't keep my promise to get on the plane and went back to search for you. I asked about you and insisted on them releasing you. They were using us against each other. I was never in any real danger. I didn't realize they drugged me until you said it just now, but they dumped me out here three days ago, too. Apparently after they found out the stone was relatively worthless, they just wanted us to get lost."

"But why not just give us back our passports, and order us to leave?"

Sam shrugged. "There is the possibility that we may complain to the authorities, I guess. But, out here, without identification, we can do nothing. By the time we either find our way out, or perish, there will be no evidence of their actions against us, or even of our having entered this country, I suspect. They probably assume that if we ever did find our way home we will not have the inclination or proof to accuse them of any wrongdoing. If we do, they will probably accuse us of being in the country without visas, or something. Our best option is to just quietly leave the country. I'm sure they are counting on just such a course of action from us."

"I'm scared, Sam. I'm really scared. I'm afraid they will change their minds, and come after us. Or, they'll be setting us up so that when we finally get to a town, we will be accused of some gross crime, and be arrested. I'm afraid . . ."

"I'm afraid," Sam interrupted her, hoping to lighten her mood, "you've been watching too much television."

"We don't have television in South Africa," she reminded him with mild rebuke.

"Well, then watching too many cheap American movies."

"I hope so," she said fervently. She smiled and turned to walk slowly toward the stream, dusting dirt and leaves from her dress. It was another beautiful, sunny day.

"You know what I find amazing?" Sam asked as he began picking up twigs.

"No," she responded meekly, as if her mind was on many other things.

"That you found me. We've been wandering in the woods for three days, and could have gone in a dozen different directions, but you found me. How did you manage that?"

"Very simply," she replied, her lips softening into a half-smile. "I could hear you."

"Hear me? That's seems impossible," Sam insisted.

"Even though we have both been in the woods for three days, we have never been very far apart. On the very first day I heard a loud pop, and a sound somewhat like a bullet whizzing through the trees."

"That was me bopping rocks!" Sam laughed, suddenly happy he had revived his childhood preoccupation with "rock bopping."

"Bopping?"

"That's what I used to call it on the farm," he explained sheepishly.

Dawn smiled broadly. "A piece of your childhood that became my salvation," she assured him. "Several times a day I heard the same 'bopping' sound. At first I thought it was someone firing a gun. It scared me to death, but I thought it had to be someone besides my kidnappers, and I decided to follow them at a distance. If it was a hunter, I didn't want to be shot by mistake. I only wanted to follow them to a road or a town."

She hesitated, and Sam waited for her to continue. "I didn't have any other means of finding another human," she said at length, her voice sounding lost again. "It seemed like my only hope. It wasn't until I smelled food cooking that I overcame my fear and tried to sneak close enough to see who it was. I was immensely relieved to see it was you, but I felt so ashamed that I almost ran away . . ."

Feeling a need to leave this subject, Sam said, "After I build the fire back up, I want to tell you about my struggle with the devil, and of my repentance. I think there is a purpose in all this for both of us, and not just some random opposition." He began blowing on the smoldering coals. They quickly came back to life.

"Do you think we will find our way home?"

A warm confidence surged through him. He straightened from where he was kneeling by the fire and smiled. "Yes I do."

Dawn felt the same assurance and replied, "I believe you."

"It won't be easy," he added with some emphasis.

Dawn's voice was resigned when she replied a moment later. "I believe that, too."

Chapter Two

Deliverance

It took hours of trying before Sam finally pulled another brook trout from the stream. This one was larger and gave them almost enough food for a satisfying breakfast. Sam cleaned his hands in the stream and carefully took his suit coat from the branch where he had hung it. It still looked fairly clean.

"You know what's odd to me?" Dawn asked as she prepared herself to move on.

"I think I can guess, but go ahead and tell me."

"This forest doesn't seem like anything I've ever heard about in England."

Sam nodded. "No fog, no ocean breezes, and relatively high elevation. I'm not sure, but I don't think England has any tall mountains, yet we're definitely in some now."

"Yes . . ." Dawn agreed without enthusiasm.

"Well, let's find out where we are. I'm sure we're still in Europe," he said.

"Why?" she wondered.

"Because the stars at night are wrong. I didn't recognize the sky at all. I know the South African sky, and the American sky. This one is different."

"Where do you think we are?"

"What is a country near England they could drive to in a single night, which also has mountains?"

"I have a vague memory of being in a helicopter, I think," Dawn said uncertainly. "We could be almost anywhere. Perhaps France?"

"If they took us in a helicopter we could be anywhere. France, or even further."

"I speak French," she commented as they started back toward the road.

"I doubt this is France."

"Why?"

Sam pushed his way through the tangle of undergrowth and held it open for Dawn. The road stood a few yards before them. There was still no sign of cars. They were standing on the road when he finally answered her question. "Because, it would be too obvious. There has to be some element of implausibility. If the suggestion is ever made, they need to be able to laugh at the idea that they hauled us that far in a single night just to get rid of us."

"Where then?"

Sam reached into his pocket and pulled out the paper money, studied it for a second, then handed it to her.

"It's a Swiss Franc," she said with some amazement.

"That's what I thought, too."

Sam and Dawn continued on wearily for several days, stopping to build fires and hunt for food. Time seemed to drag to a near-crawl, and the unending forests stretched to some parody of eternity.

They had been lost for five days when they unexpectedly heard distant rock and roll music on the wind. They both quickened their pace, and a few moments later unexpectedly walked into a fairly large village. At the edge of the town the dirt road turned to cobblestone. The shops and homes were decidedly old, made of large timbers and stone. They had steep, red-tiled roofs, and looked like an illustration from a Hansel and Gretel storybook. The people in the village were all afoot. The few cars they saw were all parked and dusty. The whole village was only several blocks long, and seemed to consist of this single row of buildings. They were primarily boutiques, clothing stores, gift shops, and ski equipment shops.

"It's a ski village," Dawn said with sudden understanding.

Sam nodded. "A tourist village. See that big lodge? Let's go there. Perhaps we can get help there." Dawn nodded silently.

As they walked, Sam put on his jacket and dusted off his pants. Because he had been careful with is jacket and tie, he looked fairly fresh. His six days growth of beard was long enough to look intentional. Dawn tried to tidy herself with somewhat less success. As long as no one got close enough to smell either of them, they would pass for tourists.

For a ski village in the middle of summer, there was an amazing number of people milling around. Behind the big lodge they could see two double chair lifts reaching further up the mountain. One of them was operating. Approximately every third chair had someone in it. It seemed as if the mountain attracted visitors all year around. Sam had to admit it was a charming village whose attractions were magical.

The sprawling lodge was built of massive logs and dominated the village. It looked like a woodland castle, and gave an enchanted quality to the scene before them. Everything about the structure was larger than life. They walked up the steps onto the covered porch. A brass plaque beside the door informed them they had arrived at the world famous Schöner Berg. An ornate set of doors stood invitingly open before them.

Inside, the room was a stunning mixture of rough logs, red velvet furnishings, and crystal. A huge crystal chandelier hung from the tall ceiling directly over an ornate grand piano. Golden lamps with silken shades stood beside French Renaissance furniture. Over the polished wooden floor lay rich Persian carpets. It took his breath away for a moment.

To the right they saw a plush restaurant almost entirely decorated in red and gold. To their left sprawled a long hotel counter of highly polished wood. Their hunger commandeered their feet, and they turned right. A waitress showed them to a seat without as much as a glance at their crumpled clothing. She said something in another language, handed them menus, smiled and left.

"What language was she speaking?" Sam asked, leaning toward Dawn.

"I don't know," she admitted. "It wasn't French, Italian, English, or Afrikaans. I speak those. Maybe German, but I don't speak German."

Sam picked up the menu and tried to interpret it. Finally, he found a page written in English. After pointing it out to Dawn, he studied it carefully. A few minutes later he pulled the note from his pocket. It was a ten Franc note. The items on the menu started at six and went as high as fifty. They found a sandwich for eight Francs, and ordered it on two plates. It was ambrosia and, truly, nothing had ever tasted more divine to either of them. They ate slowly, sipping ice-cold water.

It surprised them both that they could just barely finish their half sandwich. They sat and talked for a long time, but finally had to admit they had no idea what to do next.

When the waitress came to take away their plates Sam asked, "Excuse me, do you speak English?"

"Yes, but a little," she replied in voice heavy with guttural tones. She was young, about their age. "I did study just some English in school," she continued. "How are your holidays happening?" She placed emphasis on her words in funny places.

"We are having quite an unusual holiday," Sam answered congenially. The South African people also called vacations holidays.

"So pleased. Did you have the long walk?" she asked, nodding toward their crumpled clothing.

"Oh, yes. Well, actually, we got lost, and walked longer than we wanted to."

"So sorry, to get you lost," she said sympathetically, as if she were responsible. "Next time, we take map at hotel counter. It will not get you lost, yes?"

"Thanks. We'll take a map next time."

"So good. Is anything else wanting you to eat it?"

"No. We're fine. Thank you. What's the nearest city?"

"Bern is the closest large city."

"Is there a bigger resort nearby?" Sam asked on impulse, having no real reason to want the information.

"Why yes. The most popular is the Alpen Stein. It's on the next mountain range. It's very much biggest as this one is not."

Sam handed her his only money. She nodded and slipped away. She returned moments later with change. Sam left some of it on the table, and they walked back out into the sunshine. It was pushing into afternoon.

Dawn tugged on his sleeve. "Sam, we need to find a phone and call my Dad. He can wire us some money."

"That's a good idea," Sam agreed. He was glad for the suggestion, as he had had no idea how to get money. They returned to the hotel and, after going through three clerks, found one who spoke English. The clerk finally understood that they wanted to make a collect phone call, and directed them to a phone on a small table between two plush red chairs.

Dawn had difficulty getting an operator to understand her. At length, she put her hand over the mouthpiece. "It's ringing," she said happily.

When no answer was forthcoming the operator interrupted the call. Dawn hung up the phone unhappily. "Father's apparently not home. What about your parents?"

"They just moved to Alaska. I don't know their new number, and I think it's unlisted. I had it written in my wallet, but I don't have that any more. Let me try information." Sam took her place, and after half an hour hung up the phone in frustration. He had not been able to make anyone understand his request for information. Several had been willing to connect him to American information, but wanted long distance fees. He longed for the simple "dial zero" convenience of American telephones.

Sam stood in frustration. Dawn's eyes followed him with concern. Sam looked down at her. "I think we struck out. We can try again in a few hours. Maybe your Father will be back by then."

"Perhaps. However, I doubt my father knows anything's gone wrong. But, even so, it's odd that he didn't leave someone to answer the phone in case I called. There's almost always a maid or butler at home. In time we'll get through." Dawn's eyes filled with tears. "Oh, Sam, we just have to come up with a plan, or we're going to be sleeping outdoors and eating garbage. I'm not at all anxious to be arrested for vagrancy or panhandling in a foreign country."

Sam did his best to reassure her, even though his own assessment of the situation was bleak. They sat in dejected silence for nearly an hour before a thought suddenly came to him. Since emerging from the forest they hadn't thought to pray about their dilemma. Sam looked around. Where they sat by the phones was fairly private.

Sam bowed his head and leaned close to Dawn. He prayed aloud, speaking in a whisper. His prayer was so spiritually satisfying he had to remind himself nothing had changed yet to help them. Yet, the peace was as significant as if all was exactly as it should be. Afterward, they both felt the answer to their petition had already been granted, and all they needed to do was wait for the Lord to lay it before them.

Sam opened his eyes to rest upon the large grand piano standing majestically in the center of the large room. It was upon a small raised dais beneath the large chandelier, surrounded by a dozen plush chairs in a semicircle. Suddenly, quite unnervingly, he knew what to do. The solution was simple, yet more brash and bold than any part of him could have conceived. Yet it was the answer to their humble prayers and Sam rejoiced, even while his heart trembled.

He stood and found the English-speaking clerk. "Can I speak to a manager? One who speaks English?" The clerk frowned as if unsure one even existed, then hurried away.

"What are you going to do?" Dawn wondered.

"I'm going to put into motion the answer to our prayers," he explained happily. Dawn smiled at him, a quizzical look on her face.

A short time later an older gentleman walked briskly toward them. As he approached his eyes took in their crumpled condition. His smile was forced and seemingly superficial. "How may I assist you?" he asked pleasantly.

Sam stuck out his hand, which the manager shook. "I'm Samuel Mahoy, a musician from America. My companion and I are traveling in your country. We are apparently obliged to spend a few days in your village. We seem to now have an opportunity to rest from our tour."

The manager seemed pleased, and a bit puzzled. It was as if he were playing through his memories to find any mention of an American musician named Samuel Mahoy staying at his hotel. Sam decided to lay the rest of his plan in motion before questions or objections began flying.

"After arriving here, we find we were brought here by mistake. Our luggage and instruments have been sent to another destination, perhaps back to America, or to the Alpen Stein. We don't know. So, we have no reservations here."

"Ah, yes. I see your dilemma," the manager nodded thoughtfully. The mention of his competitor's hotel made him flinch.

"Fortunately, it is summer, and we can accommodate you. Would you like me to book you a room?"

"Thank you. We will need your best room, of course."

"Certainly," the manager said smoothly.

"We will need room service to bring most of our meals to the room, and a telephone."

"It will be as you say," he soothed. The manager made a note in a pad. "Anything else, Herr Mahoy?"

"There is something else," Sam said smoothly. "I need to practice my instruments. I would prefer a private practice room if you have one. At the Alpen Stein I would probably be doing several evening performances, but this will be much better. I will just practice."

The cash register in the manager's mind clanked happily. "Our finest piano is the large one in the lobby, which you are most welcome to use. In exchange for the use of the piano, would you allow me to announce your, um, practices? Perhaps more people would come. Would you mind if we charge admission? It is the slow season, after all. A little more revenue would be appreciated."

Sam arched his back. "I said I want to practice. If this is to be a performance, I will find no rest in it. Perhaps, I will just skip the practicing."

"No, no. Forgive me. Perhaps we could benefit one another here. As I said, it is the slow season, and our rooms stand empty. If I made your room, meals, and daytime tours complimentary, you could relax as you like during the day, and provide us with but several small, shall we say 'practices,' during the evenings? Would that be agreeable?"

Playing her part to the hilt, Dawn placed a slender hand on Sam's arm solicitously. "Don't do it, Samuel. You need your rest," she said in a silken, pouty voice.

Sam patted her hand. "Yes, my love, I do. But think of it. Perhaps if I call it a practice, and it's brief. The rest would be grand, I think. And the manager is being so generous. A few public practices would be much more relaxing than an actual performance. I've never done anything like it."

"It's up to you, as always." She smiled sweetly and gave him a long distance kiss.

31

Sam hesitated for a few moments before turning to the manager, who was anxiously awaiting his reply. "Alright, then," Sam agreed in apparent reluctance. What he was really doing was frantically trying to pump up his courage to say what had just popped into his mind. Accompanied by the glow of the Spirit, he knew the idea was right, but it was more than he could normally force from his mouth.

Sam took a deep breath. "I can promise no more than three public practices. After that, we shall see. I will expect a week's accommodations, meals and tours, all complimentary. I will expect one-half of gross ticket sales. We will reimburse you for other expenses at the end of the week from ticket sales."

"That will be acceptable," the manager said in a tightly controlled voice. "I will have the bellman show you to your room. It will take me a while to find instruments for you. Do you require any other than the piano?" He asked as he made notes.

"I will need a flute and a violin, is all," Sam replied as if bored.

"Do you have a preference concerning the instruments, such as manufacturer, or anything else I should ask for?"

"They must be the highest quality. And have the piano tuned. If it is the slightest out of tune, I will not perform, regardless of how many tickets you have sold."

"Certainly, certainly. I agree. Well, I have my afternoon cut out for me. You two enjoy your rest. Would seven o'clock be agreeable for your first performance?"

"Practice," Sam corrected him.

"Yes, of course."

"I will be down at seven."

"Splendid." The manager shook his hand, bowed to Dawn, and hurried away.

• • •

Their room was the same stunning mixture of rough and regal. The walls were hewn logs, and the furnishings French. The bedspread was an intricately stitched silken comforter the color of cream, with huge pillows of the same color. Their room was large enough to be an apartment. Dawn walked through it feigning dissatisfaction, then accepted the keys from the bellman.

The bellman held out his hand for a tip. Dawn gave him such a disapproving frown that he lowered his hand and backed out the door.

Dawn frowned as if ashamed of herself. "I'll make it up to him later," she said, then turned in a full circle, inspecting the room with a child-like smile. "This is so wonderful! Would you mind if I clean up first? I feel so filthy!"

"Please," Sam said, bowing and motioning toward the large bath. "Ladies first."

As soon as the door was closed, Sam returned to the elevator and to the lobby. There were several shops in the foyer, one of which had beautiful dresses. He found a long, lovely dress for Dawn, light blue with delicate white lace. He also bought her a pair of jeans, sweatshirt and tennis shoes. It took longer to find a pair of white dress shoes, but he was satisfied. When he explained they had lost their luggage, the sales lady became nearly indignant at the few things he had purchased for his "wife."

After asking him several specific questions about Dawn's age, weight and height, she rounded up a whole box of things, including make-up, underwear and other items. He wasn't sure how they knew Dawn's sizes, but the saleslady seemed supremely confident in her selections. Unsure what much of it was even for, and afraid to see a single price tag, Sam quit watching halfway through. In the end he had quite a bundle of things for Dawn.

For himself, Sam bought a white shirt, new tie and socks, a pair of jeans and a sweatshirt. He also bought a wristwatch. He left his suit jacket to be laundered. He insisted it be done by six. For an extra fee, they guaranteed it. He charged it all to their room.

Dawn was still in the shower when he returned. He left the clothing he had purchased for her on a chair outside the bath. He slipped into his new jeans, and called for room service to pick up his crumpled suit slacks. He ordered a meal delivered at six, and laid down. He was asleep before he got the pillows adjusted.

Sam awoke to a gentle chiming on their door. He glanced at the clock on the wall, and was surprised to see that three hours had passed in an instant.

Dawn was asleep beside him, her hair splayed out in a rainbow of luxuriant gold. She looked childlike and innocent in her sleep. At that moment she stirred and stretched slowly. He stood, walked into the next room, and opened the door. A cart filled with food was rolled in. Heavenly aromas emanated from the covered dishes. He added a generous tip to the ticket and signed it. The waiter smiled, and backed out of the room.

Dawn came out of the bedroom wearing the jeans and sweatshirt. They ate in silence, their bodies still unaccustomed to food.

Sam's suit arrived by the time he stepped from the shower. He looked clean and professional. Dawn looked stunning in her new dress. She turned smoothly to show it to him.

"Oh, Sam, thank you for buying me this dress! It's beautiful, and just what I would have picked out for myself. It was very thoughtful of you, and unexpected." She thanked him with a kiss on the cheek.

He dismissed it with a mock aristocratic wave of his wrist. "Our public demands it."

Dawn grew serious, and sat on the edge of the bed with a somewhat defeated air. "Are you up to this?" she asked skeptically.

"Truthfully, no," he admitted. "I'm not a professional performer, and they will be able to tell that. During my mission I baptized a wonderful couple who owned a music store. I must have spent a thousand hours playing in his store. I found, or maybe rediscovered, that I could play anything, in almost any way I liked. It was an amazing unveiling of this musical being within me."

"You never told me that! That makes me feel a lot better about tonight," Dawn said with relief.

Sam shrugged apologetically. "We baptized quite a few people who came to hear us. When I was younger I was ashamed of my musical ability, and I guess I just refused to let others see it. I'm confident I can entertain them tonight. I know lots of music, but I'm just as sure that I'm nowhere near a world-class musician."

Sam scratched his head thoughtfully. "That's why I insisted on this being a practice. I haven't been able to put together a program in my head. If I'm not convincing, they will cancel the whole deal, and we will be out on the street again—or worse."

Dawn stood gracefully, raising a hand in a pose of someone about to perform. "Sam, I have some voice training. I'm not a professional either, but I've been told I could be."

Sam brightened. "That's right! I've heard you sing, and you really are good. What do you know that I can play?"

"Well, I know many of the church hymns. I know some opera, and some Christmas music."

"Christmas won't help. What else?"

"Lots of things, but probably not much you would know. Wait. What about the Lord's Prayer? I can do that in Latin and English."

"Yes. That would be wonderful. Do you do Gounod's version?"

"Yes, I believe that's the arrangement I learned. Is that the most famous one?"

Sam didn't answer her question, but stood in silence for a long moment. When he looked up his eyes were confident. "Dawn, I just had an idea."

"What, Sam?"

"We have a wonderful opportunity to bless people's lives with this performance. It is obvious that Heavenly Father has intervened in our affairs. I feel strongly if we do it His way, and use this as an opportunity to bear testimony, we will be successful, because it truly is who we are. We won't be pretending, and people will recognize that.

"I feel impressed to give them music that is uplifting rather than just entertaining. What if we shift the whole emphasis to something we both love? Let's testify of the Lord's love for us with music this evening. Let's give people something to warm their hearts, and uplift their souls."

Dawn clasped her hands and pressed them to her lips, her eyes sparkling with happiness. "I know this is what we should do! It feels so right. If we fail to impress the hotel, at least we will do some good. I love the idea!"

Sam nodded, and knelt down before a plush sofa. Dawn joined him, and placed her perfectly sculpted hand atop his.

"Heavenly Father, we are so grateful for this chance to be a blessing to the people here in this hotel. We confess our dependence upon Thee, and our weakness. I know my own disobedience has plunged me into this trial, and I humble myself and beg forgiveness of Thee. No matter how great our needs, Father, we would like to bear testimony of Thy love, and Thy gospel this evening. And, we ask Thy Spirit to work upon those who hear, that they will be touched, and uplifted, and brought nearer to Thee. We thank Thee for hearing our plea, and give Thee all our love, honor, and praise. In the name of Jesus Christ, Amen."

"Amen," Dawn echoed solemnly.

During the prayer a feeling of peace had fallen over him. He knew no more of the outcome of their "practice" than before, but he knew somehow they would succeed. Even if they were pitched out of the hotel on their ears, someone among those who heard would be blessed, and eventually led to salvation because of this evening. It seemed more than sufficient, and both their hearts relaxed. Everything else seemed trivial.

The hotel management had done a thorough job of getting an audience. Sam and Dawn arrived a little early, and Sam had a few moments to inspect the instruments. As people jockeyed for the few remaining seats, he quietly tuned and warmed the instruments. The violin was very old, yet rich and vibrant. The flute was newer, and had a sweet, mellow tone which he liked very much. The big grand was perfectly tuned. He quietly played part of an intricate piece to limber his fingers. The instrument was superb. An appreciative hush fell across the audience as they listened to him warming up. By the time the manager stepped before the piano, there were a little more than a hundred people gathered.

"Good evening ladies and gentlemen, my name is Herr Johann Muhlestein, general manager of the Schöner Berg. We are pleased to welcome Samuel Mahoy, a famous musician from America, to our hotel." This he said in English, then, *"Guten Abend Damen und Herren, mein name ist Herr Johann Muhlestein, Generaldirektor des Schöner Berg. Wir freuen uns, Samuel Mahoy, ein berühmter Musiker zu begrüßen von Amerika zu unserem Hotel."*

He was answered with moderate applause. "Herr Mahoy is with us this evening unexpectedly, and has agreed to share with us a short evening of music. This is not a scheduled performance, and he prefers to call it a practice. We thank him warmly for his indulging us in this. Without further adieu, we present Samuel Mahoy."

Sam stepped forward, and bowed slightly. He held out a hand toward Dawn, and she joined him. As he spoke the manager translated. "Thank you very much. May I introduce my companion, Dawn." Again, the light applause. "Dawn rarely performs with me, yet since this is, in fact, a practice, she has graciously agreed to join me this evening. I hope you will enjoy her." Dawn bowed graciously to polite clapping.

Sam smiled genially. "Usually when I perform, I am obliged to play whatever I consider my audience wishes to hear. However, since this evening is, for me, a practice, I have set my heart upon playing what I like. Will you indulge me in this?" He was answered with the same low-key applause.

Sam sat at the piano, and adjusted his seat. The audience grew quiet. He threw his head back majestically, then forward to study the keys as if preparing himself for some great feat of musical extravagance. In reality, he had not yet decided what to play, and the longer he waited, the less sure he became. He placed his fingers upon the keys, and still had no idea what to play. He felt a restless stir from the audience. He gave a silent prayer for help, and a long-forgotten song popped into his head. It was a preposterous choice, yet it was all that came to mind.

He had been expecting to play something devotional, worshipful, or inspirational. Instead, his fingers danced across the keys in a lighthearted rendition of "Dizzy Fingers." The music was lightning fast, running up and down the keyboard in a comedy of misplaced accidentals, and playful harmonies. It was almost jazz, almost ragtime, and exactly perfect. People tapped their toes, and by the end of the performance, were clapping in time. He prolonged the piece by repeating the showy part, and ended with a sudden flourish.

The applause was spontaneous, and hearty. Sam relaxed, as did Dawn. He had won his audience, and hereafter, anything he played would be acceptable to them. He glanced at Herr Muhlestein who was beaming from ear to ear. He nodded enthusiastically toward Sam, who sent him a smile full of confidence he had not felt just seconds before.

"Thank you very much," he said, still seated at the piano. "You like American Ragtime, I see." The applause came in loud agreement.

"I do too. Ragtime is an American convention. It started in the early 1900s and continues to be a favorite in some parts of America today. Almost any song can be played in ragtime. Do you recognize this?" He played a line or two of Happy Birthday. He was pleased when the applause came back affirmative. He shifted the bass to a slow Ragtime. The people laughed and clapped. He picked up the pace, and finished the song with a vigorous splash. While they were still clapping, he played a long, minor run, flowed into a minor key, and played a heavy, booming introduction of massive nature.

"This is how Bach would have played Happy Birthday." He continued to play a thunderous bass, majestically interspersing the melody into the song.

He switched to a rousing march rendition of the same song. "This is how John Philip Sousa would have played it." Happy Birthday marched through the hall as precisely as a military brass brand.

Without waiting for a break in the applause, he transposed the song into a flowing waltz. Before he could say a word, someone shouted "Johann Strauss," from the audience. This rendition of Happy Birthday seemed to please everyone, and he played it through twice.

People were still clapping as Sam began to play the few passages he knew of the introduction to Beethoven's ninth symphony. He knew he couldn't finish what he had started, and wondered as he was playing why he had begun it. He came to an abrupt halt and turned toward the audience. A startled look was on their faces.

"Beethoven was a very sick man. I think. I'm told he suffered from constipation." A ripple of laughter flowed across the room. The manager quickly interpreted in German, and more laughter rolled toward him.

"As a matter of fact, some believe he wrote special music to celebrate his successes, and this is why we call them movements today." Sam began to play the same overture again, then interrupted himself to say, "He wrote this to celebrate his ninth."

He was still playing when the interpretation brought a peal of laughter from the crowd. When silence followed, he added, "My apologies to Victor Borga." This also brought laughter from his audience.

Sam's fingers floated across the keys, changing both mood and tempo. His heart felt full as the music changed, deepening in feeling. He changed keys, progressing through a rich succession of major sevenths, and ninths. He had never played quite this way before, and as he changed keys again, a familiar feeling came over him. Quite unexpectedly, "As the Dews from Heaven Distilling," came forth in worshipful, yet joyful harmony.

He glanced at the audience, and noticed some there with looks of recognition, a few with peace on their faces. Still playing, he said, "I see some of you know this beautiful music." A scattering of applause affirmed his suspicion. "This is the theme song of the Mormon Tabernacle Choir," he told them while still playing. Applause encouraged him to continue.

"There is another the Choir sings which I love. Do you want to hear it?" A chorus of *ja,* yes, and *oui,* signaled their happy agreement. The music switched to the Lord's Prayer. There was power in the air and as his heart sang his fingers gave life to his joy. He nodded to Dawn who walked to the side of the piano. Her voice was steady, sweet, and rich. Even knowing something of her voice, he was stunned by the beauty of the sound from her lips. She clasped her hands before her, raised her eyes to heaven, and sang in a voice more rich and vibrant than any he had heard. Tears rolled down her cheeks as she sang "For Thine is the kingdom, and the power, and the glory! Forever, Amen."

Sam stood and embraced her as the applause thundered in the large room. Few eyes were dry. A song came to mind with sudden impact. Sam leaned forward and whispered a question. She smiled and nodded. Without comment he sat, paused poignantly and began the introduction to "O Divine Redeemer."

Dawn's voice was plaintive as she began, then powerful, sure, and worshipful. He had never heard a more glorious singing of this precious and powerful music. Dawn sang it as if she, herself, had written every word. Sam's heart thrilled to the very marrow of his soul as she sang the glorious words.

Ah, turn me not away,
Receive me though unworthy,
Hear Thou my cry, Hear Thou my cry,
Behold, Lord, my distress.

Answer me from thy throne,
Haste Thee Lord to mine aid,
Thy pity shew in my deep anguish,
Thy pity shew in my deep anguish.

Let not the sword of vengeance smite me,
Though righteous Thine anger, Oh Lord.
Shield me in danger. Oh regard me.
On Thee, Lord, alone will I call!

O Divine Redeemer.
O Divine Redeemer.
I pray Thee grant me pardon,
And remember not, remember not my sins.

O Divine Redeemer, have mercy!
Help me, my Savior!

For the briefest second after the music ceased there was a silence of deep reverence, then an explosive applause which seemed to go on indefinitely.

Sam glanced at the clock and was surprised to see that over an hour had elapsed. He returned to Dawn's side, and waited for the applause to end. When it ended there was an electric silence in the air.

After thanking them for their kindness, Sam said, "It is time for us to depart. We have had a wonderful evening with you."

A rumble of polite protest came from the crowd, and the manager came forward, his hands raised, palms down, to quiet them.

"Please, my friends. Herr Mahoy, and the lovely Dawn have traveled far, and they must rest. They have consented to play again tomorrow. Please tell your friends. There will be a small admission to cover their expenses, but the performance will be longer." He glanced slyly at Sam, who nodded slightly. This brought a happy murmur from the crowd.

"Aber Sie haben nicht die Flöte noch die Violine gespielt! But you have not played the flute, nor the violin," a man protested from the first row. At least give us one small piece on one of them, then we will be content. We insist!"

"Ah!" the manager cried following his translation into English. "A command performance then!" He turned to Sam. "What do you say? I think they will not leave quietly if you refuse."

Sam nodded, and the crowd burst into applause.

Dawn turned to follow the manager away, but Sam caught her elbow. He whispered something in her ear, and she nodded. He asked something further, and again she nodded. He smiled and picked up the flute.

He turned back toward the crowd. "Since it is almost bed time, I think it fitting to play a piece I learned as a child, and one which my mother used to sing me to sleep with. Perhaps it will put you to sleep, too." The crowd laughed as he put the flute to his lips.

He played an introduction of lilting, breathy runs, which evolved from intricate to worshipful. His heart remembered his mother's voice, then his little brother, Jimmy, who had once loved this song so well. The music went on until it became subdued with reverence.

At this moment Dawn began to sing in Italian. "I am a Child of God." He had never heard the words in Italian, and found them more beautiful, more melodious, and more wondrous than ever before. He himself became a spectator, an onlooker with wondering eyes as her beautiful voice bore witness to the most important relationship one may discover in this life.

When it was over, the crowd jumped to their feet in ovation. Sam felt overwhelmed, and somewhat embarrassed. He had expected no such ovation, and certainly claimed no credit for this evening to himself. He just knew his prayer had been lavishly answered, and lives had been touched for good. They walked from the piano hand in hand, the applause still thundering behind them. It did not cease until the doors to the elevator closed between them.

Back in their room they knelt in prayer, and Dawn thanked Heavenly Father for this marvelously unexpected blessing. Just a short while ago they had been fugitives, penniless, and friendless.

Where all had been bleak and starvation seemed their future just a few hours ago, now they were being applauded and treated like celebrities. It was a fascinating turn of events.

Sam quietly made himself a bed on the long sofa, and Dawn closed the door between them. It was a night of great peace for them both.

• • •

Sam awoke slowly to a gentle chiming. He pulled on his pants and stumbled to the door. A waiter rolled a food cart into their room. Sam signed the ticket. "Complimentary" was written in big letters across the bottom. The cart contained every breakfast food know to him, and a few unknown. There was also a bottle of chilled wine, which made him smile. The waiter rolled the cart to the table and quickly laid out the food. In a few minutes he was gone. Dawn emerged a few moments later with her head wrapped in a towel. She kissed him on the cheek, and sat opposite him. After prayer, they ate a hearty breakfast.

Shortly after breakfast they reached Dawn's Father by telephone. He was tremendously relieved to find her safe. He took their address and made arrangements to deliver money and a copy of her passport by courier. Sam was still not able to reach his parents, but did get his Uncle in Alaska, who promised to relay the message. Sam was also able to reach the American Embassy in Bern, and made arrangements to get another passport. It seemed as if their troubles were nearly past. In the meantime, they had a whole day to do nothing other than relax.

The next evening's "Practice" was more successful than the first. It was attended by over two hundred people. The third and final performance was attended by upwards of four hundred people, many of them standing, with every inch of the big hall filled. As with the prior two performances, the Holy Spirit was there, and their humble petition was granted. Lives were touched, and they were able to bear witness both in song and word.

In addition to the money Dawn's father sent, their little concert tour was a monetary success. Sam learned that the people had paid upwards of fifty dollars a seat for the final performance, and many were turned away. By the time they were ready to leave the hotel, they had purchased new luggage, a fair wardrobe, plane tickets home, and had nearly a thousand dollars in traveler's checks. Sam's heart rejoiced as they waited for the train to arrive to take them down the mountain. Since the small train station was but a short walk from the hotel, the manager accompanied them, carrying Dawn's bag. He seemed subdued.

"Herr Mahoy," he finally said. By his tone Sam knew he had something serious on his mind. "Please to tell me something?"

"If I can."

"Are you really a famous musician from America?"

Sam shook his head and glanced at Dawn who was smiling coyly, awaiting his answer with obvious interest. "I didn't say I was famous."

Johann, the manager, nodded. "Yes, I recall the conversation. The distinction did not occur to me at the time. How did you come to our village? I assume you are not on tour, either?"

"I have been on tour, but only part of it was a musical tour. I was a missionary. We came here because we were kidnapped and dumped here."

"Is this so? Have you contacted the police? Are you still in danger?" Herr Muhlestein asked all in one breath.

"It was someone in English Customs who did it. We aren't sure who. We had something valuable they wanted, and eventually took from us. We feel lucky to have gotten away with our lives."

"Acht," he said and spat on the ground symbolically. "The English are mad men. I trust them less than lions." Sam laughed, and the manager smiled, but he was mostly serious. Sam was surprised Herr Muhlestein did not pump them for more details, but he seemed satisfied by that simple explanation. In fact, something more important was on the manager's mind.

"Herr Mahoy, when I first saw you sitting in my lobby, I decided before you spoke to me you were either lost or on the run. You both had that trapped and helpless look upon you. Would you like to know why I did not have you both thrown out into the street and arrested?"

Sam was startled by his candor. "Why, yes," he answered, more than a little curious.

"There were two reasons actually. The first was that despite your crumpled appearance, your suit jacket was neat and clean.

For some reason that impressed me, since you had obviously been through . . . How do you Americans say it? Through Hades, I think?

Dawn chuckled. "They do have a similar expression, I believe."

Johann smiled, pleased at having made Dawn laugh, but quickly grew serious once again. "Secondly, it was because you asked me for nothing, but waited for me to ask you. I have always found that when someone is trying to cheat you they will make their proposal first, and very convincingly. This impressed me that you were confident enough to wait for me to propose a solution to your dilemma."

"I had no idea. I just knew what I had been impressed to do."

"It is very good that you were obedient to your feelings. I routinely expel undesirables from my hotel. You will never know how close you came to being in a Swiss jail."

"Actually," Sam said thoughtfully, "we were never in any danger. We were on God's errand, and in His hands. There is no greater safety."

"I can see this is so," Herr Muhlestein agreed enthusiastically. "So, now you will continue your tour?"

Sam took Dawn's hand in his before answering. His voice was wistful. "I wish I could, but that's finished. Now we will go back to America."

"I see," Johann replied, then after a pause. "I must tell you that as soon as you began to play, I decided immediately you are not a professional musician. Don't misunderstand me, I think you play as well, but you have not the polish, you see."

Sam nodded.

The manager continued. "However, I have scarcely ever heard more beautiful, nor more heart-touching music. How can this be? Tell me what is the difference about you. Why is it that I feel happiness inside when you make the music. Many make the music of the ears. You two make the music of the hearts. This I must know why," he said emphatically.

Sam pondered this as the train slid next to the platform. "I will tell you why, and you will have to decide what the truth is. It is because with every song, we are testifying that Jesus is the Christ. Every note professes our love for Him. When people with an honest heart hear such music, it makes them happy inside. It touches their heart."

Herr Muhlestein nodded thoughtfully. "I understand this answer you make. I also believe in Jesus. But, it is a quiet place in my heart where He lives, and I do not know Him as a joy to fill my whole soul, as you do. How did you come to know Him so well?"

Sam took a step closer to him. "I will tell you because you are a good man, and because perhaps the whole purpose of our coming to this part of the world was to deliver this message to you. I came to know him because God has once again called a living prophet upon the earth, and because His true church is alive once again. Millions of people have come to know Christ in exactly the same way as I have."

"I wish this for myself and my family also, please!" he replied loudly. "Tell me where is this church, and where may I find this joy in my Christ."

"Its official name is 'The Church of Jesus Christ of Latter-day Saints.'"

"I have heard this name before. I am remembering that my wife had two young ladies that were nuns in this church come teach us one time."

"Nuns?" Dawn asked, surprised.

"Yes, they were sisters in this Latter-day Saints church, nuns," he explained soberly.

Sam chuckled. "We don't have nuns. Sister is not a title, but a means of recognizing their dedication and service as missionaries."

Their host seemed genuinely relieved. *"Acht!"* he cried, "I thought at the time they were very young to be nuns. This seems much better, yes. So, I know a little of this Church of the Latter-days. My wife very much liked and believed about it, but I did not listen so carefully to their words. They spoke in heavy American accents, and I grew weary of listening. So, I came to think it was not so true at the time the nuns came," he replied, his voice serious, yet jovial. "Is it really as you say? Has God made once again the prophets to speak?"

"With all my heart, I testify that it is so today as it was when Peter walked the earth."

"What you say both thrills and confuses me. But, I have felt something from your words, and your songs, that I have not felt before, and I promise you I will once again investigate this latter-day prophet, and this joy that lights your faces. I think this is a good thing," he concluded.

"I am convinced it is," Sam agreed as Dawn voiced similar feelings.

After exchanging addresses, the kindly manager helped them board the small, open cars.

"I now have your address, and I shall write you when I also know when I have found the prophets, and this Jesus of whom you have taught me. God bless you Samuel Mahoy, and Dawn with the angel's voice," he said as he bowed formally.

Sam's voice was subdued. He reached outside the small train and shook Johann Muhlestein's hand in a firm grip. "Thank you my friend. May the Lord bless you and keep you. May the Lord lift up His countenance upon you, and give you peace. Good-bye."

The train moved slowly away from the platform.

• • •

Neither Sam nor Dawn had ever so much as heard of a cogwheel train, let alone been on one. It looked as if it belonged in a carnival. The cars were only two persons wide, and open on all sides. One could reach out and catch leaves from slowly passing trees. On level ground, the seats reclined back almost 45 degrees, making it like sitting back in a recliner chair. The engine was a small steam engine with a large geared wheel in the exact center. Between the two rails was a cogged rail. The big gear in the engine ran on this center rail, thus propelling the train. They soon found out why this was so.

The train left the station, turned a corner, and almost immediately began a steep descent. In minutes the train was going down an incline so steep that they found themselves sitting perfectly upright in the car. Had the seats been normally reclined, they would have fallen forward out of the train.

At this steep angle, they could see over the top of the forward cars, and were able to look right into the small engine. One man was busily shoveling coal, and another was studiously watching the track ahead with his hand on several levers. The little train puffed and hissed its way for several hours to the bottom.

Upon arriving at the lower station Sam and Dawn walked a hundred yards to another terminal.

Dawn inched up to the handrail and gasped. Before them a drop of many thousands of feet yawned like the edge of the world. "Did I ever tell you I'm afraid of heights?" she whispered urgently.

Sam looked from the panorama beyond the guardrail back to her. "Are you?"

"Er, I wasn't until just a second ago," she said seriously. "Now, I think I am!"

Sam took her arm. "At least we'll die together."

"Wrong answer!" she cried and slugged his arm.

They boarded a gondola swinging on a cable that appeared far too frail for the job at hand. They began a dizzying descent from a fantastic height. They dropped quickly to a lower terminal and got out.

Dawn looked back up. "We have to go back up," she said nervously.

"Why?"

"I think my stomach's still up there."

They found their bus headed to Bern, and showed their tickets. The bus drove for several hours down steep, winding roads. They stopped twice at small villages which appeared to have been pealed from a picture postcard.

Each village had narrow cobblestone streets, a dozen small shops, two dozen ancient, Swiss chalet-style homes, and a small picturesque Catholic church. The villages all had large ornate fountains in their main squares. They were nestled against a very long lake on one side, and the steep mountains on the other.

Even the fact that they were anxious to pursue their journey home could not detract from the magical charm of the ancient countryside.

They were walking past a watchmaker's shop when Sam suddenly stopped walking.

"What's wrong!?"

"My camera! I no longer have my camera. We're in the middle of the most-photographed country on earth, and I don't have a camera!"

"You're right!" Dawn cried, looking at her watch. "We have time to get one before the bus leaves." They quickly located a shop and bought a modest camera. Sam nearly wore it out before nightfall.

Finally they arrived in Bern. They took a hair-raising taxi ride to the American Embassy, where Sam picked up his duplicate passport.

Standing outside the embassy, Dawn gripped Sam's arm to stop him from hailing a taxi. "There's no way I'm getting back into another one of those again!" she groaned. "I'm still shaking from the last ride."

Sam agreed. They finally found a bus to the airport.

It seemed like a long time since they had left South Africa. It was just over two weeks ago, yet it seemed like two months. At last they were on their way home.

Dawn finally felt like talking about her ordeal with the English customs police. It had been much worse for her than for Sam. He listened in horror as she described her experience in detail. They had been determined, thorough, and brutal. They had terrorized her for three days, deprived her of food, privacy, even sleep. They had repeatedly forced her to disrobe, submit to protracted personal indignities, and then left her without clothing for hours, shivering on a cold metal chair.

Though they left no physical scars, Dawn walked away with wounds aplenty which would take many years to heal.

Sam held her hand as she concluded her tale of terror. "I'm so sorry this happened to you," he told her through clenched teeth. "It makes me furious."

Dawn shrugged her shoulders. "I've been thinking about it—a lot, actually. In the end they won. I broke down and told them what they wanted to know. I caused us both a lot of unnecessary pain."

Sam disagreed. "But you know what I think? I think it was probably the fact that you did break which saved our lives. When they retrieved the stone from the sewage tank, they knew you had told them everything you knew. You said the stone they found was nearly worthless? Why would your father's people switch stones?"

"I've thought about that too. If they had found nothing, they would have continued to brutalize me. When the stone

48

turned out to be nearly valueless, they knew two things: First, that I had told the truth; and secondly, that someone with a lot of power and money knew that they were holding me. They let us go because they were afraid to do anything else," she concluded with certainty.

• • •

Including layovers, it took three days to fly to Alaska. During those days Sam and Dawn talked, ate and slept, all in the same seat. By the time they were able to get off the plane for good, their legs would barely support them. Halfway between Seattle and Anchorage Sam shaved and combed his hair in the tiny restroom on the plane. Dawn also freshened up, and somehow emerged looking tired but beautiful.

The Anchorage airport was surprisingly large for such a remote location. Sam watched the buildings glide by, his heart pounding in his ears. He had no idea if he would be welcomed with a loving embrace, a hero's welcome, so to speak—or met in embarrassed disgrace. It seemed almost as if he had been gone four years; two wonderful years serving the Lord, and two nightmare years trying to get home.

Finally, the plane jerked to a stop, and the rattle of seat belt buckles signaled the end of their long journey. Sam could not bring himself to stand. Tears strained to escape his eyes, and his heart seemed to skid to a stop. He felt a hand on his, and looked up into Dawn's eyes. She was standing, smiling down at him. It seemed almost as if she were a foot taller than normal, and he had the impression he was looking sharply upward to see her.

"Your family loves you," she said, as if she had read his mind. "They will always love you. You are their eldest, their beloved son, their hero. Nothing could change that, and you know I speak the truth, for the Spirit is upon me."

Sam closed his eyes and realized the warmth of the Holy Spirit was upon him as well. It vanquished all his fears, and he stood with enthusiasm. When he looked back at Dawn she had shrunk back to her normal size. He blinked twice, knowing he had just seen a miracle of sorts. He paused long enough to fervently thank Heavenly Father for His gentle mercies, and for love. Most of all, for love.

All of Sam's family were there crowded as close around the door as the velvet ropes permitted. They spotted him as he rounded the first corner, and started laughing, pointing and shouting. Mom and Dad looked nearly the same as he remembered. Mom was crying, as it should be. Dad was beaming, also as it should be.

Angela and Beth, the twins, were grown up. They were eighteen, beautiful, and dressed exactly alike. They both cried tears of joy as they waved at him.

Benjamin was thirteen, and bigger, much bigger. He had lost the softness of youth, and taken on the angles of manhood. Sam had to look twice to realize it was his little brother standing there grinning at him.

Little Rachel was eleven, and no longer so little. Of all those there to meet him, she had changed the most. She had gone from a child to a young woman, and the change was startling. Had they not sent him pictures, he could not have picked her out of a crowd. She radiated joy as she pranced from foot to foot.

Sam and his family rushed toward one another with a united shout of joy. With the rope still between them, they fell into his arms. He felt his back being patted, his arms, hands and fingers being patted and held, his face covered with kisses and tears. It was all he had imagined, and much more. It was utterly, completely perfect.

Suddenly, they were asking questions. So many questions. He tried to answer them, to tell them of his joy. No one mentioned his two-week delay. There would be a lot of fence mending, but until then, it was enough to be home.

With a sudden realization he remembered Dawn. As politely as he could, Sam untangled himself, and turned to Dawn. She was waiting almost directly behind him. He motioned for her to join him. He was surprised to see there were tears in her eyes as well. There was a wistful, almost lost expression on her face.

"Mom, Dad, everybody, this is Dawn."

There was the briefest moment of awkwardness, then his Mother gathered her in her arms. A moment later he was standing alone, watching his family make her one of their own. He had to smile, for he knew what she was experiencing. He had watched them love and welcome strangers into their home many times. It was a powerful thing, an almost palpable sense of belonging. He felt his heart sing as the expression on Dawn's face turned from lost, to loved. Suddenly, quite unexpectedly, she was home as well.

"She does look like a princess," Ben said almost to himself. As if he had said something startlingly vulgar, everyone turned toward him. He blushed, but blustered, "Well, you said she lived in a castle. Doesn't that make her a princess?"

"I suppose it does," Sam laughed. He turned toward Dawn. "How does it feel to suddenly be royalty?"

Dawn blushed deeply. "Your family is far more wonderful than you could have ever told me, Sam! It makes me feel like royalty to feel so loved and accepted." She lowered her eyes. "But, I became royalty when you baptized me, and I became a daughter of God."

It was such a perfect answer, such a noble response, that she quietly changed identity in everyone's mind. She evolved, emerged; born again, as it were. She became not just a princess, but Princess. From that moment on, it would be the only name they called her, and it thrilled her to the very center of her being.

Home—suddenly the word meant worlds more than ever before. She was home, and her soul thrilled.

Chapter Three

The Last Frontier

Sam's parents, Jim and Laura Mahoy, had brought a motor home made from an older greyhound bus to get him and Princess. By the time everyone was inside with all their baggage, the passenger section with its three rows of big chairs was fully loaded. They put Sam in the front passenger seat which had been swiveled to face backward. His mom took the opposite seat, and his Dad drove. Dawn sat in a chair behind the table, and everyone else found seats nearby. The twins took posts on either side of Dawn and held her hands in theirs. A happy chatter drowned out all else as they pulled away from the airport. Above the rumbling of the big diesel engine and happy talk, Sam could hear Princess's clarion laughter. It was like the tinkling of a silver bell on a moonless night.

Anchorage was a surprisingly bustling city. Sam marveled at all the new construction, new homes, and new roads. It seemed almost as if the city had recently awakened, and was rushing to recover from a long sleep. They drove through road construction almost the entire way, until the city suddenly ended, and a lush birch forest crowded the road on both sides. It was a beautiful, sunny day, and Sam watched the breathtaking beauty of rugged mountains so close that in winter some parts of the city were in perpetual shade.

The mountains seemed new, almost pristine, as if newly made. These were grand, majestic mountains of granite, balustraded with outcroppings of stone as unscathed by time as if cut only yesterday from virgin stone. Though deep into summer, they still sported white patches of snow snuggled into deep ravines. Everywhere he looked was green. Having so recently come from Switzerland, the comparison between these two mountain worlds was inescapable.

The Glenn highway wound its way through lush forests, until the Cook Inlet squeezed them tight up against the towering Chugach Range. For the briefest distance, it seemed as if there would be insufficient room for a road between these two unyielding forces of nature. At the last moment, the road turned left, crossed the Knik and Matanuska Rivers in a series of low bridges, and crossed the tidal flats at the mouth of the inlet.

Sam was amazed to see several moose grazing knee-deep in the lush grasses of the tidal flats. They turned left onto the Parks Highway, which almost seemed to be a black-velvet ribbon laid across the gentle rolling hills of lush birch and spruce forest. There were few businesses, few homes, and few signs of man until they approached the small city of Wasilla.

Wasilla had little to recommend itself except stark beauty. The city was unincorporated, with no commerce, no industry, and no reason for its existence except its relative closeness to Anchorage.

"Dad," Sam asked above the din of the bus. "What fuel's Alaska's economy, and where do the people in Wasilla work?"

Sam listened as his Dad explained the odd economics which made the little town work.

"The Trans-Alaska Pipeline is just being completed. It's an 800-mile engineering marvel which brought a 48" steel pipe from the furthest North shores of the state, to the tiny village of Valdez on the South.

"It crosses two major mountain ranges, including the Brooks Range, one of the most rugged in North America. It crosses four major rivers, including the Yukon, and hundreds of lesser ones. Its entire length is primarily above ground, on refrigerated pillars, and insulated its entire length. It has eleven major pump stations which use Rolls-Royce jet engines to pump the hot crude across the incredible distance. Operating to full capacity, it is capable of pumping nearly two million barrels of prime Alaska crude a day."

Sam was amazed. "That's a lot of crude. What's a barrel of crude go for?"

Jim nodded, obviously interested and conversant on the subject. "At a spot price of fifteen dollars per barrel, the pipeline pumps out thirty million dollars in gross revenues a day, nearly a billion dollars a month. Of that incredible sum, some ten percent goes directly to the State of Alaska as royalties."

Dawn was listening closely. "It's no wonder all of Alaska seems to be in a frenzy of construction everywhere you look!"

"It's really quite amazing," Jim replied. "Anchorage is nestled on a narrow strip of land between the Chugach Mountains and the Cook Inlet. After nearly ten years of booming pipeline prosperity, there's very little room left for development. People had to look toward Wasilla.

"Nearly every parcel of land which could be developed has been, and land prices were soaring. With costs so high, and the economy so vigorous, people soon looked for cheaper ground. They found it in the nearly unlimited lands of the Valley. With so much land available, prices stayed low, and the people came in droves, one hand on a shovel, the other on a mortgage. That's why I started building homes," Jim explained.

"Even though there's not much more than a grocery store and a post office, Wasilla has more than forty thousand residents. Hundred dollar bills seem more common than ones, and there are too many new homes to count."

Laura, Jim's mother spoke up. "Even so, part of the charm of Wasilla is that the dense birch forests hide most signs of development, and the valley has maintained its beauty."

At the main intersection in town, the motor home turned left, once again toward the Inlet. They drove through lush forest for five more miles before turning left onto a dirt road, right again for several miles on a very winding road, and right a short distance up a lane. They stopped before a fairly large woodframe home. It was unfinished inside and out, but Sam could see the promise of a beautiful home in its graceful lines.

The Mahoys had purchased a five-acre piece of land for not much more than a signature, a hundred dollars down, and a hundred a month. Thereafter, every dime they made went into building materials, and, though the home was not much to look at, in time it would be; until then, it was all theirs. In keeping with the Alaskan spirit of stark individualism and rugged self-sufficiency, they had no mortgage on their home.

It was the most breathtakingly beautiful setting for a home Sam had ever seen. They had cleared away a part of the dense birch forest to reveal that their property sat on a bluff overlooking the Cook Inlet. The Chugach Mountains rose majestically across the glistening waters. Anchorage sat nestled far to the right, barely visible in the afternoon sun.

Before going into the home Jim took them to his garden just south of the house. Sam could not believe his eyes. Jim showed them a row of cabbage plants with heads approaching three feet in diameter. He took them to a row of pea vines as tall as their armpits, laden with peas nearly four inches long. They pulled thick orange carrots from the rich soil as sweet as candy, and ate raspberries as big as his thumb. They walked slowly through the greenhouse and ate cucumbers as succulent as if they had been marinated in some divine nectar, and tomatoes as large as his fist.

Dawn, now Princess, had never seen a vegetable garden, let alone a garden in Alaska. By her definition, a garden had roses, sculpted shrubs and fountains. It seemed entirely novel to her that a garden could yield edibles. She walked up and down the rows, asking questions, laughing, wondering, sampling, sifting the rich loam through her hands. Jim and Princess remained in the garden several hours after Sam and all the rest had gone inside. Several times Sam glanced at them out the dining room window and caught them laughing, or saw Jim peeling a large kohlrabi with his pocketknife. He wondered how many people in this world could turn a garden into a loving introduction to a phenomenon called home.

The inside of the home lacked everything. All the floors were plywood with the exception of the kitchen, and one bathroom. Though they were obviously living in an unfinished home, there was no wanting for signs of industry. All the plywood floors had been sanded and painted. Only half of the walls had sheet rock on them, the other half were pink insulation covered with plastic. Even these had pictures, small shelves with family treasures, and signs of loving habitation. The one completely finished room in the house was the upstairs bath. It was massive, with both an oversize bathtub and a separate shower stall, accessible through different doors to be used simultaneously. It sported a laundry chute which dropped the dirty clothes into a cupboard directly above the wash machine. There were two sinks, one of which was outside the bathroom in an area always available, even when the doors were locked. There was a large closet inside the bath, and a large window overlooking the inlet. It was wonderful. Even Princess proclaimed it "magnificent," high praise from one who grew up in a castle.

Princess made a collect call to her father, and assured him all was well. What seemed like a long time after they arrived home, they found themselves all sitting in the large living room, looking out the big windows across the Inlet. Without explanation it grew quiet, and everyone drew a breath of peace and togetherness. It was one of those rare moments when for just a moment, despite visible flaws everywhere present, everything is perfect.

"Well, it's late," Jim said as he slid to his knees. Sam watched in wonder as the life-long tradition reenacted again. He could not remember a night of his youth when this very scene had not been replayed. Sam knelt, and felt Beth's hand slip into his left and Princess's into his right. Even though he was exhausted, it seemed too early for bed. He glanced at the old grandfather clock and was amazed to see it was nearly midnight. Outside it was still daylight, just moving beyond twilight. Suddenly he felt very tired.

"Sam, will you pray for us?" he heard his father ask quietly. A gentle peace settled over him as he nodded in serene silence. It was indeed good to be home.

Chapter Four

Babylon the Great

Born in Devonshire, England, to wealthy parents, Melody was the youngest of three. Winston was six years older than Marcia, and Melody three years younger than she. At nine years Winston's junior, she was truly the baby in the family.

Melody's father, Donavon Winston MacUlvaney III was the proud inheritor of the family tradition, and considerable fortune. Serving in the army in his youth had taken him all across Europe and Africa. His campaign had taken him into the tiny African country of Rhodesia, where he fell in love with the vast open spaces and arid-tropic beauty. When on the first day out in the veldt (bush lands) he had kicked up a gold nugget the size of his thumb, he knew he had discovered heaven.

He returned home, sold much of what he owned, bundled his family onto a steamer, and journeyed to their new home in South-Central Africa. Melody still remembered the two-month trek across two oceans, two continents, and three nations to arrive there.

At the time he had served in the military the little country had been a British Commonwealth, thriving economically, mineralogically wealthy, politically stable, and a veritable grab bag of opportunities. Donavon had moved his family to Rhodesia with the plan of mining gold. He had purchased a tract of land near Salisbury, staked a claim, purchased mining equipment, hired workers, and refined his first bar of gold by the time Rhodesia split politically with England by declaring independence in 1965.

At England's insistence, the United Nations immediately slapped an embargo on the fledgling country, and without the ability to sell his gold outside of Rhodesia, it became virtually worthless.

Even though independence had literally bankrupted Donavon overnight, he supported his new country's independence, more from a sense of injustice done to Rhodesia, than as an act of treason against his beloved homeland. In the end, his thinking in the matter made little difference to those who labeled him an outlaw, and stripped him of his family titles, ancestral lands, and remaining wealth. Now, besides being broke, he was also stranded in Africa.

Not one easily defeated, Donavon had loaded his gold bars into an old truck, and taking with him all his food, fuel and a small well-armed army to defend it all, he had driven nearly 1800 miles into neighboring South Africa. Much of the way there were no roads, no bridges, or signs to point the way. He followed his compass and his luck. The journey took weeks. When he finally arrived in South Africa he sold the gold for enough money to more than justify all his labors. He tarried in Africa purchasing trucks, equipment, medial supplies, books, musical instruments, furniture and diamonds. He carefully cultivated new friends, bought loyalties and secured patronage. He returned home after nearly a year's absence.

While his wild gamble had been completely successful at salvaging his fortune in their new land, tragedy had struck with mindless fury during his absence. Rebels from neighboring Botswana had swept into the poorly defended country, killing, raping and looting in the long tradition of African tribal warfare. Donavon tragically lost his wife and only son in the raid. Marcia had been raped, then allowed to escape without clothing into her father's fields. Melody, just seven at the time, had been hidden in a wine cupboard by her mother, and had watched her family's horrible fate. Had she even whimpered, or flinched, she would have certainly shared Marcia's fate.

Donavon was inconsolable, and could not forgive himself. After doing all in his power to make sure his family was safe, and healing, he had borrowed military equipment from the small Rhodesian army, collected a group of angry settlers, and retaliated by tracking the rebels to their homeland, and lynching all involved. It wasn't hard to find the guilty ones, for they had smeared themselves with the blood of their victims as a token of bravery. He simply hung every man who smelled of death. He returned a hardened, bitter man, and a national hero.

At great personal cost to his own soul, Donavon had revenged his family's losses, but healing was still decades away, and forgiveness an eternity away. His little country was immensely grateful, and deeded him ten thousand acres of rich tropical desert in token of its gratitude.

The former Brit's new kingdom included some of the greatest mineral wealth on the face of the planet, all of little value. He took the money he had recovered and drilled wells, a thing almost unheard of in that land. His wells brought forth an almost unlimited supply of life-giving water, and he put his vast holdings to the plow. He spent months clearing the land with his own hands. He laughed bitterly many times as he watched softball-sized gold nuggets roll beneath the rich red soil.

His new homeland was literally starving. Food was in scarce supply, and without a local economy, impossible to either buy or sell. Donavon planted vast tracts of wheat, barley and corn. The unstoppable Englishman traveled to Salisbury and convinced Rhodesian President Ian Smith to print currency. Donovan promised to accept the new currency in exchange for his grains, his personal possessions, lands or home.

Encouraged by Donavon's faith in Rhodesia, President Smith borrowed a printing press from South Africa, and printed their new money on newsprint. They picked the name of the most stable currency in the world, the US dollar, and named their currency accordingly, hoping a tiny portion of faith in the US dollar would rub off on Rhodesian dollars.

Donavon sold his entire crop for what amounted to basket loads of paper. This he used to pay his workers, and promised to redeem the currency for any crop he grew, or item he possessed. He treated the money with respect, bargained with suppliers for better prices, and gave nothing away. His workers took the new money to market, and exchanged the paper for scarce goods based on the rich farmer's promises. In time faith in the currency grew, and it became accepted without comment.

In the meantime, Donavon had considerable amounts of the paper money. He planted more crops including tobacco, cotton, soy, tea, and every variety of fruit tree. It seemed as if anything would grow in the red soil. In a matter of a little more than ten years, he had parleyed his investment into great wealth. By this time South Africa was accepting the Rhodesian Dollar, and Donavon traded every slip of paper he possessed for anything of value. It was during this frenzied buying that he had acquired the great stone he had eventually given Sam as a reward for saving his daughters.

During all this time Melody and Marcia struggled to recover from the horrible experiences of their youth. Their healing began the day they first picked up a violin. They had immediately exhibited unusual talent, and daddy Donavon lavished the finest teachers upon them. Soon, however, their talent exceeded the best available in that small backward country, and it was decided they should travel South to seek better education. It was with great anticipation that the two young women made plans to go away to the great metropolis to the South.

It was during this happy exodus that Sam had met them on the train as he was leaving Rhodesia following his missionary duties there. He could not have known how terrifying it was for them to once again be surrounded by African raiders. It was also little wonder that Marcia had been literally paralyzed with fear. She still remembered in far too graphic detail what it was like to be brutalized for sport, not knowing if she would ultimately live or die, but actually preferring the latter.

When Sam had laid his hands upon Marcia, her fear had evaporated as the power of the Holy Ghost bore witness of the truth of his words; she had instantly recognized the eternal significance of what had occurred. From that moment on she searched until she found the true church, and had joined with palpable joy. Her journey to healing reached a perfect climax when she stepped out of the waters of baptism on her twenty-third birthday, in Devonshire, England, her ancestral home.

When Sam gave Melody her blessing, it was powerful, yet hard to interpret. It became evident that for Melody the journey would be much longer, and fraught with peril.

The Lord, speaking through Sam, told her of a long quest that would take her to many nations, and bring her "full circle." The blessing had promised, "When you finally find what you seek, you will have returned to this moment, and it will bring you joy."

Those words were a monument in the halls of his cherished memories. They were sweet confusion that Sam would often remember with wonder; words without meaning, yet rich with power.

For Melody, those words remained troubling; food for forced forgetfulness, stony ground that refused her fervent attempts to plow. Many years would pass before she realized what precious promises awaited her in their fulfillment.

• • •

The morning following his arrival in Alaska, Sam arose early with his father and Ben. They traveled to the site of their construction project. There were two things Jim was very good at. The first, and his greatest love, was farming. But in Alaska, there was little call for commercial farming. The cost of equipment, labor, fertilizer, and everything else was too high, and food could be trucked and air freighted in cheaper than it could be raised locally.

At one time the Matanuska-Susitna Valley, which held Wasilla in its rich embrace, was the breadbasket of Alaska, and raised almost all of its staples. Numerous farms that had once been prosperously appointed with large barns, grain silos, and lush fields were all abandoned now, unused, neglected, and tumbling down, in some cases.

The other thing Jim was very good at was speculative real estate development. He had a sixth sense for a good deal, and an artist's eye for a well designed home. They pulled up to a partly framed home, one of Jim's current construction projects.

The setting, while not as dramatic as their home, was beautiful, wooded, quiet and secluded. They unloaded tools and after studying the blueprints briefly, began laying out walls. Ben went right to work, having his father's easy familiarity with tools and building.

Sam, on the other hand was on his left foot, and had to be shown everything to do. He had never built a home, and watched and learned with interest. By the time they stopped for lunch, the outside walls on the upper floor were standing, complete with windows installed. When it was time to go home, they had all the roof trusses standing.

Sam was amazed at how many muscles he had not used on his mission. Now, after a single day's work, every one of the several thousand of them was sore.

Several months later, the home was completed, and new owners were moving in. Jim stopped at the bank, deposited a sizable check, and they drove home, exhausted but happy. For the next several days they worked on their own home, adding sheet rock, installing carpet, and painting the exterior of the house. It was a happy interlude, and one they performed with loving care.

During all this time Princess wrote letters, made phone calls, and said but little of her plans. She was a delight to have around. She always seemed cheerful, willing to help, never too busy to assist, and genuinely pleased to learn new things.

She fell in love with fishing, and gamely baited hooks, hauled in salmon too large for her to lift, and amid squeals of disgust, cut and cleaned her fish. Sam watched her with growing admiration and wonder. In his eyes her new name was both a label of love and a title of distinction, both well-suited to her noble soul.

When the package arrived it was marked with customs stamps and colorful postage. Princess laughed happily as she carried the box to the kitchen table. Sensing something important in the offing, the whole family gathered around as she carefully cut the tape and opened the box. Princess grew quiet, almost reverent as she lifted the carefully packed items from the box.

Because Sam had been around her father, he immediately recognized each item as she unwrapped and laid them on a velvet cloth she had also withdrawn from the package. First came a jeweler's loop with two lenses. Next she lifted a small, but elaborate scale from the parcel. Following this she laid out tweezers of various sizes, and a handful of other tools. When she finally reached the bottom, she lifted a small leather package no larger than a box of wooden kitchen matches. She carefully unzipped the pouch and laid back the lid. Inside was a row of small white envelopes. Princess took the first in the row, laid it flat on the table, and without lifting it from the surface, deftly unfolded the edges. Inside was a thin layer of bluish tissue, and lying in the fold of the envelope, three small diamonds.

A collective gasp went up from the table, but Princess did not hear them. She was in a world where only she existed. She clamped the first stone into tweezers and lifted it to the light. Satisfied she could see no flaws, she studied it with the 10X loop, then finally with the 20X. She studied a color chart for a moment before declaring. "This is a good stone. Eye pure, with slight flaws at ten, nice color about 'I'. Good cut, good edges, a nice stone."

"What's it worth?" Benjamin asked impulsively. Without looking up she unfolded the scales, laid the stone in one dish and placed small weights on the opposite side. In a moment the scales balanced.

"It's a little larger than a third carat," she said to herself. "Stones in America are higher priced; I would judge this to be worth about four hundred dollars wholesale, nearly double that retail."

"Wow!" Benjamin said enthusiastically. "Can I look at it?"

"Sure," Princess said happily. She made sure it was clamped securely in the tweezers, and first showed Ben, then everyone present, how to look through the loop. "You hold the loop to your eye without moving it. Next you turn to the light, and move the diamond back and forth until it comes into focus. By moving it slightly you can focus on the surface of the stone, or actually inside the gem. Some internal flaws are only visible once you learn how to focus the loop inside the stone."

While they were learning to use the loop, she continued to inventory her gems. In all she had exactly fifty stones. They were all relatively small, all of the sizes in greatest demand. She confided to Sam later that their retail value was over fifty thousand dollars.

The next afternoon she and Sam drove in to Anchorage. They were between construction jobs, and Sam happily accepted her request to drive her to a meeting. She was still not comfortable with driving on what seemed to her to be the wrong side of the street.

All Sam knew of their trip was that she were going to sell some of her diamonds. Princess talked happily about diamonds on the drive to Anchorage. She directed him to an address that was more a warehouse than an office. How she had discovered this place was beyond Sam. On the outside of the building a small brass plaque held the cryptic name "Blumstein and Noble." There was no indication of what Blumstein and Noble actually did.

Princess introduced herself to a secretary, and stated she had some "quality goods" to display. The secretary left for a moment and returned to usher them into a back room. The room was very well lit, with plain, white tile floors. In a few minutes an older gentleman entered the room and introduced himself as Mr. Blumstein.

Mr. Blumstein was a short, balding man in his sixties with silver-streaked hair and a pencil-thin mustache. He wore a black, pinstriped suit that looked as if it had been pressed moments before.

Princess made no introductions, but simply laid out her wares. Mr. Blumstein sat at the small table, pulled a loop and tweezers from his breast pocket, and examined several of the stones.

"Hmmmm," he said aloud. "South African, I see. Good cut, good color, nice clarity, good size. How many do you have?"

"I have about thirty carats total, all similar," she told him.

Without examining the rest of the stones, he looked her squarely in the eye. "Your source?" he asked pointedly.

"My father is a diamond cutter in Johannesburg. These stones come through Danbers to my father, and then to me after cutting."

"How good is your supply?"

"I can bring over as much as you need. At this point I am establishing my delivery schedules and will need several months to come to full potential, but beyond that it is basically unlimited."

"I see, very good. I presume you have a sales receipt."

"I do," she said, and pulled a small certificate from her purse detailing the stones, and her right to sell them. The man was satisfied.

"Price?"

"To begin with, 75 percent of appraised wholesale by lots, 85 percent of wholesale by the piece."

The man's eyebrows went up as dollar signs appeared in his eyes. It took him less than a nanosecond to recover his composure.

"Will you place them on consignment?" he asked.

"Not at that price. For full wholesale I will place them for thirty days to begin with. In the future I will be able to extend to the customary sixty days. My apologies," she replied smoothly. Sam was amazed at her professional presentation and confident demeanor.

"Very good. I will give you 75 percent of wholesale for this lot," the man said. "I will have the stones appraised independently, and forward you a check."

"That would be acceptable," she said as she stuck out her hand. The man shook it once, looked her in the eye, and smiled.

"Pleasure doing business with you, Miss?"

"Pauley. Princess Pauley," she replied. The man's eyebrows went up slightly, and he bowed formally from the waist.

"Princess," he said simply, "May our association be long and mutually profitable."

"Thank you," she said simply. He left the stones sitting where they were, and escorted them to the front door.

"That's it?" Sam asked. "No contracts, no receipts, a handshake and you give him fifty thousand dollars worth of stones?"

"He won't cheat me," she said simply.

"You don't know him from Adam," Sam objected.

"Yes I do. He deals in diamonds. There are no dishonest diamond wholesalers."

"How can that be?"

"Because it is not allowed. You don't understand, but you will. The diamond industry is tightly regulated. It is more closely watched than you can imagine. This sale I have made is already known and approved by Danbers. If not, my father would never have acquired the stones in the first place, and I would have never received them.

"Selling diamonds is like an exclusive religion. You can only get in if you have family already inside, and to cheat another diamond merchant would be like cheating family, and is unthinkable. Should it happen, they would be kicked out, and never touch another diamond as long as they lived. My diamonds are more secure in his hands than if they were in a bank."

Princess walked through the door he held open for her, and smiled at him for his thoughtfulness. Sam smiled back. It was one of those small things which he so admired in her, that she appreciated small kindnesses, and smiled so easily. He would have opened a hundred-ton door for her to see that brief smile.

Sam helped her into the car, then got behind the wheel. "It seems odd that the first place you stopped you sold all the stones almost without effort."

Princess chuckled and turned to face him. For a moment he was lost in her beauty, and somewhere inside of him a warning bell went off. He mentally shrugged, and concentrated on her words. "My father 'suggested' I contact this man. I told you, the subwholesale diamond trade is a big family. He knew I was coming before I ever set foot in his store. He knew what stones I had, and approximately the price he would pay. He was pleased to get them because I am now his primary supplier of stones."

• • •

Exactly three days later an envelope came in the mail addressed to "Princess Gems." Sam read the name and smiled. He knew the name was the creation of Mr. Blumstein. Yet somehow it said all that needed to be said. Princess laughed when she read the name, and asked if Sam would drive her to the bank. He gladly agreed.

One might expect a small city bank to have little exposure to international banking, yet when Princess declared her intent to make a deposit into a Swiss account, the bank manager smiled and handed her a deposit form. It was a full sheet of paper. She handed Sam the check after endorsing it, and began filling out the rather lengthy deposit form. He gasped when he read the amount, which was for $22,000. It was the largest amount of money he had ever seen. He felt as if he should be glancing over his shoulders for robbers.

Sam was deep in thought when she slid the paper over to him and handed him the pen.

"What's this?" he asked.

She pointed to a section of the form labeled "Account holder." "You sign by the 'X'," she said simply.

"Why? This is your money, not mine," he objected. He noticed the bank manager trying to suppress a smile. It apparently seemed unlikely that anyone would refuse so much money.

"Do you trust me?" she asked simply.

"Absolutely."

"Then sign. I'll explain when it's time. Until then, I just need you to trust me."

Sam twirled the pen in his fingers while he studied her face, which, he decided, was just as pretty with a frown on it as a smile. He quickly signed the document and the banker whisked it away. In minutes they were back in the car.

Every few weeks another package arrived for Princess. After a while the family lost interest, and just the two of them sorted through the stones. The first few months the stones were carefully graded and sorted so that every stone in the batch was similar in size and value. As the quantities became larger, the stones became more varied, until no two were exactly alike.

"Isn't it dangerous to have that many diamonds here at home in a cardboard box?" Sam asked, suddenly wary.

"That brings up the next subject. We need an office in a secure building. We also need several safety deposit boxes in different banks. Sooner or later, someone is going to find out we have the stones here, and make an attempt to steal them. They will easily succeed the way we keep them now."

"Well, I don't see a problem with getting an office. I'll help you find an office tomorrow afternoon after work if you like. You may enjoy having your own office anyway," he said. It sounded like fun.

"You don't quite understand. The office isn't for me. It's for us. I can't handle everything that's going to be taking place. We will need to hire a bookkeeper, arrange for armored car delivery of stones, all kinds of things. We need to make trips overseas to secure new delivery routes, better prices. I am tempted to go to Asia and purchase colored stones. This is much bigger than I can handle alone. I really need your help, if you'll have me as your partner."

Sam was stunned. Since the first small parcel of diamonds had arrived, he had considered this her business. It even bore her name. The idea of working for Princess had never occurred to him, let alone working with her as a partner. It made his head buzz.

She took his silence as a rejection and turned away from him, busying herself with a stone under a loop. A quick glance at her revealed a glistening tear hovering in her eye.

"Why are you doing this?" Sam asked.

"What do you mean?" she replied without looking away from her stone.

"Why are you setting up this business and involving me in it? We both know you don't need the money. Your Father restored all your assets he took away before your baptism. You have more money than I could ever hope to make in a lifetime. You have your father's inheritance on top of this business.

"Besides, you know I'm planning to go away to college next spring, and you mentioned going to college too. You put my name on the Swiss bank account without explanation, and now you are involving me in your business. Why are you doing all this? You said several months ago you'd explain it when the time was right. Maybe now would be a good time."

Princess turned toward him. A blink sent a single tear streaking down her cheek. He reached out and brushed it away. As he did so she leaned her face into his fingers. For a moment he found it difficult to breathe.

"The time isn't right," she said cryptically.

"Let me ask you something else, then. Are you doing this for yourself, or for me?"

"For myself," she replied, then smiled and added. "Well, mostly for me. I have another motive, but it's of no consequence right now."

"And you really need my help? You're not just making that up to be generous or something."

Princess turned to look him full in the face. "I honestly need your help, and I am trying to be generous. I owe you a lot, but this is not repayment for that. I don't know. It's just that I want you to be with me in something I feel is very important."

"You're not going to tell me why." It was not a question.

"No," she replied simply.

"I didn't think so." He realized he was bumping into that part of Princess's personality that was very stubborn. Well, so was he, just on different matters, and not nearly to her level. She was a curious combination of generous to a fault, and as stubborn as a rusted, make that, welded hinge. When something was important to her, nothing, that is no earthly thing, could make her budge. It made Sam chuckle that she could be more headstrong than he was.

"What are you laughing about?" Princess asked suspiciously.

"That you are more stubborn than I am."

"Get used to it," she replied cheerfully but without any attempt at apology.

"I'll do it," he said without further delay.

"Thank you," she replied as if he had given her a great gift. Her smile was so beaming he wondered anew what deep plot she was brewing. It was something of great significance to her. He thought it may be some time before he knew what it was, if ever.

The following afternoon they found an office above the National Bank of Anchorage, which occupied a new building in the middle of Wasilla. It was exactly what she needed. They would have easy access to their safety deposit boxes, and the building was unusually secure. They made arrangements to have a quality security system installed. Princess paid the lease a year in advance.

Their new office consisted of a lobby and three large offices. It was bare except for carpeting. They spent several days in Anchorage arranging for office furniture. Princess insisted they rent the furniture, rather than purchase it. Since he knew she had access to considerable sums of money, it surprised him. However, he considered it pointless to debate the issue. Since he had no idea what her agenda was, he could not guess at her motives for the decisions she made. He decided to simply trust her.

Accordingly, Sam took the first office, Princess the second, and a bookkeeper the third. Princess had been involved in the diamond trade since her youth. After her mother's death at age eight, it was her main tie with her father. His life was diamonds, and she had made it hers in an instinctual need to connect with him. She showed a genuine aptitude for the business which her father had recognized, fondly kindled and encouraged. All of her current wealth stemmed from prior involvement in the trade. Though only twenty-two years old now, she possessed her father's prodigious knowledge of the diamond trade.

It was precisely six months from their return to America that they purchased tickets and returned to South Africa. It was a whirlwind trip which began at Princess's childhood castle, and then on to diamond mines in Germiston, diamond cutting houses in Johannesburg, and finally the diamond works in West Africa. By the time they returned home, Sam could describe every aspect of a diamond's journey from a mine two miles beneath the earth's surface, to a woman's finger. It was a fascinating, exhausting journey.

Of all he learned, of all he saw, of all things made plain to him in this long journey, the greatest of these was the preciousness of Princess's soul. Over the course of the past year he had seen her in every condition possible: happy, sad, excited, terrified, disappointed, fresh, exhausted, healthy, sick, laughing and weeping. No matter the circumstances, she radiated a noble quality that seemed unassailable. There was no thin veneer, no cheap facade to Princess. She was simply a princess, both in name and quality.

The plane was four hours out of England, and Princess had fallen asleep beside him. They had flown first class for the express purpose of "giving him more leg room." It was one of a thousand thoughtful things she just did for him. He was tired, and his mind and body demanded sleep, but he was too troubled to rest. He tried reading the scriptures, but his eyes passed over the words. His mind did not register their meaning, for his thoughts were upon another puzzle so pressing it refused to give him peace.

It was barely ten days ago that they had walked up to that imposing front door of her father's castle together. As the heavy door groaned open, it was almost as if those first moments played out again when he had first stood there as a missionary. He looked across that vast room, and could almost see Dawn walking through it in her swimsuit and gossamer robe. As the evening progressed from laughter, through dinner, and to small talk, certain words seemed to trigger flashes of memory for

Sam, and he would be transported away with a memory of her. He saw her serving tea in her father's study, leading them through the secret passages of the castle, serving them cinnamon rolls and cold milk in the vast kitchen after a missionary discussion. In his mind, he listened again with wonder to her golden answers to their missionary questions, and saw the tears stream down her face as she acknowledged for the first time that she knew it was true.

By far, Sam's most powerful memory was of that eternal moment when he had pronounced the words of divine cleansing, and lowered her into the waters of her baptism. She had looked at him, her intense blue eyes lovingly fastened to his, only closing as the waters washed over her. As she emerged, her eyes reopened to his as if no thing in eternity could separate them. How he thrilled then, to her purity, to the spiritual feast it was to teach and baptize her, to the shear joy of that unity that forever binds a spiritual child with her first teacher.

Now, nearly a year later, they were once again on a plane, headed toward his home, now her home. They had spent nearly every intervening day together, either living in his parent's home, or working in the same office. Each day had revealed a new side of her inner beauty, until he was awed into silence.

It was true she was flawed in some ways, but the flaws were like the tiny specs of flint he had learned to find in the most perfect diamond. The flaws did much more than signify imperfection. Truly, one great flaw lowered the value of an otherwise precious stone, but many small flaws attested to the fact that this is indeed a diamond. A flawless stone did not exist in nature, and any stone without some imperfection was labeled valueless as a cheap laboratory creation.

It was not her flaws he constantly saw, but the brilliance of the diamond surrounding them. Any mortal can put on a perfect facade for a period of time, and like the laboratory mockery, its sparkle is artificial. But there was no façade in Princess. Her flaws were naked, visible, and honest. Sam saw her flaws as evidence of the fact that this was her soul, utterly unadorned, in bright light, under a 20X loop. It was this, and a thousand other brilliantly special things, which made him love her.

But, this was not the puzzle now twisting his soul into knots. What puzzled Sam nearly to insanity was that he had come to love her with great intensity, but he had not fallen "in love" with her.

He knew it was a distinction worthy of some great philosopher's treatise or a poet's inspired lyrics; it was a distinction smaller than dust, yet greater than the vastness of space. It bound him to her forever, and in the same mighty stroke, separated them for eternity.

Still greater than his dilemma was hers, for there was little doubt she was not encumbered by this subtle, yet steely distinction. Her every gesture spoke of her love for him in a way he recognized in the deepest, most precious part of his soul. She made every effort to hide it, to treat him as a friend, or perhaps a sibling. And though manhood had placed the usual brown paper bag over his head in regard to female subtlety, the message had slowly seeped into his heart after countless hours, days and weeks of exposure to it. Princess loved him.

It brought tears to his eyes, and anguish to his soul to know that one day soon he must tell her he did not love her in a romantic way. He knew it would tear a great hole in her noble heart and simultaneously tear a hole in his own.

"Oh, Father," he heard himself cry out in the silent anguish of his soul. "Thou knowest how I love Thee, and how I love to feel Thy arms around me. Thou knowest how in the simpleness of my heart I have longed to be a blessing to Thy daughter. Oh, Father, how it pains me to know that I must tell Thy precious daughter that I can't love her the way she needs and deserves. I have no idea why this is, and I would give all, Father, to spare her that hurt. Father, I . . ." his prayer was interrupted by a stirring next to him. He turned to watch Princess lean over until her head rested on his shoulder. Long blond hair spilled over his shoulder and a smile played briefly across her lips. It was almost more than he could stand. His heart cried out in love for her, yet he ran into that brick wall that refused her entrance any further.

A flash of pure truth suddenly penetrated Sam's thoughts as cleanly as a beam of light through total blackness. He saw the wall which her love had hit, and recognized for the first time that he, himself, had constructed it.

It was not a fixture of his nature, but a construct alien to the landscape of his soul. Every way Sam looked at it he saw his handiwork, his thinking, and his peculiar craftsmanship. Almost with a palpable feel of stone on his fingers he picked up a brick and looked at it from every side. It was made of cold resolve. It was the color of his mission, and the texture of the mission rules. It was every female on his mission whose feminine call had gone unanswered. With great relief he mentally tossed that brick away. It had outlived its purpose.

He examined another, and saw it was made of the same stone as Princess's castle home, from the very first time he had ever seen her. It was the color of her swimsuit, and the softness of her skin. On impulse he brought it to his nose, and smelled the sweetness of her perfume as the movement of the big door wafted it to his nose. He knew why he had placed this brick on the wall, and tossed it aside.

Brick after brick he examined. He found dozens of them the texture of the missionary lesson guide. Each was the color of a different piece of clothing she had worn. There was one for every missionary lesson he had taught her, one for every time he had forced himself to see inside her soul and outside her skin.

He was surprised to find many the color of pine trees, and the texture of rough-hewn logs. They had crystal for ends, and gold for corners. He lifted one to his ear, and heard her voice singing those angelic evening performances in Switzerland. He found one for every time he had looked at her, loved her, and remembered who she was, and who he was.

He found one with velvet sides, textured like silken bed sheets, the color of her hair as it spilled across the pillow beside him. It smelled of expensive soap, and freshly scrubbed skin. He turned it over in his hands and savored its softness and beauty, and rejoiced that he had made it a part of his wall. With joy he mentally tossed it aside, and watched it vanish to non-existence.

There were dozens of bricks made of Alaskan birch wood, the color of her bathrobe, the texture of her skin. There was one that smelled of shampoo and swirling steam from a hot bath. Dozens of them he had put into the wall in his father's home, each a little different, each adding to the thickness of the wall keeping her out. There was one slick like porcelain, the smell of chlorine, moist to the touch, the color of her swimsuit atop the pinkness of her skin.

Each of these he examined with care, savoring the memory, remembering their function, valuing their purpose then, and each he tossed aside. At length no wall stood, no barrier prohibited her. He looked around, searching, hoping, waiting for her love to try the wall again.

He rejoiced that now it could pass, now it was free—no, in reality, now he was free. The contemplation of the happy moment when she came and found the wall gone thrilled him, and he laughed. The sound of his own voice delighted him, and he laughed again.

Something moved against his shoulder, and that peculiar sensation of sudden awakening surrounded him. He hadn't realized he had fallen asleep. He blinked opened his eyes to see her sleepy face pulled into a puzzled smile.

"You were laughing in your sleep," she said, then chuckled softly at the memory.

"I was dreaming, I guess." He explained, and found his eyes drinking in her beauty in a way he had never allowed before.

She pushed herself away from him as if she had been trying to focus on something too close. Her smile turned to happy puzzlement. She blushed. "Why are you looking at me that way?" she demanded happily, yet confused.

"Don't you recognize this look on someone's face?"

"No," she responded playfully. "Should I?"

"You'd better get used to it."

"Why? What does it mean?"

"It's the look of love, Princess. It means that I have loved you from the first moment I saw you, and that my life will never be complete unless you are an eternal part of it."

"Sam!" Princess stammered. She fumbled nervously with her hands, her eyes darting from his face to her hands. "I think you're still asleep." She finally managed to say.

"Then I wish to never awaken. If this is a dream, let me dream it through out eternity." He reached out, took her hand and brought it to his lips. Twin tears streaked down her cheeks.

"Don't tease me. I couldn't stand it if . . ."

"Dawn." His voice softened, and he touched her cheek lovingly. "Princess, I love you. I think I have always loved you.

Before this world began I loved you, and as long as the smallest speck of dust exists anywhere in all eternity, my love for you will be what it's made of." His eyes clouded with tears, and his hands trembled. Tears fell on her hand as he pressed each finger to his lips and kissed it tenderly.

"I know this is unexpected," Sam continued. "And I know we have talked of little other than the Gospel and diamonds. But I will burst if I wait another second!

"Princess . . ." He paused to regain control of his voice. "Princess, will you stay with me for the rest of eternity? Will you make my journey through this dismal world meaningful, and marry me?"

The sound that came from her lips was at once a cry of joy, a laugh of sweetness, and the sound of bitterness escaping once and for all. She looked at him, her face wet with tears, her lips moving, trying to say the right words, but they would not come. She laid her face against his chest and wept. At first they were tears of happiness, then tears of long-held fear, suddenly, unexpectedly released. He held her gently against his chest, his cheek on her head as she cried until only sweetness remained.

Finally, she raised her head, and rubbed away tears with both hands. She smiled and tried to speak, but her mouth contorted again with emotion. When she did speak, it was so small he nearly had to read her lips.

"Yes," she whispered, then with great happiness, "Yes, a thousand times yes, an eternity filled with Yes! My answer has always been yes. I just feel like I have been waiting a million years for you to ask me the right question." Her voice was soft and breathless.

Princess's face was very close. Sam placed his hand on her cheek. She turned her face and kissed his palm. "Perhaps," he said gazing into her eyes with an intensity that was both new and intoxicating, "Perhaps if one counts the premortal world, it has been that long. Since you have had to wait so long, do you mind if I ask you again?"

She shook her head wordlessly, a beautiful smile glowing upon her face. How like an angel she seemed to him at that moment. Sam swallowed hard, his heart pounding nearly beyond control.

"Princess, will you make me the happiest man among all of God's creations, and marry me?"

"Oh, yes!" she cried, "I will," and fell into his arms.

Without explanation, without warning, without regard for the sanctity of what had just occurred, a passenger nearby began to clap, then another, and another. As seconds turned to minutes, and whispers to shouts, their section, then the whole plane erupted into applause. People cheered, some of them whistled, many laughed, and a few cried. Princess, and her beloved prince nestled down into their seats, oblivious to anything but one another, and the miracle of perfect love.

Chapter Five

Love as Soft as Butterflies

On the morning of June 14, 1975, Sam waited nervously in the long hall below the Salt Lake Temple, his clothing entirely white. His heart raced like a chariot of fire, and his eyes continually pooled with tears. He had tried all his life to imagine this moment, this frightening, celestial moment. He had rehearsed and replayed this image in his mind a thousand times, and each had been less in every respect than what he felt now.

Sam had imagined less fear, less nervousness, less love, less shear joy. A rustle of skirts to him was like the parting of the veil, and he turned to see the most heavenly of all God's creations coming toward him in a wedding dress. Oh how he strained to imprint that image in his mind, to remember every detail, every nuance of her beauty, the glow of her righteousness, the halo of love that surrounded her face. He wanted to be able to replay this moment every day of his life, and remember, remember the intensity of the love now filling his soul to overflowing.

Surrounded by his mother, family and friends, Princess walked toward him like a glorious preview of the Second Coming. Her dress was rich and full, entirely made of lace with thousands of lace rosebuds in an intricate pattern. He marveled, wondered, and felt his heart race. She was lovelier than any dream mortal man could devise, awake or asleep, and she came to him, to him of all people.

He reached out to her and felt her silken hands slide into both of his. He pulled her to him, and was immediately hindered by billowing lace. He laughed to himself, for joy, for happiness, for love, and leaned forward to kiss her lightly. Her face was radiant with joy. Her lips moved without making a sound. "I love you," she said. It was the most perfect thing she could have said.

Princess had received her endowments that morning; he had been there, heard her say the words, repeated them with her at the dividing of worlds, and seen her step through the eternities to meet him. "Glorious" was too small a word to describe that moment, and the promises more rich and eternally profound than he had ever realized before. The symbolism was rich and eternally significant. He wondered what it all meant, and longed for the day when the promises were all granted.

Almost as if the world skipped a step, Sam found himself holding Princess's hands across the altar, her face a halo of love and serenity. He listened to the words of the ceremony with rapt attention, trapping them in his mind and heart. He had never heard such beautiful words, such profound promises and pronouncements. It was as if the Savior Himself were pronouncing those vast promises, and he knew, as he had never known anything else before, that they were true.

Was it a minute, an hour, an eternity later that he heard God's authorized spokesman say those words which made her his for time and all eternity? He leaned across the altar, cradled her face in both hands, and kissed her as if all his love had to be expressed in that single act. He heard, saw, felt, knew nothing else but she who was his forever, until a hand on his shoulder demanded his attention. His father laughed and suggested saving some for later. He chuckled, and reluctantly surrendered her face. She opened her eyes to his as if awakening from a dream, her eyes childlike with utter joy.

So much happened in the next few hours that the newlyweds almost had no time to see one another. They zoomed from place to place, breakfast to lunch, to friends' houses, to home, to receptions, to photos, to gifts, to thank-yous, to goodbyes, to darkness in the wee hours of night.

When at last they climbed into their car and drove away, they were exhausted beyond relief. They drove the short distance to the Hotel Utah exactly east of the Salt Lake Temple, checked in, knelt in prayer beside their bed, and fell atop it fully clothed, sound asleep.

Sam awoke with a start to the warmth of sunlight in the room. He sat up in a daze. It took several moments to remember where he was and how he had gotten there. A memory seized him spellbound for a split second before he turned to the bed behind him. Only a white wedding dress lay there carefully arranged. It was then that he realized the door to the bathroom was closed. He could hear soft movements from beyond, and felt his heart quicken with . . . anticipation? Fear? Passion? So complex were these emotions that the only one he was entirely sure of was love. On his side of that door, and on hers, love was the power of life.

The door stayed closed a very long time until he wondered if it might actually be vacant, and his Princess fled from the room. He lifted the phone and ordered breakfast for two. He had practically lived in the same house with his new bride for the last year, and knew exactly what she liked. He ordered it all, with every side and trimming he could think of. It was more food than ten people could eat.

The door to the bathroom clicked softly just as he hung up the phone. It opened slowly and an angel stepped softly into the room. For a moment his heart stopped, his eyes glued themselves open, and he felt his face heating up. He had never seen so lovely a creature as his Princess as she walked slowly toward him. He stood to meet her and she came to him, her arms open wide.

They held one another for nearly an eternity, their hearts melting into a single inseparable whole. He kissed her, softly, slowly, tenderly, until the world ceased to exist except her love, which she gave to him completely, utterly, passionately, and perfectly.

• • •

Neither had a recollection of having received or eaten breakfast and lunch, yet the carts of half-eaten food testified to the reality of their having done so.

It was hard to do, very hard. Anyone who has tried it will testify that it is nearly impossible to pack a suitcase when you can't look at the luggage because your eyes are glued in near worship to another's face. But, somehow, perhaps as a result of a miracle, they both left the room with most of their possessions.

His last comment to his bride as they closed the door to their honeymoon suite was; "I wonder what housekeeping is going to think when they see the mess we left behind."

"They're going to be jealous," she replied shyly.

He sighed. She laughed softly, like a wind chime in the distance. She looped her arm through his.

"They should be, my Princess. If they knew, they surely would be."

"I'm going to hear you say that when you are eighty years old," she whispered in his ear. He felt a thrill of delight travel up his back. He couldn't help sighing again, for in the fabric of his soul, he believed her, and it thrilled him through and through.

• • •

As far as their family knew, they were flying to Hawaii for two weeks. In reality, Hawaii was a jump on their way to Paris, Switzerland, Greece, and finally, South Africa. Having been raised a struggling farmer's son, it was hard for him to adjust to the idea that the least of their concerns was financial. In the eight months since Princess had started importing diamonds they, actually she, had done far better than good.

His demure bride, however, had grown up in affluence, and seemed perfectly at ease with the astronomical prices demanded to dip one's tongue in the syrupy sweetness of luxury.

They flew, ate, slept, and honeymooned first class. They spent more money during those two weeks than he could have earned in a year of building houses. It didn't really matter, for life had been good beyond reason, beyond their wildest dreams, beyond any hope of permanency. It was a walk in the full sunshine of utter happiness, and wild joy. It was paradise, and they rejoiced in its perfectness.

• • •

The Atlantic's cold waters churned thirty thousand feet below them as Sam hovered somewhere between sleep and wakefulness. He had been watching Princess sleep for almost an hour, and it seemed as if she grew more precious with each breath she drew. She was lying on her side facing him, and he found that he could not sleep with her this close.

Their honeymoon had been more glorious than anything he could have imagined. He had been invited with passion into a new and glorious world previously unknown to him, and he found himself in a constant state of giddy happiness. Being married was everything he had hoped it would be, and a thousand times better. Without reservation, he considered himself the luckiest man alive.

At that moment Princess's eyes flickered open, and a smile transformed her face when she realized he had been watching her. Her hand gently touched his cheek, and flopped sleepily back into her lap.

"Why do you watch me so much. You could give a girl a complex," she said, her voice a little indistinct from sleep. It made him think of her as a sleepy little child, and he chuckled.

"I find I can't sleep with you near when there is light in the room."

"Oh? Why not?" she wondered, straightening and stretching in her seat.

"Because, I feel like we're the luckiest people on earth," he replied after a moment's silence.

"I don't want to even think like that." Her voice was suddenly sober.

"How come?"

"Well, because luck is fickle, and temporary, and eventually turns bad. I don't want to be lucky. I just want to enjoy the good things while they are mine. That would be sufficient for me."

"Me, too," he agreed. "But is that really what you believe? That happiness is temporary?"

"On some level I do, I guess. I've been here before. Well, not nearly this happy, and not nearly this in love, but I've seen happiness turn to tragedy. More than once," she concluded quietly.

"Like when your Mother died?" Sam asked.

"Yes."

"And, when your father kicked you out of the house?"

"Why are you bringing up these unhappy memories at such a happy moment. I don't want to think about those things." Her voice sounded pouty, not angry.

"Sorry. I only wanted to understand your personal philosophy about happiness."

"I understand. I'm really not angry. I don't think I could be angry with you. Let's just change the subject." This she said with a hand on his knee. It felt very good there, and he placed his hand atop hers to soak up as much of her as he could.

"Are you afraid of happiness?" He asked.

She gave him a stern look, then smiled. "I thought we were going to change the subject."

"Are you?" he asked, ignoring her protest.

"My love, I could give you a thousand-word essay on my attitude about happiness."

"Distill it to one word."

"Just one?"

"Please," he said.

She took that moment to readjust her skirt, and push a loose strand of hair out of her face.

Princess opened her mouth, her face suggesting a long explanation.

"Just one word," he reminded her.

"In a word. Yes," she said forcefully, throwing her hands into the air in frustration. Then more subdued, "I sometimes get the feeling that God does not want me to be happy very long. Every time something gets wonderful, it goes away, usually violently. I guess whenever I feel strong happiness I begin to resent God, because I fear He is going to take it away from me. It's almost as if God does not want me to be happy about anything except Him. It makes it hard for me to have great faith in Him sometimes. Does that make you think less of me?"

"Nothing you can say could make me think less of you."

"See? See why I love you? You always know the perfect thing to say to make my heart sing." Princess sat quietly for a while. Sam wanted to ask her more, and to assure her that he would never let tragedy strike her again. But, he knew it was not within his power to promise such a thing, and honesty kept his mouth closed. Still, he felt pained for her unhappy outlook on things.

Finally, she looked him squarely in the eyes. "Tell me something? Are you afraid of happiness?"

Even though he had broached the subject, Sam was still taken back when it was his turn. He had to think hard to come up with the correct answer. Most of all, he had to push aside some pride to give her an honest answer.

"Afraid isn't the right word, I think. I'm . . ." he began, but she wagged a finger in his face.

"In a single word," she insisted.

"Then I would have to say, no."

"Really? I'm surprised. From the stories you tell, you have had some awful things happen to you, too."

"Not really," he disagreed.

"Oh? What about Jimmy's death. What about those guys beating you up at the lake, and trying to rape your sister. What about being whipped on your mission and thrown in jail. What about those things? Don't they make you doubt that any happiness can be permanent?"

Something occurred to him, and he asked a new question rather than answering hers. "Is that why you are so intense and passionate about enjoying life, and love, and money, and beauty, because you think they will all end abruptly?"

"Not fair!" she said.

"The court directs the witness to answer the question," he said sternly.

Princess smiled and sat up rigidly in her seat. "Yes, your Rudeness. I am guilty. I intend to squeeze every milliliter of happiness from my life while it is available to me. I'm passionate about things because they don't last."

"That's kind of sad," he allowed.

"Tripe," she said sternly. It made him laugh. Tripe is a filthy-tasting dish made from the lining of sheep stomach. It tastes so bad that it had become a common curse to define something as utter garbage, yet intended to be consumed. Sam had eaten, or more correctly, had *tried* to eat, tripe in Africa, the curse was very graphic to him.

"You owe me an answer," she insisted.

"What was the question?"

"Haven't the awful things in your life given you the sense that happiness is temporary?"

"Oh. Yes, kind of."

"Then, how can you say you are not afraid of happiness? You know it won't last, and the happier you become, the more devastating the inevitable disaster is."

Sam turned as far as he could in his seat until their knees were touching. He took her hand, and gently massaged it as he tried to answer her question. "There was a time in my life when I agreed with you. I sometimes went to the extent of avoiding happiness because I didn't want to experience the misery and unhappiness I thought would inevitably follow."

"Yes, yes, that's how I am sometimes. But, you said that's how you used to be. What's different now?"

"I discovered what true happiness is," he replied.

"Really? Tell me what it is," she said playfully.

Sam laid his head back in his seat. "True happiness is finally understanding who you are in God's eyes. It is thereafter knowing you are worthy and acceptable before the Lord, and feeling His love to the marrow of your bones."

Princess almost looked disappointed. "I thought you were going to say something incredibly romantic. You know, like loving me was true happiness."

"Loving you is the most wonderful emotion I have ever experienced, and by far the sweetest thing that has happened to me in my lifetime."

"That's what I thought you were going to say the first time," she said happily. But, her mood turned serious. "I don't understand why having my love isn't the ultimate happiness."

"I know you don't. And, I'm not sure I can explain it in a way you can understand. I'm not sure anyone can understand it without experiencing it. But, your feeling that God will take away any happiness you achieve is a part of what it is I am trying to say."

"Keep trying until I get it," she said. It made him laugh.

"Okay. Suppose you were a parent and had a beautiful little girl about four years old."

"Hmmm, I like this scenario. I plan to make it come true."

"Me too. Well, suppose this beautiful daughter of ours discovered chocolate. The first time she tasted it she fell in love with it, and thought chocolate was the ultimate happiness in life. As her mother, would you forbid her to eat chocolate."

"No, of course not."

"Let's add to the picture. In time your daughter became so addicted to chocolate that she thought it was the most wonderful thing on earth."

Princes laughed. "Who's been telling you about my childhood? I was like that once."

"Aha, a true confession!"

Princess laughed. "Get on with your story! This imaginary daughter sounds adorable."

"It gets better though. Your daughter refuses to eat anything except chocolate. You can see that her health will be affected by her addiction. Would you become concerned? Would you begin to restrict the amount of chocolate she could have?"

"Yes, of course."

"Do you think your daughter would understand, or appreciate your restricting her chocolate diet."

"I'm sure she would fight against it."

"Might she not think you were mean, or cruel?"

"I know I would if I were that child."

"But, since you have greater wisdom, and you love your daughter enough to risk making her hate you, you take away the very thing she thinks is necessary for her happiness."

Princess sat quietly for a moment before replying. "I hadn't thought about it that way. I can see why Heavenly Father would do that, even if we don't understand that this thing of happiness is hurting us. What I don't understand is how having a loving home, or a baby brother still alive, or other things that appear to be good, would be harmful to us."

Sam clasped his hands and shoved them into his lap, arching his shoulders; then he relaxed. "Princess, I don't know the answers to all these things. I'm not claiming to know why everything happens, or if those things we lose were actually bad for us. What I do know is that in order for us to achieve the ultimate happiness, the eternal type of happiness that we are capable of, we must be absolutely focused on righteousness. I think what happens isn't so much that everything we lose was bad for us, but that we still are not aligned with a celestial reward.

"Perhaps it's just that our temporary joys make us complacent, and make us think we have all we need. It seems to me that our trials keep us from being lulled into immobility. I know that when I am comfortable and happy in my life, I don't want anything to change, even if it means progressing to greater happiness."

Princess nodded her head, albeit somewhat uncertainly. "I can understand that. I'll have to think some more about it. But it still doesn't seem fair."

"At times it certainly doesn't—perhaps even most of the time. I think that's the purpose faith serves in our trials, to give us the assurance that our trials have a greater purpose and will ultimately exalt us if we bear them well.

"Speaking from my own life's experience, my sweet wife, I have gained tremendous blessings from every trial I endured. I wouldn't change any aspect of my life. As near as I can tell, my life in its present form is the most perfect it can be in. It would terrify me to think of taking some other path that might lead to some other outcome in my life. Though it's been hard, it's brought me great blessings, not the least of which is loving you."

Princess smiled, leaned forward and kissed him on the forehead. "You keep reminding me why I love you," she said. "However, you do admit that happiness is temporary, and sometimes ends abruptly, even tragically. But you're not afraid of happiness because you believe the outcome of your trials will be wonderful in the end."

"Princess, I can honestly say that I have enjoyed every year of my life more than the one before it. I can also honestly say that each year has been harder than the one before."

"So, just because we're deliriously happy together, you don't fear that it will come to a tragic end?"

"It may."

"Oh! That wasn't the right answer," she cried as she punched him on the shoulder.

"No, but it is the truth. And the truth of this whole discussion is that no matter what happens, as long as we are faithful and obedient, all things will work together for our ultimate, eternal happiness.

"I expect to say that I have enjoyed every year of my life more than the one before—when I'm a hundred years old!"

"I hope I'm there to hear you say it," she said pointedly.

"If you aren't there I won't be able to say it, because it won't be the truth."

"Now," she asserted, a beaming smile on her face, "*that* was the right answer!"

Chapter Six

Summer of Joy

"It sure looks bigger in reality than on paper," Princess admitted as she stood outside the massive log structure that was soon to be their home. Sam had to agree, it did look too big. They had poured over the plans for months, moving walls, adjusting window sizes, moving bathrooms, shrinking, enlarging. It had been a happy, yet frustrating experience for them both. Their backgrounds were so varied, that their vision of the perfect home was quite different.

Princess had been raised in a castle, literally. She had been waited on by servants, pampered beyond reason, spoiled rotten, and indulged in every whim. Sam had been raised in a small home on a farm. He had worked hard, been taught discipline, temperance, sharing, and had received but few of his greatest desires.

One would have thought then, that Princess would have wanted another castle home, and Sam a smaller, more functional home. However, it was an odd twist that this was not so. Sam wanted what he had never had; a large home, with many rooms, secret passageways, a formal dining hall, and many garages.

Princess wanted what Sam took for granted, closeness, love, family, a strong sense of home. Since she had not found these in her castle, she feared to move into another one.

Their compromise had produced a home not entirely unlike the Swiss hotel; rough-hewn logs and crystal chandeliers. It looked comfortable, homey and peaceful to her, and big and successful to Sam. Its rooms were small enough to be livable, and large enough to be spacious. One side of the house was a four-bedroom home not unlike any other. The other side was a collection of rooms not clearly defined in their purpose. They just existed for the purpose of being, for the purpose of having, for the simple process of living with excess. The rooms were appropriately connected by a hidden hall, and cleverly crafted secret doors. There was even a room that could only be entered through the secret hall. To add a splash of functionality to soften the sense of foolishness he felt, Sam also made the secret hall the quickest and safest way to leave the big home in the case of a fire. This was the unused East wing in his castle, and he valued every empty square inch.

Princess decorated the livable part of her home in warmth, lace, and love. His side of their castle was rich, luxuriant, velvet, and crystal. Yet it suited them, and heaven knew they could afford it.

Their log mansion sat beside beautiful Lake Helen, on one end of a twenty-acre paradise of dense Birch forest. Sam had the area around the home cleared and planted in grass and formal gardens. Princess had the area near the lake cleared of under-brush, planted in grass, and left to its natural beauty. She had sand hauled in for a small beach, and a boat dock built. Walking from one side of the house to the other, one passed from exquisite formal gardens to the lush grasses and virgin forest. In many ways it pleased them both, and symbolized their jigsaw puzzle love.

Sam had an airstrip cleared near the house and bought a single engine plane. In 1975 Alaska had more private aircraft per capita than any other place on earth. With its low altitude, cool dense air, and vast expanses of unpopulated land, it made a perfect location for small aircraft.

They moved into their new home October 31, 1975, Halloween day. Sam's whole family showed up to help them move. Even though they had been married less than a year, they had acquired a considerable array of possessions. Especially after they decided to build the log castle, they had purchased anything they thought might go well in their new home. They were both amazed at how much of it was just junk, and had no real place in their new abode.

A light snow fell most of the day as they unloaded the big truck. They had backed the truck into the big garage, and had a warm place to unload the boxes. They carried them down the ramp of the truck, up two steps into the laundry room, through the family room, past the kitchen, dining room and breakfast nook, through the living room, past the study, and up a broad circular flight of stairs to the bedrooms.

Sam was regretting the size of his home long before he carried the last box inside. While the men finished up the last of it, Princess and Sam's mother slipped away to make a treat. Mom had brought an apple pie, and Princess made Red Bush tea. His family had all come to appreciate its rich, herbal flavor. Apple pie was unknown in South Africa, and to Sam's knowledge had never been served with Red Bush tea. They found the two made a delightful combination.

It was nearly midnight before everyone left, and they flopped down exhausted on the big sofa in the main living room. They silently surveyed their accomplishments, and were pleased. In all, they had come a long way, and it seemed wonderful to finally have a home of their own. Before them a natural rock fireplace rose a full two stories. On either side of it stood a bookshelf recessed into the walls. Behind them a large grand piano stood on an oval oriental rug. Another set of sofas surrounded the opposite side of the piano. Various groupings of Victorian chairs were scattered around the room. The ceiling was high with large open beams. Beautiful woodwork had been laid diagonally across the big beams. The effect was truly stunning.

"I am so tired," Princess mumbled to herself. "I think I'll go to bed." She smiled at him, and levered herself to the edge of the sofa.

"I'll help you make the bed," he offered. He knew their bedding was still in boxes.

"That's nice, but your mom and I already did that. All I have to do is go pass out between the sheets."

Sam laughed, then sighed. "When are you going to tell me?"

"Tell you what?" she asked innocently as she stood.

"Your big secret."

"You mean about the diamond business?"

"No, about our family," he said.

"I don't know any secrets about your family."

"You don't understand, my love. Yours and my family. Us."

"Oh? Do you think I'm keeping a secret from you?" She asked mischievously.

"Either you are keeping a secret from me, or you don't know yourself."

"Know what, you silly? What are you talking about."

"Are you sure you want me to say it? I thought it was something women wanted to do themselves," he said in all seriousness.

"What *are* you talking about?" she demanded, her curiosity piqued.

"Why, I'm talking about your being pregnant," he said happily.

"I'm not!"

"Yes you are."

"If I was I would know it before you. Why do you say that?"

"I say it because it's so."

"You can be such a tease sometimes. I'm going to bed."

"Wait," he said and caught up with her part way up the stairs. She received him happily, and wrapped her arms around his neck. Princess by nature was a snugly person and never seemed to tire of physical affection. It was another of her many virtues which made her priceless in his heart.

"I may be wrong, but I don't think so. I watched my Mom have four babies. Every time I knew she was expecting before she told the family. I could tell."

"How?" she asked, her head cocked to a side, her brow furrowed.

"Well, there's a different look about a mother to be. It's a new softness, a gentleness not there before, a kind of glow. It's the way they walk and move, a new peace, a kind of reverence, I guess. For about a week I have been seeing that in you, and I have been wondering when you were going to tell me."

"You amaze me," she said, and since she was standing on a step above him, kissed him on the forehead. "I have been feeling different, and kind of sickish in the mornings. I actually have a doctor's appointment next Monday. You speak with great conviction about something that is an unknown to me. Maybe you're right. Maybe not."

"I'm right," he replied with emphasis.

"Are you ready to be a daddy?" she asked, her face lowered, a hint of a pout on her lips.

"I can think of nothing finer. What about you?"

"I'm not ready to become a daddy," she said, then laughed at her own joke.

"You've got to learn to keep a straight face," he said.

"I know. I'm working on it. To be honest, I'm scared."

"Of being pregnant?"

"Well, that too, but mostly I'm scared of being a mother."

"Why, my love?"

"Because my mother died when I was young. Somehow I have always assumed the same thing would happen to me."

"I can see how one might come to that conclusion as a child. But, surely, as an adult you can see that your mother's death didn't set a precedent. Her circumstances were unique to her. There's no reason to believe the same thing could or would happen to you."

"I know all that, of course. But, ever since I was a child, every time I thought of the day when I too would have children, I have had this feeling that my life would end shortly thereafter. I suppose it may be a childhood delusion, but it's always been there. I guess I have ceased to question it anymore." There was resignation and sadness in her voice. She deeply believed what she was saying, and it disturbed Sam.

"You said children. Does this mean that you think you will have more than one before you are going to die?"

"Well, yes, I guess. I have always thought that I would have several before I was called home."

"Okay then," Sam said, acting much more cheerful than he felt. "This is baby number one, so nothing is going to happen. Before baby number two comes, we will work on your bad attitude about living. At any rate, I don't think there's anything to it at all."

Princess brightened somewhat. "I know it sounds silly, but I've told myself everything you just said, and it doesn't help. It's probably nothing, but it bothers me. Sometime appropriate would you give me a blessing? I'd like that."

"I will, I promise," he said, wishing there was anything he could say to take away her fear.

"I just hope I'm a good mother," she added seriously. "I haven't had a role model, really. I was raised by an English nanny. She was wonderful to me, but not the same as a Mother. I really want to be a good mother."

"I can't imagine you being anything other than a perfect mother. I'll give you a pointer though."

Princess nodded seriously. He paused for effect, cleared his throat, then continued, "The most important thing to being a great mommy is to pamper the new baby's daddy," he said with exaggerated seriousness.

Princess laughed. It was a silken, joyful sound. She stepped down to his level. "Let's start your pampering right now."

•   •   •

Melody had gone on to study music in South Africa. It was a tearful and frightening transition for her. This time she flew from Rhodesia with Marcia by her side. Their studies lasted approximately a year. After a brief visit to Rhodesia they packed again and headed to England. Marcia's talent was technically superior to Melody's. Marcia's technique and prowess showed great promise, but for Marcia the violin was merely an instrument.

Melody's music was charged with emotion. Her violin was far more than music; it was a love affair. She played with what some described as genius. Her instructors considered the missing technical skills something that could be learned, and her love of the violin divinely inspired. Hence, Melody showed greater promise and was courted by prestigious orchestras. Marcia studied until she met and married a warm and loving Englishman.

Melody returned to Rhodesia after two years in England's finest music schools. Her timing was unfortunate, for she had returned on the exact day the rebels once again attacked their home.

This time, however, her father, Donavon was prepared. He had quietly purchased a small army, complete with cannons, armored personnel carriers, one WWI vintage tank, and a considerable supply of small arms and ammunition. Melody had loaded guns for what seemed like days on end as her father, and a few faithful friends, defended their fortress-like home.

On the sixth day of the attack Melody fell asleep on the couch in utter exhaustion. All had traded turns taking short naps, but the strain was most telling on her, and her father had ordered her to sleep. She awoke with a start to the feel of someone nearby. Her eyes fluttered open to see her father kneeling beside her. Tears were streaming down his face; yet, when he saw her awake, he quickly fumbled with something in his hands. She knew very well what it was.

"Daddy, I know you can't bear the thought of me being captured by the rebels, but I don't want you to kill me, even out of love, even if you know in your very heart of hearts that it's the best thing to do. Do you understand?"

"Oh, Baby, I'm sorry you saw that," he whispered, and stroked a grizzled hand through her soft hair. "During the night they brought up an army tank. Until now I thought we could hold out. It's only a matter of hours before the sun comes up, and they attack. There's no way we can defend ourselves. Forgive me, precious one, but I couldn't bear to have them take you and . . . and . . ."

"And do things to me like they did my mother, and Marcia," she finished for him. He merely nodded without looking at her.

She sat up and wrapped her arms around his neck, laying her head on his broad shoulder. He held her tightly, and wept for not much more than ten seconds. With a sudden resolve so typical of him, he straightened, kissed her on the cheek and smiled as if nothing at all was amiss.

Melody was frightened by the sudden change. "Daddy, I want you to listen to me. I know you have already decided to do what you think is unavoidable, but I want you to consider my words, then reconsider your decision. Will you do that?"

"It's the least I could do," he admitted, still kneeling a short distance from her. She placed a soft hand on either cheek, and kissed him on the forehead.

"When I was on the train and you came to rescue me, do you remember that?"

"I remember it bloody well," he said grimly.

"There came a time when bullets were smashing into our cabin, glass was flying everywhere, and we could hear the rebels just outside our window. We knew it was but a few minutes before we would be captured, and they would begin . . . well, you understand."

"I was certain I would be too late," he said with a grimace.

"At that moment when we could not possibly survive, that Mormon missionary who was with us . . ."

"Elder Mahoy," Donavon supplied.

" . . .Elder Mahoy gave me a blessing."

"You told me about it, but not many details, honey."

"He wrote it down. It's actually fairly short. What it said in essence was that we would not be harmed by the attackers, but that it was a type of other trials that I would have in my life. The important part is that he promised me that I would survive them—all of them—including this one. Do you see what I mean?"

"Do you believe what the blessing said?" her father asked intensely.

"I do, with all my heart. When he gave it to me I felt a great warmth rush through me, and a sense of peace I had never felt before. I feel that same peace now, Daddy, and I want you to honor my faith, and not try to save me by . . ." She couldn't bring herself to say it.

"I have never felt such a peace, or rush of warmth. I've heard others describe it though. Your mother spoke of it . . ." He seemed lost in memories for a split second, his eyes focused on distant scenes. He quickly returned his attention to Melody. "I will make you a promise."

"Okay," she replied.

"I will wait until the rebels are actually in the house, and coming for you. But, I promise you, I will not let them take you alive. It's the best I can do, my precious child."

"I understand Daddy, and I thank you for that. But, there's one other thing you need to understand."

"Which is?"

"If the rebels kill me, I will be dead."

"That seems apparent," he said, and chuckled with dark humor.

"If you kill me, you'll be dead."

"What do you mean?"

"As awful as it seems to both of us for me to be tortured and killed, it would be much, much worse if you killed me, even to save me. My blood would be on your hands, and you would not be guiltless. I'm afraid you could not come where mama and I would be, and that would be the greatest tragedy of all," she said emotionally.

"I'm afraid my hands are already stained with many people's blood, child. One more, as an act of mercy, couldn't make a difference."

Melody persisted. "Tell me, tell me what my heart already knows. Have you ever killed someone except in the line of duty, or in defense of what was rightfully yours?"

"No, of course not," he attested.

"Then, killing me would be an act of horrible, unforgivable shedding of innocent blood. Oh, Daddy, don't you see, the Bible says a person who sheds innocent blood can't ever go to heaven. Please, Daddy, for your sake, for Mama's sake, for my sake, please rethink this, I beg you."

Donavon's shoulders hung low; his face became a forsaken mask, and he hung his head. She had never seen him so defeated. Even while he could not accept allowing his youngest daughter to be brutalized, he loved her too much to deny her this request. Unknown to her, he silently vowed to stay by her side until they either both escaped, or both perished. It wouldn't be his bullet that spared her, but he would not draw his last breath until she had been spared in one way or another. It was a solution far too risky to give him any peace. And, it cost him more courage than he actually possessed to agree to risk her so needlessly. But, it was how it would be.

He stood and looked down at her still sitting before him. "I will do as you say. No matter how awful it seems, I will not interfere by taking your life." Then added, "I never break my word."

"Thank you, Daddy," Melody cried with tears of gratitude. She jumped to her feet and embraced him fiercely. He held her for a moment, nodded, spun on one heel, and marched away, barking orders as he stomped into the other room.

During all this time, months of negotiations had been underway in Salisbury for the unconditional surrender of Ian Smith's government to the new communist-backed government seeking to take its place. Ian Smith finally capitulated to stop the killing, and a truce was set in place.

The so-called truce was nothing more than an unconditional surrender of the former British citizens to their indige-
nous neighbors, many of whom had chafed under the apparent
unequal distribution of wealth. Now in power, their former
employees began a systematic punishment of those upon whom
they had relied for so many years for their welfare.

Thousands of British farmers, business owners, owners of
industry and merchants were forced from their homes and businesses at gun point. Their daughters and wives were ravaged
before their eyes, their sons murdered, and they were either
jailed as enemies of the state, or executed on the spot.

A week of relative calm came and went as the new government enacted laws outlawing persons of British descent
from ownership of land larger than one acre, or buildings larger
than one thousand square feet. All other properties were immediately forfeit and subject to resettlement. All mortgages and
financial obligations on the land were to remain the burden of
the former owners, who would be jailed if they were not
immediately paid in full, in cash.

Food became scarce as those taking over the vast farms
and factories neglected to plant crops, or simply lacked the
expertise to run the equipment. Famine loomed, the economy
plummeted, and anger raged. Those in power loudly blamed
the prior government of Ian Smith, and by association, all of
British descent; and mobs, with the sanction and assistance
of government troops, began systematically killing their former
employers.

Thousands of former British citizens escaped across the
border into neighboring Botswana, hoping to make their way
into South Africa. Less than half of them made it. Surrounded
on every side by hostile troops, Donavon and all with him were
not able to sneak away. Though a proud man, and as stubborn
as hardened concrete, he would have gladly abandoned all to
spirit Melody away to safety.

The day following the enactment of these new laws saw
the fiercest fighting yet. The tank was brought forward and fired
three shells. One overshot the house, the second blew away the
whole south corner, killing two defenders, and the third blasted
completely through the front of the house and out the back

without exploding. It left a three-foot hole in the front, and a ten-foot hole in the back. Miraculously, no one else was killed. Inexplicably, they never fired the big gun again. Melody would never know that the fourth shell had partially fired, killing the tank crew, and jamming the shell in the barrel beyond repair.

The shooting stopped suddenly about seven P.M., and Melody found herself deafened from the shelling. A man approached cautiously with a white flag and informed them everyone but Donavon could leave in safety if they would leave their home and possessions and never return. For the safety of his daughter, Donavon agreed and had surrendered his weapons, his fortune, his home, and his life before Melody could object.

Melody and the others were allowed to escape in a battered old truck with two flat tires. They drove away not knowing what would become of Donavon.

The last Donavon saw of Melody, she was crying hysterically, clawing at the back window of the truck.

The last Melody saw of her father, he was surrounded by armed guards in military uniforms, his eyes fixed upon her. As soon as he was certain she was truly being set free, his chin rose defiantly. He smiled broadly and turned to face his captors.

Donavon was immediately arrested as an enemy to the new state of Zimbabwe. When asked how he would plead, he said "bloody guilty," with great feeling. Minutes later he was hanged on his own front porch. He was noble to the end, and as a last request asked to wax his mustache. The amazed soldiers watched as he carefully waxed and curled his great mustache, fitted the rope carefully around his own neck to avoid disturbing it, and nodded. He was buried in an unmarked grave in his own front yard with an odd smile on his face.

Melody learned of her father's fate a few days later at the same time she learned she had also been declared an enemy of the state. She was smuggled out of Zimbabwe on an airplane inside a mailbag, taking with her great faith, bitter memories, and her violin.

• • •

The day after Princess and Sam moved into their log castle Sam's parents' home was burglarized, or rather, vandalized. The only evidence was a big diamond shape scratched onto the mirror hanging above the living room sofa. The diamond shape was carefully faceted and faced to look like a real diamond. The number "22" had been deeply etched beneath it.

They all felt violated, and careful precautions were taken to preclude another break in. The police were truly stumped by the weird vandalism, and the fact that the door had been professionally picked. There was nothing else to suggest a motive. Robbery was ruled out as nothing had been taken.

Sam and Princess returned home in deep silence. Neither needed to ask the other if they knew what the "22" represented. It was the exact weight of the diamond they had attempted to transport through England many months ago. The fact that only a diamond could cut the carefully drawn image in glass, and the number below it incontrovertibly connected it to the lost gem.

Suddenly, what was forgotten history was terrifyingly present. They had no one to whom they could turn for advice or protection. They were on their own, and what minutes before had been the number before 23, was now a looming, invisible threat in their lives. They both knew the reason his dad's home had been vandalized. It was a warning, and it meant they still wanted the stone.

• • •

Princess found she loved being pregnant. From the beginning she felt a deep sense of love and unity for the precious life she carried. As her tummy grew in size, her love grew to match. Each day she became more anxious to finally meet the sweet spirit inside her. She would find herself talking to her unborn baby, and then blush and stop in embarrassment.

Sam came home unexpectedly one Friday afternoon and found her sitting in the rocking chair, singing Primary songs to her baby. Between each hymn she stopped and told her baby the meaning of the words, and how important it was to understand. Sam listened a long time as tears trickled down his cheeks. He felt as if he had quietly stepped into the celestial room in the temple, and interrupted an angel singing to her child. How he valued that moment in years to come, and how sweet its memory was in his soul.

"How long have you been standing there?" Princess asked when she finally realized he had been listening to her.

"Minutes," he answered, then amended it to "A lifetime."

Princess blushed, and turned away from him quickly. "I didn't know you were there. You caught me being silly."

"I caught you being the perfect mother you were concerned about. Our baby is so lucky, how could you call yourself silly?"

"I just love this baby so much," she said, rubbing her tummy tenderly. "Sometimes my heart has to express it. I find that singing fulfills my need to express my love. But, I . . . I hadn't planned on you seeing me."

"I shall always treasure the memory of watching you sitting there singing softly. It is a moment of joy I would not want to have missed."

Princess smiled softly at him, and looked down with a tender twinkle in her eye. "Baby, I want you to meet the person I love most in this whole world. His name is Samuel, and he's your Father. He loves you just as much as I do, and one day, he is going to teach you how to grow up strong in faith and goodness. Listen my child, listen as Mommy and Daddy sing to you." Tenderly, quietly, she began to sing, "I am a child of God, and He has sent me here . . ."

Sam started to sing with her, but memories toppled in upon him, and his voice broke. He had vivid memories of singing this precious song to his little brother the morning he had died. He had loved Jimmy with all his being. Somehow, singing it again to a child tugged at his heartstrings beyond endurance.

He stood and walked to the big piano. Softly, ever so softly, and with every fiber of love he possessed, he played the precious hymn as she sang the words to the child of their love. In some way unknown, unrecognized, and unexplainable, something healed deep within his soul. When the music came to a reverent end, he was enriched beyond his understanding.

For Princess, this was a moment of sweet awakening. For the first time it became sweet and acceptable to be a mommy. It was her carte blanche to be a tenderhearted Mommy who talked to her children in loving baby talk, quietly sang songs, read nursery rhymes, and expressed unabashed love.

Suddenly, she was free of the restraints of the stuffy societal morays of the luxurious wealthy who had been her role models. In ways too important for her to understand, she evolved from a woman to a mother, and the change was liberating beyond expectation. Even though she did not understand the glorious change which had overcome her, she did rejoice in its purity.

• • •

Since their marriage, Sam had given little thought to anything other than Princess and their growing business. It came as a shock, then, when his father asked if he would come to the church. Jim, his Father, had been serving as bishop of the new Wasilla ward since its creation two years ago.

The Wasilla ward boundaries extended from the city limits of Palmer to the outskirts of Fairbanks, over three hundred miles to the north. The ward extended thirty miles south, and four hundred miles east to Valdez, the new terminus of the Trans-Alaska Pipeline. With nearly twelve thousand square miles of area, their task was daunting.

Sam wasn't sure if he should be suspicious or afraid as his father closed the door behind them, and offered him a chair.

"Thanks for coming, Sam. I know you are wondering why I couldn't talk to you at home, but I wanted this to be official. I hope you don't mind."

"Sure, Dad. What do you need?"

"It's not what I need, but what the Lord needs." The Spirit to begin to burn in Sam's soul. He sat up straighter.

"As you know, my first counselor is moving from Alaska. I have spent many days fasting and praying to know who the Lord has prepared to fill this position. Each time the answer came to me I didn't have sufficient faith to accept it, I guess. Time after time I have gone back to the Lord to seek a reaffirmation of His will. At last, the Lord has confirmed His will in such a way that I am left a bit chagrined for my slowness to respond."

Sam didn't know what to say but was beginning to feel considerable suspense over his father's words. "What is it Dad? You're making me nervous."

"I am calling Brother Linus to be my counselor. As you know, he is presently my elder's quorum president. So, I'm in need of a faithful priesthood holder to fill that position. I have submitted your name to the stake, and received authority to ask you to be my new elder's quorum president. There will be an official call by a member of the stake presidency, of course. But since you're my son, I asked if I could tell you myself and was given permission to do so."

"Wow. For a moment I had thought you were going to ask me to be your counselor. I was wondering how the people would react to that. They would probably think you did it because I was your son, not because I was who the Lord wanted."

"I think that is the very reason I have been so slow to hearken to His words. I wanted to be sure this call was correct. Now that I know it is, I am anxious to work with you. Whether or not the people accept you in this position is up to them, and largely up to how you labor in your calling."

"It is an odd situation. I don't think I've ever heard of a son being an elder's quorum president to his father."

"Me either. Well, will you do it?"

"Yes. Certainly. However, I want to talk to Princess first. I already know how she'll feel. But let me talk to her, and I'll let you know."

"I understand. I'm proud of you, son, and I know you will make a faithful elder's quorum president. If you accept, I'd like to put you to work immediately. You could be set apart by a member of the stake presidency this coming Sunday. Thank you for being a faithful member, and a wonderful son."

Sam had forgotten what it felt like to have the mantle of authority settle upon his shoulders. On his mission, his authority had been limited, and the burden was light to be born. The mantle of responsibility of being the elder's quorum president was a burden of considerable consequence.

His first task was to find two brethren to serve as his counselors. He studied the list of elders and was dismayed to find nearly ninety names, all but six of them inactive. Of those six, all but one already held responsible positions in the ward. The sixth came to church but refused to accept any positions. Most of the ninety had no addresses or phone numbers. They were merely names on a list. He prayerfully selected two brethren he had never met, drove to their homes, and succeeded in calling them to be his counselors. From the day of their calling, both brethren remained stalwart in the church and faithfully labored with him in the daunting task of creating a brotherhood from a list of unwilling names.

• • •

The rebel soldiers had been ordered to let all leave except Donavon and his family. In their haste to capture the man responsible for leading the retaliatory raid into their own villages, the generals had not identified Melody as Donavon's daughter. She had moved out nearly two years prior, and her presence was unexpected. Several of those attacking their home were former employees, who recognized her but said nothing, fearing implied guilt by prior association. Her release and subsequent escape from the country cost at least three of these former so-called friends, and one officer, their lives.

Their orders were to search all those leaving the farm to insure they were taking nothing valuable with them. When it came Melody's turn to be searched, their attention turned from finding valuables, to having their hands on her body. As repugnant as their rough groping was, it was totally ineffective, and she left with a small collection of gems embedded in a plastic clip in her hair. It was not a lot, but it would just be sufficient to see her to England.

Donavon had had many friends in South Africa—mostly people who had profited substantially from his frenzied purchases during the years of his wealth. She quietly contacted these until she found one willing to help her—for a price of course.

Melody booked passage on a steamer. She did not have a passport and could not pass through customs at any airport. Discrete inquiries found a captain of a small freighter who would take anyone anywhere for a price. Once he learned she was a refugee from Rhodesia his sympathies were aroused, and he accommodated her comfortably on the long voyage. He, however, did not lower his price.

The passage to England was uneventful except that she had nothing but her violin and the clothing she wore. She was forced to wash her dress in the sink in her cabin and let it dry before she could once again emerge. During the two-week voyage she spent many sweaty days cooped up inside her cabin waiting for her long black dress to dry in the humid heat.

Her arrival in England was unceremonious. She simply walked off the gangway and down a narrow street. There was no one there to meet her, no one she could contact, and nowhere to go. It was true that Marcia was in England, but Melody was not even sure what city she was in. Since Marcia had joined the Church she had moved to a new apartment closer to the chapel, which had been some thirty miles away in a different city. Which city, Melody could not even guess.

Melody's only money was a few South African rand. Even in a large bank, it was difficult to exchange rand for pounds. No bank anywhere would exchange less than one hundred rand, and she had far less than that. They were, for all intents and purposes, worthless pieces of paper.

When she had asked the captain of the ship to exchange them for any amount of local currency, he had laughed at her, and told her there were better ways for a beautiful young woman to make money, "If ye know wha' I mean, missie," he said as he winked at her. More than merely leaving, she had fled from his ship in disgust.

Melody's only real advantage was in the simple fact that they had landed in England in the morning hours. She had eaten her last meal aboard ship a few hours ago, and would not be in desperate need of either food or lodging for most of the day. It was not much, but it would have to be enough.

The ship had landed her in the port of Swansea, Wales, a sizable city, yet not a usual destination for ships bearing passengers. As a result, the waterfront was a narrow strip of piers and warehouses jammed against the ocean. It was an ideal location for anyone without a passport because there were no customs agents within three hundred miles.

A few blocks inland all trace of the waterfront vanished into a dirty slum. Melody kept to the busiest streets she could find, and felt very grateful she was not making this foot journey at night. Many people stared, a few asked questions, several even offered directions. Not a soul threatened her. She walked swiftly toward the busier part of the city, not sure what she planned to do, but compelled to escape the squalor of this section of the city.

In a short time she began passing small shops, clothing stores, and other signs of culture. By the time she found the main business district she was very tired, thirsty, hungry, and disheartened. She had been able to keep her courage up while she had a goal, but now she was without a clue as to what she should do.

The young, frightened refugee sat on a bench near a small park and kicked off her shoes. Her feet ached from the long, hot walk. She watched the bustle of the big city, and studied the faces of people walking by. Though fearful, she was very glad to be safely among people who had no intention of either exploiting her desperation, capitalizing on her beauty, or arresting her for her political leanings.

While she rested, Melody took stock of her assets. They were pitifully few. She had nothing, knew no one, and had no passport, no work papers, no money, and no way of getting any. She was unwilling to prostitute her body for money, and could not think of anything else she had except her violin.

Thinking of the precious instrument brought her a concern, and she opened it for the first time since boarding the ship. She had packed it with several bags of table salt to keep it dry. These she pulled from the case and set aside. She lifted the instrument and turned it over to inspect it. Thoughts of having to sell or pawn it filled her with sadness.

The afternoon sun reflected off the highly polished surface in rich reds and browns. When she was satisfied it was in perfect condition, she plucked at the strings to satisfy herself that they had not grown limp from moisture.

"Do you know any Mozart?" she heard a man's voice ask her. She looked up to see an old, kindly-faced gentleman leaning on a cane. He was not much taller than she, and spoke with what seemed to be a German or Swiss accent. She quickly concluded his question was completely innocent, and meant nothing more than the actual words he spoke.

"I do," she replied. Then as if struck by her instructor's baton, she suddenly realized what he was asking. He wanted to hear some Mozart, not just learn whether she knew any.

She stood slowly, looked around self-consciously, and quietly tightened the strings until they were in perfect pitch. She suspended her bow over the strings without any sure idea what she would play.

At that moment a lively polka, well loved, and oft played, came to mind. It was too showy, she thought, and tried to force it from her mind, but it persisted. Without any other thought than to quickly get this over with, she drew the bow quickly downward. The music danced out into the park, its clarion tones and obvious quality apparent to everyone who heard. As she played, other passersby walked up slowly. Initially she played simply to fulfill his request, but shortly she was playing for the simple joy of the music, and for the great peace it filtered into her soul.

The polka ended happily, and people clapped. Melody opened her eyes to see about ten people applauding. She curtsied politely, which looked very old fashioned in England and brought a chuckle of delight from those watching.

The old man who had requested the piece stepped forward and dropped a five-pound note into her open case. She looked at it in surprise and almost handed it back. She didn't want him to pay her for her music. She had accommodated his request as a favor.

As if he had just purchased a ticket to a concert, he requested another piece by Strauss, the beautiful Emperor Waltz. It was a piece she had played many times, though never as a solo. However, it was well within her range of talent to improvise as she played. She played with fervor, and a man and woman began waltzing on the grass.

Others dropped in paper money and coins, and made their requests. She had so much fun playing for such a happy and appreciative audience, that she had not noticed her case filling with bills and coins. The older gentleman who had first asked her to play stepped forward and stacked most of the bills, leaving a few in the case. He folded them carefully, and handed them to her.

"Never leave too many in the case, and always leave just a few. Come here during lunch time and afternoon to early evening only. Never stay after seven p.m. There's a clean little hotel called

The Royal Roost several blocks north on Queens Avenue, with a little café in the lobby. I'll come check on you tomorrow." So saying, he bowed slightly, took one step backward, turned and walked quickly away. Though the walking stick clicked on the pavement, it seemed as if he hardly needed it. His instructions surprised her, yet she was grateful for the advice, and did exactly as he suggested.

The lunch hour ended shortly thereafter, and people simply stopped walking in the park. She counted her little pile of bills and was amazed to find over one hundred pounds in various notes. With a racing heart she walked north and found the hotel and café. She ate a simple meal, hired a small room, and fell onto her bed in exhaustion.

That evening Melody played from five P.M. to seven, exactly as the old gentleman had suggested. During that time she made another 126 pounds. That evening the park was alive with jugglers, mimes, musicians, pundits of politics, and hucksters of religion. She was in good company, and enjoyed the fact that she was one of many doing the same thing.

The following day the old gentleman reappeared as promised. He paid her another five pounds after she had played several of his requests. He nodded, smiled and limped away without a word.

That evening she started early, eager to find the best spot. She played with extra fervor, and found her take growing larger. When seven o'clock came, people were still listening, and she played on until nearly eight.

After finishing the final number, Melody noticed that at least half of those listening were ragged young men who were looking at her in the wrong way. She quickly packed her instrument and started away. For a moment she was lost in the evening rush of people, but when she turned onto Queens Avenue, they were there before her. She turned around and found herself facing more of them.

$\bullet \quad \bullet \quad \bullet$

As the mantle of his office fell upon Sam something unexpected occurred, and that was the beginnings of the sure understanding of the Lord's will concerning His quorum.

Sam began to exercise himself in obedience, and small miracles began to occur. After all, it was the Lord's priesthood, and however important his calling as elder's quorum president might be, it was subservient to He whose priesthood it was. As he obeyed, Sam's faith grew in the Lord's willingness to use him as His servant, and miracles began to occur.

Friday evening found Sam driving home from work. It was late, and he was tired. It was his habit to visit a different member of the ward each day on his drive home from work. Sam had made it his goal to know every member of his quorum by the end of the year. Even though their ward area was immense, those for whom Sam actually had addresses lived within an hour's drive from his home. His ambition was to visit a new member of his quorum every day on the way home from work. However, because he was especially tired this evening, he had convinced himself to go straight home.

The long shadows of summer were warming the verdant green landscape as Sam made his way home. He drove slowly, enjoying the idea of coming home an hour earlier and surprising Princess. As he approached the turn off to a small subdivision he felt a sudden urging to turn in. He signaled, slowed, and turned into the subdivision. Under the urging of the Spirit he turned left, then right, and then left into a driveway. He was pleased to see the name of a family he recognized. He had not previously known where they lived. This would be a pleasant visit, since they were active in the church, and stalwarts in the ward.

As he approached the house it felt cold and dark, as if someone had left a window open to a winter breeze. He rang the bell and waited.

"Oh, Brother Mahoy," Sister Williams said in an ironic tone. "I'm surprised to see you here? What can I do for you?"

"Sister Williams, I'm here because the Lord sent me. May I come in?"

She hesitated. "Well, sure. Brother Williams is in the living room," she said, gesturing that direction. Sam walked the three steps into the living room to find Brother Williams sitting on the sofa hunched over. He stood slowly as Sam entered and came around the coffee table to shake his hand. There was an atmosphere of tension and sadness in the air which chilled Sam.

"President Mahoy, to what do we owe this visit? Here, take a seat," he said, pointing toward a large chair.

"You owe it to the Lord, Brother Williams. I was on my way home and was directed to swing in. You will have to tell me why I'm here."

Brother Williams glanced at his wife, and then sat back on the couch, resuming the cowered posture Sam had seen upon first entering.

"Well," Sister Williams began. "Perhaps it's just as well. We sent the kids away for the evening so we could have time to ourselves. We have been sitting here all afternoon discussing our divorce."

An electric moment came and went. "I see," Sam replied, suddenly filled with the Spirit, energized with truth, and the mantle of his office. "As you are aware, I am your quorum president, and have priesthood stewardship over your family.

"I know that sometimes couples split up, and sometimes it's not only justifiable, but also necessary. I don't know what has brought you to this dilemma, and don't mean to be judgmental in any way. However, since the Lord interrupted my journey home to come visit you at this critical moment, how do you suppose He views your plans to divorce?"

It was a startling question, and Sister Williams lowered her head, her eyes pooling with tears. Sam thought her reaction was one of sadness, but quickly changed that estimate to defiance and frustration. Brother Williams straightened as if a new hope had suddenly entered him. "I would say, He doesn't want us to split up," he said with conviction.

"Why do you say that?" Sam asked.

"Well, he wouldn't send you over here to urge us on, or to help us break up. It could only be that he disapproves."

"What do you think, Sister Williams?" Sam asked quietly.

She seemed stunned into silence. Her mouth moved, but no words came out. The Spirit moved within him, and he knew it had been her idea, and upon her insistence they were considering divorce. She wanted out and was reluctant to have that plan aborted.

"Sister Williams, do you mind if I ask you a question or two?" Sam asked. Without looking up she shook her head from side to side.

"Do you love the Lord?"

Her head snapped up, then lowered slowly. With fervor she said, "I do."

"Do you think He loves you?"

"Oh yes, I know He does," she replied with equal emphasis.

"If He asked you to give up your life for Him, would you do it?"

"In a heartbeat," she said, and she meant it.

"Would your eternal reward be better or worse for having given your all to obey His will?"

"Better by far," she replied.

"Let me ask you again. In the light of His having sent me here to your home, what is His attitude toward your divorce?"

"I think he is repelled and sickened by the idea," she said. The intensity of her answer surprised both Sam and Brother Williams.

"Regardless of whether you understand why, are you willing to have faith in His love for you, and obey Him in this matter of your divorce?"

"Do you really think we can be happy?" she asked pointedly.

"That isn't the question. The question is one of obedience. Even so, do you really think he would send you down a path designed to make you unhappy?" Sam asked with tenderness. She did not answer his question.

Sam stood and walked to the kitchen, picked up a wooden chair and set it near the sofa.

"Sister Williams, I have a blessing for you, if you'll receive it." She looked startled, then stood and walked slowly to the chair. She glanced up at him before she sat. Tears streaked down her cheeks. Her face was sober, resigned, and fearful.

Sam placed his hands on her head and waited for the glow of the Spirit to fill him. After a long moment it came upon him so powerfully it gave him a sense of great courage. It took him a moment to recognize that it was courage he was feeling. This was the second time he had felt this empowering emotion in response to the Holy Spirit. The first time had been on a train in the bush lands of Botswana, expecting to die at any moment.

"Sister Anna Williams, in the name of Jesus Christ, and by

His holy priesthood, I give you a blessing this day according to the will of God, and under the direction of His Holy Spirit. For your sake, and as a witness unto you of the source of your anger and adverse will, I rebuke the power of evil within you and command it to depart.

"Sister Williams, you are a precious daughter of Heavenly Father, beloved of Him, and glorious in His sight. All God's children, with the exception of Christ himself, have at times succumbed to the influences of darkness. This is not an indictment against your goodness, or an indication of your worth, but is a result of poor choices on your part. You have long listened to the anger within you until you have accepted this anger as your own. Yet, you are not an angry spirit, and have been tricked into thinking of your anger as justified, or worthy, at times, even righteous.

"Feel the liberty of being free, and rejoice in the purity of your native sweetness. It has been many years since you last felt it this pure and strong. I admonish you that from this day, and on throughout your life, that you rebuke this dark influence whenever it presents itself. Never again yield to its fury, for the choice is yours.

"Without doubt, and according to divine law, it will return. Satan and his angels have a divinely decreed right to infest our minds and hearts. Your anger will return after a brief absence caused by this blessing. But, know that it is within your power to keep it from taking residence in your soul again. The choice was, is, and forever will be, yours.

"Your lack of happiness literally has nothing to do with your marriage but is a function of your yielding to the influences of darkness. Awaken your spirit, put on your beautiful garments, adorn your spirit with flowers and sweet perfume, and go forth henceforth in the glow of your premortal beauty. For great you were, and great you are, and glorious shall be you reward hereafter if you heed the council of this day.

"I seal upon you this blessing according to divine guidance, and according to the stewardship of my office, in the name of Jesus Christ, Amen."

Sam hadn't realized until he said the word Amen that she was sobbing. She stood to find her husband standing before her with open arms. She fell into them with a sob. Sam heard her whispered apologies as Brother Williams soothed his wife with words of love.

"Brother Williams," Sam said at the appropriate moment. "It's your turn." For just a moment Brother Williams looked surprised, as if there was no need. Yet, there was much power in the room, and he nodded in submission and took the chair.

"Brother Williams, in the name of Jesus Christ, and according to His will I also give you a blessing, a promise, and a warning. You are not blameless in the darkness that has overcome your home. This is your stewardship, and you have walked away in fear and resignation when you should have been fearless in doing that which is right. You have let your fear of your wife's anger drive you from your position as head of this home. In the name of Jesus Christ I command you to reclaim it. It is your right to preside, and you must act in that responsibility in order to be exalted. Even though this anger originated from your wife, your response to it has been far less valiant than it should have been.

"You are a noble son of God, and a spirit of intelligence and unusual faith. Your love for your wife extends beyond this world, and has literally existed for millennia. Had you allowed your timidity and fear to end this love relationship which has existed so long, and has been a delight to your Heavenly Father, you would not have found true happiness in this world, nor the world to come. My visit here today has been as much to save you from this eternal blunder, as to save your love from destruction.

"Arise, awake, and stand in the office where you have been called. Love your wife without reservation or qualification. Expect nothing, give everything. Teach your children by precept and example. Perform your church duties faithfully, and you shall open your eyes one day in the Celestial Kingdom of our God surrounded by your glorified wife and children and loved ones who shall for an eternity rise up and call you blessed.

"I seal upon you these blessings in the name of Jesus Christ, Amen."

Sam raised his hands from Brother Williams head and walked directly to the door. They did not notice him leave as they held one another and wept. Sam basked in the glow of the Spirit for days thereafter. It was the first time he had experienced the pure joy of perfect service. The distinction had never occurred to him before. Always before he had done as best he could. This time, for the first time, he had done precisely as Jesus Christ would have done had he been there Himself. He had acted with absolute honor, and rendered that service which is perfect and eternal. Had Christ Himself visited this troubled family, He would have done precisely the same. For the first time his service had truly been in the name of Jesus Christ, and it thrilled him beyond comprehension.

• • •

"Princess, can we talk a minute?" he asked as he wrapped his arms around her waist from behind. They were just finishing cleaning up the kitchen. Sam enjoyed working in the kitchen with her. This kind of surprised him, because he had hated it as a child. But there were two great paybacks for helping Princess. First, he got to be around her that much longer. Second, no matter how many times he helped, she never seemed to expect it, and was always truly grateful.

"Love to," she said as she dried her hands.

They walked to the sofa facing the piano and sat so that their knees were touching. Sam was thoughtful for a moment before speaking. "I learned something today, and I wanted to share it with you while it was fresh on my mind."

"Tell me about it," she replied with interest.

"Well, I made a stop at a member's home under the direction of the Holy Spirit. It was wonderful."

"You've done that before," she observed. "I know how hard you try to be completely obedient to the promptings you receive."

"Well, I do most of the time," he said. "But, tonight something was different. It was almost as if I was a spectator there. I went in and the Spirit was so strong that I knew exactly what to do, and what to say. I gave them both blessings, and the words were profound and I know will be honored by the Lord. The startling thing is that as I was leaving I had this overwhelming sense of pleasure from the Lord. I have never felt such power."

"What kind of power do you mean?"

"It was the kind of power that comes from absolute faith. If God would have commanded me to move a mountain

I would have simply turned and ordered it to move. And, it *would have*. That's the thing that's so startling. I know for an absolute fact that it would have moved. If He would have told me to raise the dead, or stop the world from turning, or to call down a pillar of fire, it would have happened. I have never felt faith like that. It was absolute."

"Wow," she said as she placed a hand on his knee. "I've never felt anything like that."

"Until tonight, I hadn't either. Actually, that isn't the part I wanted to talk about."

"There's something better?" she asked, a little astonished.

"I don't think better, just important. You see, I know why it happened. I know why this absolute faith came to me."

"I'd like to hear what that was. I want to try it."

"It was because for the briefest moment in time I was absolutely obedient. I had placed my life, my will, my whole being into His hands. I have flawlessly obeyed every prompting I have received for weeks. And, as a result of walking in the Spirit so closely day and night for weeks, I finally arrived at the point where I could do precisely as Christ would have done had he been there himself."

Princess laid her hand atop his and looked into his eyes. "I think I understand what you are saying. It's kind of like becoming so obedient that your acts actually become identical with what the Savior would do if he were there himself."

Sam nodded, leaned back in the sofa and crossed his legs loosely. After a moment he said. "That's exactly the way I see it. It was fantastic, Princess! It was the most spiritually fulfilling experience of my life. I have finally tasted the sweet fruits of service, and it is sweet beyond my ability to comprehend it. It has filled me with an overwhelming desire to have this blessing again, and again."

"I have no doubt but you will," she replied with surety.

"I hope so. The interesting thing is how difficult it seemed to achieve, and how many small obediences it took to qualify for this great blessing. However, now that I have experienced it, it seems so natural and beautiful, and simple. It makes me wonder why I took so long getting to this point." He studied his hands for a moment before continuing. "It occurs to me that this is the fullest meaning of the phrase, 'In the name of Jesus Christ.'"

"That's an interesting thought. I'll bet it is," Princess agreed. She loved having these conversations with Sam not only for the spiritual blessing they were to her, but because she got to experience the most profoundly significant part of her spouse. She did everything she could think of to make these discussions last longer. "We seem to say 'In the name of Jesus Christ,' for about every act we perform in the Church."

"That's true," Sam responded thoughtfully. He interlaced his fingers behind his head and stared at the ceiling. "I'm sure the way it's used in the Church is completely acceptable to Heavenly Father. But, it makes me wonder if that phrase doesn't actually carry a much heavier burden of meaning. And, if it does, it makes me wonder if we shouldn't be seeking to fulfill its higher implications."

Sam's voice took on a tone of wonderment. "The way we use it it's almost like saying 'Okay, that's all I wanted to say,' rather than, 'I have just spoken by revelation, and the words I spoke were from Jesus Christ Himself.' There's a big difference between the two."

Princess glanced at her husband, and then returned her gaze to the highly polished side of the grand piano. She could see their combined reflections in the curve of its glossy blackness. Their reflections almost seemed to merge into a single image. It felt symbolic to her at that moment. "I remember wondering about this very thing when I was taking the missionary lessons. Can't remember the missionary's name who taught me, but he made a comment that may be valid."

"You never can tell what a missionary might say in the heat of a teaching frenzy," Sam said with a tone of feigned cynicism.

"True, so true," she agreed in mock seriousness. "Anyway, that nameless missionary said that many things were true on various levels. He said that even in the Church things were understood on different levels, and each level could be true. Even the child who stands up and closes a talk he read in the name of Jesus Christ, even when he didn't understand a word he just read, is still speaking in Christ's name."

"I believe that," Sam allowed. "I'm just concerned that it

has taken me so many years to gain a higher understanding of the meaning of those words. In reality, to hear someone truly, correctly say 'In the name of Jesus Christ' at the end of a talk, should literally send chills of spiritual ecstasy up our spines. We should correctly interpret that benediction to mean 'I have spoken as Christ would have had He been here Himself.' To correctly make such a statement would have a profound effect upon every listener."

Princess scooted toward him and laid her head on his chest. He wrapped an arm around her and kissed the crown of her head. "I get those sometimes," she said softly.

"What?"

"Thrills of spiritual ecstasy up my spine," she replied just as softly.

"Really? When?" He laid his cheek on the top of her head.

"Whenever I think of spending eternity with you."

Chapter Seven

The Threshing Floor

"What do you want?" Melody demanded as bravely as possible, her voice tremulous with fear.

"We wan' yer money, sweetie," one of them said.

"An, maybe we wan' somethin' moah, too," a bigger one announced with a grin. "You are about the prettiest bloody organ grindah ah've evah seen. It's obvious yer not from around heah, an, ya didn' know ya had te pay us, in order te play in our pahk. But, ya do, see?"

"I didn't know that. I honestly didn't" Melody said quickly, terrified. "I can pay. How much do you want? I'll pay you, just please don't hurt me."

"Oh, ye'll bloody pay, missie. But, ya messed up, an' ya gotta pay it all, or we gonna bust up yeh little fittle, and have some othah fun with ya. So give it all ovah. Now!" he shouted.

Melody jumped and dug handfuls of bills from the pockets of her dress. She was about to hand them over when upon sudden impulse, she tossed them into the air. The bills scattered in the light evening breeze. Her attackers cursed, and dove after the substantial quantity of fluttering money. Melody turned instantly and ran the opposite direction.

"Hey!" someone shouted. "She's gettin' away! Scooter! Devin! Catch the wench. We ain't done wi' 'er!" he ordered. Instantly, two of them sprang after her. One glance over her shoulder told her they were significantly faster than she, and her heart fell. She raced toward the nearest intersection where she could see cars passing in the approaching dusk. She knew she could not possibly beat them there.

A mere two paces separated them when a side door in one of the buildings opened and an old gentleman stepped backwards into the street.

"Good night, Melvin," he called into the building, and pulled the door closed with a bang. He turned just in time to catch her in his arms. She nearly knocked him over, but he spun around nimbly and kept them both standing. As he spun around his cane from flew into the air and came down hard on the right shoulder of one of her pursuers. The action was so sudden it appeared an accident. The young thug fell to the ground groaning, clutching his shoulder.

"Oh! So sorry!" he exclaimed, bending over the young man on the ground. "I was in such a dither to have this handsome young lady crash into me, that I'm afraid I've dashed you with my cane. Are you all right?" he asked earnestly.

The ruffian still standing took a dancing step toward him, his hands punctuating the air in jabs of anger. "Hey, old man! You beta' walk awai' from this, oah' . . . what the bloo . . .!" His curse was cut off when the old man's cane flashed out and cracked loudly against his left knee. The street thug crumpled to the cobblestones with a yelp.

"I'm so sorry! I'm just mortified. It seems my cane doesn't like you. Perhaps you'd best leave, so my cane doesn't express its unhappiness with you any further, hmm?" he said in a voice of perfect calmness.

With the sudden appearance of this unexpected help, Melody's fear had turned from fear for herself, to fear for the old gentleman. However, upon seeing his composure, and the speed and precision with which his able cane expressed its dislike for her assailants, she grew calmer.

"Let's leave these gentlemen to nurse their wounds, shall we?" he said casually to her. He took her elbow and they walked slowly away as if taking a stroll to enjoy the cool of the evening. He did not look back, but merely chatted amiably about the weather until they reached the intersection and turned toward her hotel.

"I thought I suggested you not stay in the park after seven," he said as pleasantly as he had discussed the weather. It wasn't until that moment that she recognized him as the same gentleman who had first asked her to play Mozart in the park. He was dressed differently tonight, and was wearing a hat.

"It's you!" Melody said in amazement, looping her arm a little tighter around his.

"You didn't recognize me? I'm abashed," he winked, then chuckled happily. "You do remember my instructions," he asked.

"I'm sorry. I guess I got greedy, and stayed longer. I am sorry," she replied contritely, almost the same as she might have if he had been her father.

"Well, no harm done, except you lost all your money. I see you did retain your instrument," he noted happily, indicating the violin case still securely tucked under her arm.

"Yes, I'm very lucky to not lose it. I really have no other . . ." she stopped, embarrassed to admit it was her only hope for survival.

"You do play so very well," the mysterious gentleman said cheerfully as they stopped at the bottom of the steps to her hotel.

"There you are my dear. Now, if you like, there's another park exactly four blocks east of here. I suggest you perform there tomorrow, and then come back here the following day. Follow that pattern, and don't get greedy, and all will be well. Are you quite able to make it to your room?"

"I am. I'm truly indebted to you, sir." She paused, cocking her head to one side, partly in apology, yet also in interest. "I don't even know your name. I'm Melody, Melody MacUlvaney." She offered her hand, which he took in a warm, sure grip. She was surprised to find his hands strong and steady. It seemed inappropriate to his age and heightened her curiosity regarding him.

His smile was warm, his voice cheery. "Melody. What a beautiful and fitting name for one who plays so beautifully, and who is so beautiful as well. I am thoroughly charmed to meet you. Well, Melody, I bid you a very good evening," he said. Lifting his bowler from his head, he nodded formally and turned back the direction they had come.

"Good evening, and thanks again," she called to him. Without turning around, he raised his cane in the air, and twirled it slightly in response. It was almost as if he were saying "no big deal." It made her chuckle.

It wasn't until she was safely inside her room that Melody realized he had not told her his name.

The old gentleman met her each morning regardless of which park she played in. After four days she had sufficient money to move on. Her most pressing need was to find her sister. She still had no idea how to accomplish that.

• • •

Princess went into labor late on the afternoon of July 3, 1976. They rushed to the hospital in Palmer, a short thirty-minute drive away. They were admitted to the maternity ward, checked in, and assigned a room in a matter of minutes. Princess changed into a gown and settled in for a long, frustrating wait.

Sam's mother arrived minutes later, and walked past Sam with little more than a concerned smile. She placed her hand on her daughter-in-law's forehead, smiled at her in a knowing way, and was thereafter in charge. Even the nurses bowed to her authority. Sam held onto his wife's other hand and spooned chunks of ice into her mouth. It was the extent of his duties. In a way, he was glad for the calm confidence his mother brought into the room. He certainly knew Princess appreciated it. Beneath his wife's calm exterior, she was terrified.

In another way, in a way too instinctual to even understand, he resented it. This was his baby being born, his night of joy and fear, wonder of wonders, and he was reduced to spooning ice as if he had suddenly become a moron barely able to do anything more complicated. It was almost as if he was the criminal who had caused his beloved wife this pain in her life, and he was not to be trusted with anything more important, lest he mess that up too.

To his astonishment, the more intense the labor became, and the more his beloved cried out in pain through clenched teeth, the more he felt isolated from the only women he had ever loved. It was as if the very process of birth climaxed in an irony of rejection of the poor fool who had contributed to the pregnancy.

But Sam wanted with all his heart to be there and knew his feelings were childish, no matter how many millennia men had been feeling them. Every time she became paralyzed in pain, and then fell back on her bed in sweaty exhaustion, he felt as if another thread had been torn from his heart. The only thing that kept tears from coursing down his own cheeks was the odd need he felt to present a courageous face.

Time became a blur of Princess's pain, his tangled emotions, and ice cubes. When he finally realized something was wrong, he was the last one in the room to comprehend it. The clock on the wall said 8:02 A.M. Princess had been in hard labor for sixteen hours. Yet the baby was not ready to be born. The heart monitor on the baby showed it was in distress. Doctors began coming through the door with increasing frequency, then huddling outside to consult one another.

Finally, a woman in a white coat walked through the door and approached Princess's bed. Sam stood as she entered. Somehow, everyone knew this was a pivotal moment, and this new woman was here for something important.

"Princess. Mr. Mahoy. My name is Doctor Sally Green," she said in a conversational tone. "Before the next contraction begins, I need to talk to you."

Princess pushed a pillow behind her head so she sat a little more upright. Her face was ashen, her hair soaked with sweat. Her hands trembled as she shook the doctor's hand. "What's going to happen?" was her only question to the doctor.

"You are not progressing as expected. The baby should have been born by now. Both you and the baby have reached a critical stage. You both may be in shock. I have consulted with your attending physician, and we feel it is time to deliver your baby by Cesarean. Do you know what this means?"

"Yes," Princess replied calmly, though Sam thought there was an increase of fear in her eyes. "I know what a Cesarean operation is. Do you know how to do them?"

"I am an obstetric surgeon. I have performed many Cesareans. There is nothing for you to worry about. The hospital is equipped for the operation, and I am ready to perform it. All I need is your consent and we will begin. You will be given anesthesia. You will wake up in what will seem to you like minutes later, and it will be all over."

"That sounds wonderful," Princess said weakly.

"Good. Let's begin then," Doctor Green said as she turned to give instructions to the two nurses standing behind her.

"No," Princess said emphatically. The room fell into immediately, heavy silence.

"Excuse me? What did you say?" Dr. Green asked in a shocked tone.

"I said—no."

"But, Mrs. Mahoy, if we don't do this procedure, I cannot guarantee your baby's safety. I think it is essential for your own welfare as well."

"I'm sure it is," Princess replied wearily.

"Then, why do you object to the procedure?"

"I don't object to the procedure," Princess began, but her reply was cut off by the onslaught of a tremendous labor pain. She doubled over, then relaxed and puffed through her teeth. The contraction lasted nearly two minutes, which seemed to all present like two eternities.

"Please continue to explain your objection," Doctor Green urged as soon as Princess fell back onto the sweaty sheets.

"I don't object to the procedure. I object to you doing it," Princess replied, her voice small, but determined.

"I am the only qualified surgeon in this hospital. It's a small hospital, and there is no one else here. I don't understand."

"I object on the grounds that you perform elective abortions. I don't want the same hands who take life from babies, to give life to my baby. I don't mean to be rude, but I am not willing to have you operate on me, or my baby."

Doctor Green walked up to the side of the bed and leaned over until she and Princess were eye to eye. "If I don't operate, I believe you and your baby will die. I'm sorry you object to my abortion practice. In my opinion it is immaterial. We don't have time to debate the moral issues surrounding abortions. You and your baby don't have any time left. I suggest you set aside your prejudice and let me help you. Do you understand?"

Princess did not blink an eye as she replied. "It's you who does not understand, Dr. Green. This baby inside me is no more precious than any of the hundreds you have killed in the pursuit of making money.

"If I let you deliver this baby, you will walk away feeling justified in your heart because you saved one. Because of that, you will go on to kill more, perhaps hundreds or thousands more. Don't you see? I can't let my baby's life grant you justification for killing others. If my baby's death will save a thousand other little babies, then it's a small price."

Sam was nearly beside himself with panic, and pushed himself between the doctor and his wife. His first impulse was to beg her to reconsider, to let the doctor help, not to sacrifice herself in a battle she could not win. His objections were stilled when he saw the calm determination in her eyes. Anything he might have said was swept away as another contraction gripped her.

"I regret your decision. If I had time, I would seek a judge's order to force you to let me operate. But there is no time. I will remain in the hospital for a time if you change your mind," she said, and turned to leave.

Princess spoke through teeth clamped tight in pain. Her voice was nearly impossible to understand, yet the message was heard very clearly by the doctor. "Perhaps in a short time I will meet our Eternal Judge personally. The idea brings me peace. One of these days you will meet Him, too, and it terrifies me for you."

Her words brought the doctor to an abrupt halt. She stood there for the briefest time as if frozen in mid-stride. Just as suddenly, she lifted her chin and left the room.

As soon as she was gone everyone began speaking at once. Sam, his mom, and nurses all began pleading with Princess. She simply ignored them, a look of ashen calm on her face. One of the nurses began weeping and rushed from the room. Another wiped Princess's forehead gently, then walked slowly from the room.

"I'll be right back," Sam whispered to Princess, who seemed not to hear, and hurried from the room. He found a pay phone and made a dozen calls. His request was the same every time.

They began arriving only a few minutes later. About the third person to enter was his father, Jim Mahoy. Others came, many others. Less than thirty minutes after his first call almost a dozen priesthood holders surrounded Princess's bed. Sam was moved upon to ask his father to be voice in the blessing. Princess smiled as they placed their hands upon her and upon one another until they were all joined in the power of the priesthood.

Jim began in a whisper. "Princess, beloved daughter of God. We the elders of Israel combine our faith, and in the name of the Holy Messiah, and by the power of the Melchizedek Priesthood, we bless you with this one great blessing. You and your babies will survive this ordeal, and all will be as it should be. I seal this blessing upon you in the name of Jesus Christ, Amen."

A chorus of Amens was interrupted by the abrupt opening of the door to the small room. Doctor Green scuttled into the room with another doctor in tow by the sleeve. She plowed through the press of priesthood holders until she stood beside the bed.

"This is Doctor Green, my husband. He is a pediatric physician and has performed many delicate operations. He has never done an abortion and is philosophically opposed to them. He has assisted me in many Cesareans and has agreed to do it while I direct his every move. I will stand back and assist only. Will that satisfy your objection?" She sounded breathless, angry, and frustrated all at once. Her husband looked as if he had just been abducted by aliens.

A collective sigh of relief went up from the overfilled room.

"No," Princess replied breathlessly.

"Why not!?" the woman demanded angrily. "I won't be doing the operation, just assisting."

"Because your soul is still in jeopardy. You learn nothing. You still feel vindicated, and you still perform abortions. Nothing has changed."

"I can't stand here and let you and your baby die!"

"Babies," the Sam's father corrected.

"What?" At least four voices asked simultaneously.

"I said, there is more than one baby at risk. Babies. She is carrying twins."

"How could you know that?"

"I learned it in the blessing. Twins," he said with absolute surety.

Dr. Green had a look of panic on her face. "If that's true, it's even worse. I couldn't live with myself if I let you and your babies die. It isn't right!"

"Why are my babies any different? Women who opt for an abortion chose their baby's death. I choose the same for my own reasons. It's the same thing."

"It isn't the same!" Dr. Green objected loudly. "What you are doing just isn't right."

Princess's voice was breathy, barely a whisper. "Explain it to me. Why isn't it right?"

"Because your babies have a right to . . ." She stopped short.

"They have the right to live. I know they do, and I want that for them. But so do the thousands of others you will kill in your practice. Don't you see they all have the right to live."

"This is not the right time for philosophy!" She shouted. "You have very little time left."

"I have an eternity left. It's you who are out of time."

Tears began to spill down the doctor's cheek. "I don't want to be responsible for your death. I couldn't live with myself."

"I don't want to be responsible for the death of countless more. I couldn't live with myself," Princess replied, her strength gone. Another contraction gripped her, but she was too weak to deal with it and simply laid back, her eyes rolled up into her head. She had now been in labor nearly twenty hours.

"I will make you a deal," The doctor said loudly, hoping to get through to Princess.

Princess replied without opening her eyes. "You must make it with God. I will know when it is enough."

The doctor pushed herself away from the bed in frustration, spun around, and walked toward the door plowing into people with every step. She turned and returned to the bed in the same manner.

"Okay," she said.

"Whatever your deal is, it's not enough," Princess replied after a moment.

The doctor threw up her hands and repeated her assault on those in the room with greater energy. She stopped at the far side of the room, and placed her head in her hands.

Everyone waited with pounding hearts. All knew, including Doctor Green, that it was the final time she could make her arrangements with God. There was no more time for Princess and her babies. It was many minutes before she walked slowly back to Princess's bed. Time seemed to stand still, as if hours had passed in terrible waiting.

"Princess," she asked quietly. "Is it enough?"

Princess remained quiet, almost as if she had not heard. After a long moment she slowly moved her lips. "It is enough," they formed, almost without sound.

Doctor Green came to life, and began ordering people like a storm trooper. In less than two minutes Princess was under anesthesia and being prepped for the operation. The last thing Doctor Green said to Sam as she bolted past him was, "I'm afraid we have waited too long."

Before the double doors slammed behind her she heard him say, "God will guide you. She will live."

The doctor stopped and turned back toward him. She nodded before disappearing beyond. When he had said it he knew it with absolute surety.

As soon as the doctor disappeared, doubt began to assail him.

• • •

Saturday morning Melody's kindly old friend stood and listened to her entire morning concert. Afterwards he gave her ten pounds, roughly thirty US dollars. As people began to drift away he remained. It pleased her, for over the last few days she had begun to realize how much she owed him. She wanted to thank him, and also to pepper him with questions. She had it in her mind to loop her arm through his, and not release him until he had satisfied her curiosity. She was just brash enough to do it.

"Beautiful concert, Melody," he said with his light, continental accent.

"I'm pleased you enjoyed it. Would you have time to walk me to my hotel?"

"Delighted, my dear," he replied. "There's something I'd like to ask you."

"I have a question or two for you, too," she admitted, feeling smug that her plans were coming to pass so easily.

The old gentleman's face was kindly as he asked. "Why are you still here in Swansea? Don't you have sufficient funds to complete your journey?"

She found it an odd but insightful question. "Actually, thanks to you, I have more than enough. I'm still here because

I don't know where my sister lives. She's in England some-where, but she moved recently, and I don't know her address. I don't even know what city she's in."

"Why did she move without informing you?" he asked congenially.

Melody debated whether to give him a simple answer, or the long version. There was a lot of prejudice against Marcia's new religion, and she didn't want to offend or alienate her new friend by mentioning it.

"She just joined a new church, and she moved to be nearer to the chapel. I had her new address at one time, but I left home rather suddenly and didn't think to pick up the paper. I can't remember what city it was. England has so many oddly named cities."

"It does indeed. What church did you say she joined?"

"I didn't," she said, then added almost apologetically, "It was the Mormon church."

"Truly? I may know someone who can help. As a matter of fact, they're right there," he said, pointing across the park toward a small gathering of people.

It was so common for people to cluster around a per-former or actor, that Melody rarely paid much attention to little gatherings. She turned her attention to the group he indicated and saw a young man in a business suit and small black derby standing on a box, speaking. It seemed that someone in the audience was giving him a hard time.

"Who are they?" she asked.

"Why, they're Mormon missionaries," he said, his tone implying everyone on earth knew who they were. She gave him a remonstrative glance, and he hunched his shoulders as if she really should have known.

She gathered up her meager possessions and walked toward the gathering. She turned to ask her friend another question, but he was no longer near. She could see his gray head bobbing slowly away in the distance. She thought it odd that he had not even said good-bye.

"I don't know how many wives Brigham Young had," one of the missionaries was saying in an exasperated tone.

"How can you be a missionary for the Mormon church and not know?" the heckler wanted to know.

"Tell you what," the young man said in a heavy American accent. "When I get to heaven, I'll ask him."

"He's not in Heaven!" the heckler called back. This brought a roar of laughter from the crowd.

"Then you ask him," the missionary shot back. This brought an even greater roar of laughter. The heckler lost interest and left the group. After that, the missionaries delivered a message to the crowd that Melody found uplifting. It was, in fact, her first exposure to LDS doctrine. In the years since meeting Sam on the train, she had either not had the opportunity, or had not taken advantage of the ones she had had to learn more.

The crowd was dispersing and the two missionaries were just turning to leave when Melody interrupted them. "Excuse me," she said shyly.

They both turned toward her. They were slightly older than she, about nineteen or twenty, she guessed. One of them was tall and quite good-looking. The shorter one was freckle-faced and red-haired. He seemed to be their spokesman, and smiled at her. "Can we help you?"

"I don't know," she replied honestly. "I'm looking for my sister who just joined your church."

"What's her name?" he asked.

"Marcia MacUlvaney."

"Is she in this area?"

"I don't know what city she lives in."

"That makes it harder," he said soberly. "It's a big mission."

"I guess it was a long shot," she said sadly. "She's recently from Rhodesia, Africa," she added, hoping it would make a difference, "and she plays the violin."

"Elder," the taller one said, "Do you suppose that's the young woman President Farnsworthy spoke of at the last zone conference? Wasn't that a lady from Africa who played the violin?"

"Hey, I think he did say she was from Africa. It's worth checking into. Miss, if we can find a pay phone, I can call President and see if that girl is your sister. What do you think?"

"I would be ever so grateful. Please."

"Great!" the freckle-faced Elder said, sticking his hand toward her enthusiastically. "I'm Elder Johnston, and my companion here is Elder Fleur. We're both from America."

Melody shook both their hands with a sense of amusement mingled with gratitude. They were unusually helpful, as sincere as the Pope, and certainly seemed harmless.

"I'm pleased to meet you both."

"There's a post office a short distance from here," Elder Johnston suggested. "We could find a phone there. If we hurry we will probably catch our mission president still in his office."

"Thank you," she said as she took a place walking beside Elder Johnston as they hurried toward the middle of town. Nearby turned out to be nearly a quarter mile away. Her legs were aching from trying to keep up with them by the time they arrived.

Melody talked to President Farnsworthy, and they decided the woman in question probably was her sister; however, President Farnsworthy had no idea where she actually lived. He promised to find out. He would call the missionaries, and they would deliver the message to her. President Farnsworthy assured her she would have her sister's address sometime soon, possibly even tomorrow.

The missionaries were kind enough to escort her the considerable distance back to her hotel. During the whole journey they talked excitedly about someone named Smith, who had seen an angel, and had been given a golden book. They talked with so much animation in their thick accents that Melody had difficulty understanding their speech, and soon found herself lost. She was quite unsure what they were talking about, except that they believed it with all their hearts.

She made a shallow connection between the book Sam had given her father, and the gold book from the angel. Melody had never read the book, since Marcia had taken it with her when she left for England. If she had not, it would now be in the possession of the Rhodesian rebel army.

It took most of a week for the missionaries to deliver her sister's address. Each evening they met her in the park and escorted her to her hotel. During their walks they talked enthusiastically about various gospel topics. At first Melody tolerated it because they were helping her find her sister. After a time she began to enjoy these brief talks, and looked forward to them. The odd thing was that since the missionaries had begun escorting her home, she had not seen her friend, the older gentleman without a name.

Saturday she played in the park from noon to four p.m. By now she had a small following of people who regularly came to the park to hear her play. It was rare for one of such extraordinary talent to be a street musician, and her impromptu concerts drew fairly large crowds. She found that she collected so much money in a four-hour concert that she could not carry it home, and even feared being robbed. After several hours she closed her violin case, and refused further gifts.

The missionaries showed up around three, and politely worked their way through the crowd until they were nearly in front. They watched her closely, and closed their eyes in appreciation when she played especially beautiful passages.

Melody decided to give the two elders a treat, and searched through her memory for some music they might enjoy. She remembered a hymn her sister had played over and over after joining the Mormon Church. It seemed perfect.

Waiting for the applause to die down, Melody lowered her violin. Thinking she was through, a collective sigh of disappointment drifted across the gathering. "I have one more piece to play today. It's a church hymn, a song especially for my two friends. I hope you enjoy it."

Melody raised her bow, paused, and brought it down in a long minor strain that seemed to weep with anguish. Slowly, with tender care she played the music. She glanced up and saw tears in the eyes of both missionaries. She did not know the words, but they did, and they began to sing, quietly at first, and then with gusto. Elder Fleur had a rich baritone voice. It rose up in impassioned strains, and she felt the hair rising on her arms as a thrill of spiritual yearning passed through her such as she had never felt before. It was as if her soul had suddenly discovered it was emaciated from life-long starvation, and had just tasted its first sip of the very nectar of the gods.

> Come, come ye saints. No toil or labor fear.
> But with joy, wend your way.
> Though hard to you, this journey may appear,
> Grace shall be, as your day.

Gird up your loins, fresh courage take
Our God will never us forsake.
And soon we'll have this tale to tell,
All is well. All is well.

The music died in the autumn breeze, and Melody lowered her bow to appreciative applause. She had sat in grand halls and heard the world's finest voices. She had played in orchestras as virtuoso tenors thrilled thousands. But she had never heard anything like this.

This young missionary's voice wasn't trained. She knew he hadn't sat at the feet of a master teacher, and practiced scales endlessly until his voice was flawless. She doubted he had sung for more than a hundred people in any one room. Yet, she had never heard someone sing with more joy and passion. His voice had reached far beyond the furthest ears in a large concert hall. It had reached deep within the soul of all who heard.

It was the second time simple music had touched her soul at its greatest depth. The first time was on a train in Africa. The parallel between then and now was inescapable; both times the music had unexpectedly come from a young Mormon missionary.

People wandered away reluctantly. Melody laid her violin atop the pile of bills and succeeded in closing it only after stuffing several hands full into her pockets.

Elder Fleur waited until she looked up before speaking. His voice was husky with emotion. "Thanks, Sister MacUlvaney," he said, mispronouncing her name slightly.

"You're welcome, Elder." It tickled her that they insisted on calling her sister. It made her feel like a nun from a convent. Yet nothing she could say would dissuade them; She had finally given up.

"You were right," he continued. "It is one of my favorite songs. I hope you don't mind that I sang it. I didn't mean to butt in, but it just welled up in my throat, and I either had to sing, or burst," he explained.

Melody placed a slender hand on his arm. "I loved that you sang," she assured him. "I have to say that you have a beautiful voice."

Elder Fleur seemed quite abashed by the idea. "Oh, gosh.

I don't know. I just love to sing. I know I can make a lot of noise, but that's about it."

"Don't be so modest," she admonished happily. "You do have a beautiful voice. Even without training you caused the hair to rise on my arms."

"I always thought that was a bad thing," he replied with wide eyes.

"No!" she laughed. "No, what I mean is you touched my heart. I think what touched me was how much you love that song, more than how fine your voice is."

"Sister MacUlvaney," he replied earnestly, "It isn't that I love that song."

"What then?" she asked, genuinely perplexed.

"It's that I love the Lord. This song causes all my hope and faith to come in great bursts of happiness. That's what you're hearing; not my appreciation for a tune, but my love of all it stands for."

His words entered her heart with power. "I stand corrected," Melody said and bowed toward him from the waist. When she arose she could see he was genuinely perplexed by her response. She laughed, her voice not unlike sleigh bells on a windless winter's eve. She turned to walk and beckoned them to join her.

She stepped between them, handed her violin to Elder Johnston, and took each by an elbow. "As much as I know about music," she told them, "You have added a dimension I never realized before."

"What's that," they asked almost in unison.

"Great music expresses great passion. I have always known this. What you taught me is that the nearer the passion of the performer mirrors the passion of the composer, the greater, and more life-altering a performance becomes. I think we heard you sing just as the composer might have sung had he been here."

"That's a wonderful thought," Elder Fleur replied after another few steps, then turned to look at her. "I was just puzzled about why you bowed to me."

Melody stopped walking. Both young missionaries stopped, turning to face her. "To me, music is everything," she explained. "It is the food I drink, and the air I breathe. Music comforts me, feeds me, and gives my soul wings. Yet, I have never understood what you just revealed to me. What you taught me would be somewhat analogous to when one of your investigators accepts what you teach them. I bowed because it is the way I was taught as a child to acknowledge when someone has given me a great gift."

Both missionaries stared at her with wide eyes, then as if they had rehearsed it many times, they both bowed to her.

"What's this!?" she laughed.

Elder Johnston's eyes sparkled as he replied, "Pay-backs."

"Yeah," Elder Fleur added. "Every single time we see you playing in the park we leave blessed and spiritually fed. Whenever we feel discouraged, we come to the park because your music sustains us and feeds our souls. You see, you have given us a great gift as well; not once, but many times."

Having received plaudits all her life for her beauty, charm and considerable talent, Melody was still not prepared for their reply. Her eyes misted. She smiled happily and brushed a tear away with the back of her fingers. "Thank you," she said very softly.

Elder Johnston was about to say something else, when he suddenly remembered. "Oh! I almost forgot. We've got your sister's address," he said happily, and held out a copy of the Book of Mormon.

"What's this?" she asked with mock suspicion. She had twice refused to take a Book of Mormon.

Elder Johnston smiled slyly. "Well, we wrote the address in the fly leaf. See?" he said, holding open the book. There was an address, and a telephone number. Her heart leaped and she reached for the book, but he pulled it back.

"I know this is blackmail," he said in all seriousness. "But, I want you to have this book because it's true, not because it's got your sister's address inside. I don't care if you believe in it or not, I just want you to know why I want to give it to you. This book will eventually help you complete your life's journey. It will take you full circle. It is the most precious thing I possess, and I want you to have it." So saying, he held out the book.

Melody took the book in both hands, then shook her head in wonder. "What did you say?"

"Er—I'm not sure what . . ."

"I mean, about this book taking me full circle?" she inquired, her eyes narrowing.

"Yes, I think I said that. Did it offend you?"

Melody shook her head vigorously. "Not at all! Is this a common expression with Mormon missionaries?"

Both Elders looked at each other, then shook their heads. It was Elder Fleur who said, "I've never heard anyone say it before just now."

Melody looked at the book, thumbed to her sister's address, then looked back at Elder Johnston. "Why did you say that? What does 'it will take you full circle' mean, do you think?"

The young missionary shrugged. "Honestly, Sister Mac-Ulvaney, I have no idea. I was speaking from my heart, and the Spirit was upon me, and I just said it. I'm sorry, but I can't give you an explanation other than that it was the right thing to say."

Melody stared at him in deep thought before replying. "Elder Johnston, it was probably the only thing you could have said to make me accept this book—other than just to get my sister's address." She closed the Book of Mormon and held it before her with both hands.

"Thank you, Elders. I will not forget what you have said. I believe you when you say this book is precious. I couldn't have said that one minute ago. Perhaps in time I will understand why you said what you did. Until then, I will accept your words on faith."

Her eyes focused on a far distant memory. "I knew another young missionary in Africa named Elder Mahoy, who used those very words in a blessing he gave me. I believe that blessing saved my life. Some day I hope to understand both his words, and yours."

Elder Fleur's voice was husky. "That's really great, Sister MacUlvaney. Without knowing anything specific about your life, I can promise you in the name of Jesus Christ that this book is essential to your finding what you seek. I just know it with all my heart." His accent was a heavy American drawl, and it strummed pleasant memories in her heart.

"Thank you, Elder. I believe it is, too. Now, I just need to find out how."

They escorted her directly to the pay phone near the post office and she called the number they had written in the book. Her heart nearly stopped when she heard her sister's voice on the phone.

"Marcia!" she cried. But, before she could speak even one joyous word, she remembered that Marcia did not know. She had to swallow three times before she could make a sound come from her lips.

"Oh Marcia," she wailed. "Daddy is dead!"

• • •

The operation lasted three agonizing hours. When Doctor Green once again emerged through the double doors her face was drawn and weary. Except for his faith, Sam would have collapsed in an agony of sorrow. As it was, the look on her face was enough to tear at his fragile hope. Tears sprang to his eyes, and an terrible foreboding gripped his soul. He felt his knees folding beneath him. The doctor grabbed both his shoulders and lowered him back to his chair.

"Your faith has seen you this far. Don't give up yet," she said cryptically. "Princess has survived the operation. She shouldn't have. Three times she nearly bled to death, and three times we revived her. The second time we had no more blood. One of the nurses was her blood type and gave blood right there in the operating room. Each time I was on the verge of giving up, but something more powerful than logic urged me on.

"In the end, I would have to say that regardless of the seriousness of the procedure we performed, there was never any chance of her not making it. Her God has quite obviously delivered her from the jaws of death. She will have a long recovery, but she will be fine.

"We don't know what effect the severe blood loss will have on her, if any. She may suffer some memory loss, perhaps slight personality shifts, though I doubt anything severe. You can relax, Mr. Mahoy. You are the proud recipient of three miracles."

Sam sagged in his chair, his heart soaring in relief and silent prayers of thanksgiving. He didn't hear what else the doctor said until his father nudged him.

"What?"

Dr. Green was leaning forward, smiling. "I said, two of your miracles are identical twin daughters. They are perfectly healthy."

Sam was so amazed that his legs refused to support him further, and he dropped into his chair, stunned. "When can I see them?" He demanded.

Dr. Green frowned thoughtfully. "Princess is still under anesthesia. The babies will be in isolation for at least twenty-four hours. I suggest you go home and get some rest. Your wife won't be seeing anyone for at least twelve hours. Go get some rest."

Sam struggled to stand, and shook the doctor's hand. "Thank you very much for giving me back my wife, and new babies."

Dr. Green looked at him with some irony in her face. She merely nodded, and turned away as if in a hurry to be elsewhere.

Sam's family herded him to his car. His mind was in a fog of colliding thoughts and emotions. He would have happily gone home and slept for a small eternity, but was shocked to full awareness the instant he saw the driver's side window. Scratched deeply in the glass was a large "22."

Someone took him home and put him to bed. He slept for several hours in death-like exhaustion. But, the implication of the hated numerals on his car at the hospital, so near his family, terrified him. He hurried back to the hospital as soon as his mind and body could function.

They named the girls Lisa Laura Mahoy, with her middle name after Sam's mother, and Bonnie Marie Mahoy, her middle name after Princess's mother. Princess came home three weeks later. She was still too weak to care for the baby girls by herself. Sam's Mother moved in with them to help. The babies thrived.

Princess seemed barely to have the will to survive. She had to be urged to eat, urged to sit up, urged to breathe it seemed. She seemed to have little energy for her babies, though a look of love came on her face when she saw them. The first turning point toward recovery came when Grandmother Mahoy carried the twin girls to her, one in each arm. Princess was lying in bed, staring up at the ceiling.

"Princess, I have in my arms two little angels who have loved you since before time began. They depend on you for life itself. You have to eat, if for no other reason that so that your can nurse them. You chose life for them; now follow through on that commitment. You nursed them in the hospital, and they have thrived on your gift. But, I refuse to feed these precious little ones cow's milk, not when you have the milk of life to give them."

Princess's face changed. She smiled weakly, and without a word she struggled to sit up. Sam hurried to help her, but a warning look held him back. She pushed herself to a sitting position, a look of pain on her face. She held out her arms and took one of the babies. The little one fumbled anxiously, and with a little help, began nursing noisily. Mother Mahoy propped a pillow under Princess's elbow to support her arm, which trembled from the weight of the baby. The other little one soon found her meal on the other side, and began drinking as daintily as her sister was noisy. A smile formed on Princess's lips as she looked from one tiny face to another, an expression of love on her face.

Sam took a seat on the edge of the bed to watch this precious moment. In response, Princess shot him a withering glance. He stood as if shot by an arrow and left the room quietly. He went to his study and wept. He wept for happiness, sadness, joy, and tragedy. It was all more than he could endure. It was the first time Princess had ever looked at him with anything other than enduring love.

Princess slowly recovered, each day a little stronger. It was almost as if the babies fed her even as she fed them. In time she regained her health, and Mother Mahoy went home. But even after Doctor Green pronounced her physically well, Princess's former feelings of endearment for Sam seemed partly forgotten, or lost, or perhaps discarded.

• • •

That November the ward was divided and the Wasilla Second ward was formed. Sam and Princess lived within the boundaries of the new ward, while his parents stayed in the former. His father remained bishop of the old ward. Sam was immediately called to be elder's quorum president in the new ward. He rejoiced in the opportunity to serve, and pressed forward with determination. He and Bishop Dowling spent many evenings going from home to home, using somewhat the same methods his own father had used for so many years to build the wards in Downey and in Wasilla.

January of that year brought the worst winter storm ever recorded in the Matanuska Valley. On January 15th the temperature dropped to twenty-three below zero and a deep snow fell. The odd thing was that it was too cold to snow; usually it will not snow when the temperature is below freezing. The snow was light and crystalline, almost glass-like, and it fell until several feet of fine powder lay on the ground like so much glitter. Almost midnight on the next day the wind began to blow. It whipped up until the winds exceeded 120 miles per hour with gusts to 150. The big log house trembled as the winds hammered against it. The winds continued to pound the valley for nearly two weeks.

Sam's new home was thick and sturdy, but it was also large and hard to heat without electricity. The power went out within the first hour of the windstorm. Sam bundled up and brought in wood to stoke the big stove in the living room. The heat seemed to rise to the ceiling, leaving the floor cold and drafty. He brought Princess and the babies into the room with the stove and hung blankets in the doorway and across the stairs. The room slowly became tolerable, but hardly comfortable.

With no electricity they were left in darkness, and Sam quickly found he was unprepared for such things. Having only lived there for a few months he had yet to complete their food storage. They suddenly found themselves rationing things like matches, toilet paper, diapers, toothpaste, and drinking water. They had only a few candles and one kerosene lantern with one small bottle of fuel. The only thing that worked to their advantage was that their kitchen stove was propane and they had a full tank of fuel. Sam lit the oven and left the door open. He carefully monitored the level in the tank which went down much quicker than he liked.

Princess seemed to accept the situation with a stoic sense of fate. She kept the babies wrapped against her body for warmth and cared for them as best she could. Sam melted snow for water and chopped wood. They ate everything in the house until all they had was wheat, beans and canned goods of various unappetizing varieties. Sam ground the wheat to flour in a hand mill, and cooked it as many different ways as he could. The toilets in the house were frozen solid, and he set up a privy in the corner of the big room separated by curtains. Many times a day he took the bucket outside and emptied it.

The wind blew the powdery snow into great drifts as hard as concrete. One side of their house had a drift to the roof line. The drift grew around the house until the front door was blocked, then the windows. The only way to exit the house was through the garage doors. Every time he raised a garage door it felt as if the wind would take away the whole garage. The structure whined, and the roof rattled from the strain. He decided it was no longer safe to open those big doors.

Sam pried open the front door and shoveled a tunnel through the drift. After about ten feet he turned left and dug another six feet before breaking through. The opening faced away from the wind, and he could come and go without sending a gust of wind and snow into the house. Had he not had a sick wife and two newborn daughters, it might almost have been an adventure. Princess was getting sick of wheat and beans, and her milk was slowly dropping off for want of adequate drinking water. After two weeks they were on the last 15 percent of their propane tank. Sam reluctantly shut it off as a source of heat.

The winds died down to 40 mph on February 1st.

Sam knew they desperately needed supplies, and dressed up in everything he could put on. It was still nearly 30 below zero; with the wind chill it was well over 100 below zero.

"Princess, I'm going to try to get into town today," he said, walking up behind her. He placed his hands on her shoulders and kneaded them gently.

"Sam, please be careful. But come back in when you decide what you're going to do, so I don't worry, okay?"

"Of course. I'll go see if the Jeep will start."

"Be careful," she urged.

He made his way to the four-wheel drive Jeep. He had unwisely parked it outside the night of the big blow. It was buried in three feet of rock hard snow. He chipped open an area sufficient to open the driver's door. When he hit the starter the engine would not turn over, but gave off a screaming sound. He raised the hood and found the engine compartment completely white. Only the air cleaner was above the snow.

After warming himself by chopping some more wood, he returned with a screwdriver and chipped the snow out of the engine compartment. As soon as the fan was clear the faithful old engine roared to life. The cabin immediately filled with exhaust. He shut it off and dug away the snow from the tailpipe. By this time it was dark again, and he gave up.

The next day the wind was still blowing. He found the truck drifted back in, but this time the snow that had blown in was powdery. Sam started the truck, observed there was only a quarter tank of fuel, and shut it back off. With his snow shovel he chipped a narrow path through the solid drift until he came to an area nearly free of snow. In the fickle nature of snowdrifts, his truck was buried nearly three feet deep, and a hundred feet away, the ground was bare. He chipped ice-like snow for a whole day.

It was just twilight when he started the jeep and drove it without trouble onto bare road. In an Alaskan winter, twilight is around 3 in the afternoon. He went back inside to warm up.

"I've got the Jeep on the road. I'm going to make a quick trip into town," he informed her as he piled more wood by the stove.

"Is the road open? Can you make it into town?"

"It has drifts, but seems to be passable. If I encounter anything too big I'll turn around and come back."

Holding Lisa in her arms, Princess walked to the door with him. She was wearing Levis over pajamas, with a warm bathrobe over all that. She had one of his baseball caps on her head, and looked like a refugee. "Remember diapers, and please be careful."

"I will. Don't worry."

He brought with him a shovel, a candle and a blanket. He drove a short distance down their lane before encountering another drift several feet deep blocking the road. He got out and walked across the drift. It was as hard as stone. Carefully, he drove up onto it. It easily supported the weight of the jeep. The other side was an abrupt drop off of three feet. It had turned dark by the time he was able to dig a ramp off of it and drive onto solid ground.

Turning left was the shortest way into town. In the headlights of the truck he could see many small drifts, while the other direction seemed to have larger ones. Favoring the most direct route, he turned left. The first drift he came to was powdery. It dissipated in the wind as he drove through it. Each drift he came to was powdery and easy to get through, though the larger ones required some speed to blast through them.

He was about a hundred years from the intersection with the main highway when he came to a massive wall of snow. He got out and inspected what looked like the side of a mountain. The drift was taller than the telephone poles, and stretched as far as he could see in either direction. It was simply impassable. Had he not been shivering in 100-below temperatures, and desperate to get food for his family, he would have been amazed. As it was, he was disappointed to the point of explosive anger. He struggled to regain his emotional stability, and climbed back into the truck. He was nearly on an eighth of a tank. Under normal circumstances, it would be plenty to get him into town.

Sam turned around and retraced his tracks, now blown nearly to nonexistence in the wind. He passed their drive, and felt an urging to return home. He wondered if it was the Spirit or his own thinking, but shrugged it off. All he could think about was food for his family. The thought of Princess smiling at him as he carried in bags of groceries warmed him, and once again, he drove past their drive. She hadn't smiled at him much at all since the babies were born, and he was willing to brave winds and storms, or dragons if necessary, to have the joy of it again.

The road beyond their driveway was nearly bare. He could see the brown gravel underneath the layer of snow slithering across the road like a thousand white snakes driven by the winds. He came to the first big drift and eased the front of the Jeep into it. It was soft but too deep to drive through, and he got stuck. He easily backed out and got a short run at it. The snowdrift exploded into white fury, and vanished in the brisk wind. He drove through onto hard ground. The next drift was smaller and likewise vanished when he hit it. Drift after drift gave way to him, until he thought little of finding another crossing the road.

The biting cold was frosting his windshield even with the defroster blowing full blast. He periodically scraped the inside. The fuel gauge continued its plunge toward 'E'.

"Heavenly Father, I really need some help," he prayed out loud. "Please let me bring home food for my family."

Five miles passed with no major problems, his sense of success grew, and he thanked the Lord. The road turned right, and he only had another mile to go until he came to the highway. He was certain he would have no problems on the highway. He had been listening to the radio. Power had been restored to the city of Wasilla. The main roads were being maintained, and stores were open. Secondary roads would be opened as soon as the winds died down.

As these thoughts were going through his mind he came to another drift. It was somewhat larger than the others and sloped on the side facing him. He stopped and pushed open the door. The wind slammed it back shut before he could get out. The wind had picked up considerably. The world of cold on the other side of the glass caused him to shiver. The Jeep rocked as it was buffeted by the wind. He suddenly felt very weary and decided not to brave the slamming cold to inspect the drift on foot.

An urging inside warned him against it, which he ignored. He backed up the Jeep and mentally judged what speed he would need to break through the drift. He decided on about 25 mph. He backed up a little further and began forward. He carefully adjusted his speed until it was just under 25. The drift approached, and he steered toward the lowest part. He came onto the drift and waited for it to explode.

Without warning the Jeep launched into the air. His head snapped forward, hitting the steering wheel as the Jeep took flight. He flew through the air for a dozen feet before landing with a jarring impact on the other side. Sam's head snapped back, and his neck screamed in pain. He slammed on the brakes and came to a stop. The engine was still running, but the Jeep sat at an odd angle. He took inventory of himself, and decided he was all right, though his face was bleeding slightly above his brow, and his back and neck hurt.

Refusing to give up, he shut off the truck and climbed back out. Hours passed in a frantic scramble between bone-numbing digging, and partly warming himself in the Jeep. He lost track of time. Outside, the wind pierced through him like nails shot from a gun. He did not dare run the truck long enough to warm himself completely. The wind was stronger now, and the path filled in as fast as he could dig. Despair slowly settled over him.

Sam returned to the Jeep. He had been working in the headlights without the motor running, and for a frightening moment it seemed as if the faithful truck would not start. At the last possible moment the engine barked to life and he slapped himself to keep warm until heat came from the truck. He knew he could push himself no further, and steely fear swept over him.

He turned on the headlights and saw that the digging he had just done had blown back in. He laughed aloud with dark humor, then laid his head back. Something sharp snapped in his neck, and he shouted in pain. For the first time he realized he was seriously injured. Cold sweat beaded on his forehead as he slowly went into shock.

Faced with his own mortality for the first time in his life, Sam was startled to find that his greatest regret was regarding Princess. He did not want to die without having restored her love to his life. He pondered what the twins might become without him, but knew they would be cared for and loved. He pondered every aspect of his life, and found himself surprisingly in good repair. The only loose end he truly regretted was the inexplicable loss of Princess's love. This loss, he decided, was greater than the apparently imminent loss of his own life.

As only the howling of the storm disturbed the quiet of the cold truck, his heart soared in prayer. No sooner had he begun to pray than the Holy Spirit swept over him, and he felt peace. Tears filled his eyes as he poured out his soul in prayer, not begging for physical salvation, but in words of love and worship. Without asking, without begging, with no more than a feeling of peace, he knew all would be well. He turned off the headlights and let darkness surround him.

The engine coughed and died. He did not try to restart it. Instead, he turned off the key. The blower quickly became cold, and he turned it off as well. Cold invaded the cabin immediately. He listened to the wind and estimated that it was almost up to 100 again. He tucked his hands under his arms and prayed as feeling first left his toes, then his feet, then legs. He knew he was dying, and yet fear was not the emotion he felt—it was joy; joy that soon he would have the privilege of worshipping at the Savior's feet.

At first his benumbed mind thought it was the rumble of an earthquake. He felt it in his pants before he heard it. He decided it was an avalanche, yet he was nowhere near a mountain or hillside. He opened his eyes to what appeared to be a hurricane coming directly toward him. The hurricane had two blinding lights above and on either side of it. His mind struggled to comprehend, to understand what it might be. It roared even louder than the wind, and screamed as it sent snow and ice furiously in every direction. He decided his mind was playing tricks on him, and nearly closed his eyes when he felt a surge of warmth and a clear command.

"Turn on the lights," it said. He reached out and fumbled without feeling for the light button. It stuck to his fingers as he pulled on it. The headlights of the jeep flared into the night, and the hurricane stopped with a lurch just in front of his Jeep. Sam watched with stupid interest as the hurricane paused, then grew silent. As he watched, it died away, and magically became the gaping mouth of a giant beast with huge yellow teeth slowly turning in his headlights. He simply stared at it in dumb fascination.

A hand rubbed away the frost from the side window. A face appeared and quickly vanished. He heard voices and heard a shovel banging against his door. In a few moments his door was yanked open and Sam was swallowed by the wind. He felt irritated that whoever it was had opened the door and let in the wind. Someone grabbed his arm and yanked him out into the storm. He would have resisted, but he was too cold. Hands fumbled all over him, and he was lifted. It seemed like his feet were directly over his head, and snow blew into his pant legs. It was an odd sensation.

The next Sam knew, he was upright again and being pushed up a ladder. He tried to help and managed to climb. In a short while he was sitting in a large cabin with hot air blowing in his face. Someone shoved a cup against his lips and he swallowed a gulp of burning liquid. It tasted awful, and he wondered if they were trying to kill him. But the heat hit his stomach and flared outward. It felt so good that he took another swallow of the foul liquid. It burned his mouth and throat, but the warmth was magical.

Someone was talking on a radio, reporting something about a buried Jeep. Someone else asked his name, and he tried to remember it. He took another swallow and almost as if a light switch had been snapped on, he remembered. With sudden panic he became fully aware, and couldn't help himself from yelling.

"Hey, you're okay. Here take another swallow of coffee." Sam looked into the concerned face of a young man. He was wearing a military uniform. Sam looked around himself and decided he was in the cab of a big machine. From the fact that everything was drab green, it was a military machine. He took another swallow of the hot liquid before it registered that it was coffee. He handed back the cup and nodded his thanks.

"Judist Priest, we almost ground you to pieces!" the older man said as soon as he hung the radio microphone back up. "You okay?"

"I think so. Where am I. What is this?"

"It's one of the National Guard's biggest snow blowers. We've been working for weeks to open up the back roads. We didn't see your truck until you turned on the lights. Another two feet and we would have ground you to shrapnel," he said with deep concern in his voice. Sam leaned forward and couldn't even see the top of the Jeep over the big blower. The huge blower was a mere two feet from the front of the truck. Its vicious mouth was ten feet wide, and capable of chewing up an automobile without much more than a cough. Sam shivered inwardly, and sent a prayer of thanks for the urging to turn on the lights.

Sam noticed that both men were sweating. They had turned the heaters in the cabin up full blast to thaw him out.

"Mr. Mahoy, we need to take you to a hospital," the senior of the two insisted.

Sam shook his head. "I'm feeling much better, thanks to you. My family is out of food, and I need to get back."

"I can't force you to go," the man said, "but I think it unwise to not treat your injuries immediately. I can see that your neck hurts."

"I will be fine. I promise, I'll get medical attention as soon as possible."

"It's your call, Mr. Mahoy. I'm just so darn glad we didn't . . ." He shook his head

In about an hour he recovered enough to climb back out of the big machine. He was amazed to see how his Jeep was dwarfed by the big machine a mere twenty-four inches from his bumper. They backed up and tied a chain to his truck. The little jeep hopped effortlessly onto smooth ground. They gave him a spare can of gas.

"You'd be surprised how many stranded motorists we have dragged out of snow drifts. We were ordered to carry extra gas, courtesy of the U.S. government." The needle read half a tank when he climbed back in. He started the engine and waited until heat once again came from the blower. He could feel everything but his feet, which he was able to move stiffly, so they weren't frozen, just very cold.

The soldiers backed the big machine out of his way. The road was flat and smooth before him. Nearly four hours after his engine had died, he was once again able to continue his journey. He just happened to glance in his rearview mirror just as the big snow blower roared back to life, belching a column of snow and ice into the air. The drift that had thrown him into the sky vaporized into the night.

A few minutes later Sam pulled up to the brightly lit grocery store. He purchased many bags of food and milk, paper diapers, candles, kerosene, another lamp, matches, and toilet paper. He resisted the urge to buy the whole store.

The poor little Jeep was sitting so low to the ground that the wheels almost rubbed the wheel wells. In the bright lights of the parking lot he inspected the damage. Three of the springs were broken, the forth hopelessly bent. He got out the bumper jack and jacked it up. He had several pieces of 2x4 which he laid between the frame and axle. He found some bailing wire and tied them in place.

He had to stop twice to put the blocks back in place. He finally arrived home about ten o'clock at night. He had left around three. His labors to dig out the driveway were wasted. It had all blown back in, and he had to park by the road. He walked the long lane to his home carrying his treasures.

Princess was waiting for him and threw open the door. Her face was a picture of relief. She took the packages from him and he returned to the Jeep for the remainder. When Sam finally arrived with the final load he was nearly as cold as when the National Guard had rescued him. His speech was slurred, and he was having difficulty concentrating. The wind had resumed its former ferocity.

Princess sat him by the stove and pulled off his gloves and boots. She massaged his feet and wrapped them in towels warmed on the stove. She worked on him for nearly an hour before he began to feel warm again and his shivering stopped.

"Thank you, Princess. I'm okay now, I think," he said, his speech nearly normal.

"Oh, Sam, I was so worried! I was afraid you had gotten into trouble. The babies and I said many prayers for you," she said earnestly.

"I did, actually. I got stuck and ran out of gas and nearly froze."

"Oh no! Sam, I was afraid something had happened. How did you get out?"

"The National Guard came along."

"Truly?" she asked in disbelief.

"They did, they were clearing the roads and pulled the Jeep out of the drift. I broke all four springs hitting a snowdrift. I thought I was a goner." He left out the part about almost being ground to hamburger by their snow blower.

"I'm so *grateful* you're okay!"

"Thanks for worrying about me, and for warming me back up. It felt wonderful to have you care about me again."

Princess looked at him with a blank expression before turning away. "What did you bring us?" she asked in an obvious effort to change the subject.

• • •

Princess made regular visits to Dr. Green with the babies, and they seemed to be thriving. Sam decided to contact the doctor himself. Princess said very little about her appointments, and Sam was concerned. Even though she was much better physically, there was a vast change in her personality. Dr. Green invited him to come and talk about his fears.

Doctor Green's office was near the hospital. Sam arrived after hours and had to wait nearly an hour for the last patient to leave. The waiting room was decorated like a nursery, obviously for the comfort of expectant mothers. He could hardly believe this was the office of an abortionist. But that wasn't what he was here to discuss.

The doctor shook his hand and ushered him into a large office. Her office was all business and had none of the feminine trappings of the outer rooms. He felt as if he had entered a lawyer's office. Doctor Green took a seat behind a big walnut desk and came directly to the point.

"Mr. Mahoy, I understand you have concerns about your wife's health. How may I help?"

Sam cleared his throat and nodded. "It's not her physical health I'm concerned about. She seems to have had a personality change. She no longer seems to care about things she formerly loved." He wanted to say people but felt more comfortable saying it this way.

"I see. Has this all happened since the babies were born?"

"Yes. It has been sudden and dramatic."

"Hmm. Does she treat you differently?"

"Very much so."

The doctor frowned and leaned forward, steepling her hands on her desk. "I see. Let me make a couple observations. First, pregnancy and birth require tremendous physiological changes in a female's body. Hormones change, body chemistry changes, her diet and routine all change. In addition to this, there are tremendous emotional burdens associated with giving birth. Sometimes there is a deep depression that lingers for several months following delivery. In the vast majority of cases these things wear off in a few months and the mother returns to normal."

"I know about those things," Sam interjected. "She was wonderful during the pregnancy, and seemed anxious for the baby to come. The changes have all been since the birth. It's been three months now. She just isn't the same person." Sam felt as if he were whining, and had to struggle to keep tears from his eyes.

"Yes, I see," she said. "During the operation your wife lost a lot of blood. Several times her heart stopped and she had to be revived. These times were brief, but it is entirely possible that she suffered some minor brain impairment. In almost all cases related to blood loss, the impairment shows up first in small personality changes. In severe cases, there is loss of motor skills, or memory. She doesn't exhibit memory loss does she?"

"Not that I can tell. But she hardly talks to me any more."

"I'm going to recommend that you take Princess to a specialist. He is not a psychologist but a doctor who deals specifically with long-term illnesses of this type. His methods are unusual and even controversial but are highly effective. I don't know if anything can be done to help Princess regain her former feelings, but he may be able to help." With this she jotted a name and number on a prescription pad.

Sam took the slip and stood. He was about to leave when a thought occurred to him. "Doctor, I want to thank you for saving Princess and my babies. I know it was a traumatic affair for you. Anyway, thank you very much."

The doctor seemed to struggle with indecision before she motioned him back into his chair. Sam sat down uncomfortably.

"In all candor Mr. Mahoy, your wife's behavior has troubled me deeply. What she did was either very brave, or incredibly stupid. I haven't decided which. She was willing to die rather than let me save her." She shook her head and appeared to be viewing the scene again in her mind.

After a moment she continued. "When I went to medical school they taught us repeatedly that a fetus was only tissue, that there was no more life in it than in your finger or foot. Because of my training I have had no qualms about performing abortions and have done so many times. I don't especially enjoy doing it and send new patients requesting an abortion to another doctor. But when an established patient requests it, I have obliged them.

"As you know there has been a great uproar in recent years about abortions. There are many who want to make it illegal. It made me angry that some group of people wants to shove their moral system down my throat and tell me what I can, or can't do. As a result, I have performed more abortions in the last two years than I would have otherwise; perhaps as many as three times more.

"However, I have never been so unhappy in my life. It seemed to me as if every time I returned from a procedure of this type, I felt more and more unable to care about the mothers and their babies who wanted a live birth. I began to view them as carrying unliving tissue inside them, and I felt indifferent toward their babies, whom they loved deeply. I have lost some patients because of my attitude."

She sighed, then went on as if telling this story for the first time. "It had come to the point that I had almost decided to go into abortion practice exclusively. There is certainly more money in it and less risk of lawsuits. There is much demand, and many reasons to do such a thing. As a matter of fact, I had decided in favor of dropping my obstetric practice the very day I was called in to work with Princess. The reason I'm telling you all this is so you will understand my circumstances prior to meeting your wife."

"Sure," was all Sam could think to say.

"I felt both relieved and deeply troubled by my decision. I reasoned that in ten years I could retire wealthy from my abortion practice. It would take twice that long to achieve the same end with my regular practice. Yet when I realized Princess was willing to die rather than let me operate on her, I was stung. I was struck with such deep self-loathing that I could barely function. I know I displayed it as anger toward Princess, but it was really anger toward myself. I wanted her to recant, to let me help her."

There was a long pause. Dr. Green looked at her hands, which she laid flat on the desk. "She was right, you know. If I would have performed that operation on her I would have felt vindicated. My skills saved precious lives and eliminated unwanted tissue in the same noble stroke. What she actually did was force me to reevaluate my own morality. She forced me to look deep enough into my soul to see that I did not like what was there."

Sam cleared his throat nervously. He wasn't sure why she was telling him all this. "So," he asked. "Can you share what your decision was?"

"It wasn't a decision," she declared. "Princess said I had to make a deal with God. The first time I came back I had decided to reevaluate my position. Princess would not accept that. Even not knowing what my decision was, she would not accept it. When I went away the second time I realized if I was not sincere in my negotiations with God, and if it was not 100 percent right, Princess and her babies were going to die. The thought of my trading their lives for my financial gain was so bitter in my mind that I literally felt ill."

The doctor stood and walked to the window so that her back was to Sam. She stared out the window at the towering mountains just beyond.

When she finally spoke, her voice was subdued. "When I returned the second time I had made a deal with God. I told Him that if He would let me save Princess's life and her babies, I would keep my obstetric practice and not switch to abortion work. Just in case that wasn't enough, I also promised to only perform an abortion in limited cases where the mother's life was at stake. Any others I would send to another doctor.

"When I returned to Princess's bedside I knew it would be enough. I was not even surprised when she nodded. I wasn't sure we had not waited too long, though."

"It was a frightening and confusing event," Sam confided. "I'm extremely grateful you were able to come to a decision which allowed you to save her. It makes my gratitude doubly significant."

The doctor walked around the desk. Sam stood and accepted her hand. "So am I," she said softly. There was a brief hesitation before she added, "I am very grateful to Princess, Sam. Please tell her that. Tell her that, once again, I like what I see in the mirror."

• • •

Sam had dubious feelings as he escorted Princess to the door to Doctor Spenard's office. It was small and somewhat shabby compared to Doctor Green's. It was obvious he cared much less for fine trappings and acquiring wealth. Princess blushed when she shook his hand. He was in his thirties, medium height, and dark-haired. He had a thin mustache and bright blue eyes. His speech was animated and upbeat. He seemed larger than life. Even Sam thought he was good looking and was impressed with his optimistic appraisal of Princess's condition.

After a thorough exam which Sam attended, the doctor proposed a form of oxygen therapy which involved removing quantities of her blood, infusing it with oxygen, and injecting it back into her. He recommended the treatment three times a week.

Dr. Spenard sat on a small stool and faced Sam directly. "I've never tried this therapy in a case such as this, but I'm optimistic Princess will benefit from it."

Sam nodded and took Princess's hand.

"It stands to reason that if oxygen depravation has caused minor brain damage, then oxygen enrichment may reverse it," he told them confidently, "I suggest we try it. It is somewhat expensive."

Sam nodded. "That's not a problem." In addition, the doctor prescribed an extensive diet change and megavitamin therapy along with long exposure to sunlight and moderate exercise. They left his office feeling hopeful.

On the way home Princess unexpectedly began to cry. "Sam," she said after she regained her composure. "I know I've changed since the babies were born. I don't know why. I just don't feel the same. I'm so sorry. I really miss the wonderful feelings we had before. I desperately want them back. Will you forgive me and be patient with me?"

Sam fought back strong emotions. It was the first time she had acknowledged anything amiss. "Princess, I will always love you, no matter what. I will wait as long as it takes," he said with a lump in his throat. She smiled at him the way she used to. It warmed his soul.

Princess returned from her first treatment animated and happy. She laughed and seemed enthusiastic for the first time in months. She described her session with the doctor in glowing terms.

Princess continued her treatments every other day and Sam returned to work. The business had run itself nearly without him for months. He returned to find things badly needing his attention. He had left affairs pretty much in the hands of his salesman and the bookkeeper. He threw himself into his work with passion, feeling optimistic about everything for the first time in months. In a short time sales surged as word spread about the great deals he was offering. In reality, it was the first time a subwholesaler had done business in Alaska, and the market responded with near greed to the lower prices.

In a short time the opportunity came to expand into Washington and Oregon. Sam flew down for a couple weeks to investigate. He returned having signed a contract with several diamond wholesalers potentially worth millions.

Princess continued with her treatments faithfully. After each treatment she felt stronger and upbeat, but the effect wore off before the next treatment. She was afraid to stop taking them. On the day Sam returned home she came home from a treatment depressed.

"Doctor Spenard says I'm not responding to the treatments. The effect appears to be temporary. He wants to try something else."

"Damn!" Sam said loudly. He had truly hoped it would help. Princess's eyes opened wide in shock. "I'm sorry," he added contritely. "I just really wanted this to work! What does he suggest?"

Princess dropped her purse onto the couch and took Bonnie from Sam's arms. "Well, he thinks I may have a chronic blood infection called Epstein Barr virus. I have heard about it before. It drains a person's energy and causes depression."

"I've never heard of it," Sam admitted. "Why would you get a virus during an operation? Is there a cure?"

"Well, there really is no cure. There is a treatment. It involves a low-stress lifestyle, absolutely no sugar, and very little red meat. There is also some medicine you take with it."

"No sugar?" Sam asked a bit alarmed. He was particularly fond of sweets, as was Princess.

"None whatsoever, he says."

"Gosh. What do you want to do?"

"There's one other thing I haven't mentioned."

"What's that?" Sam wondered. From her voice he could tell she was reluctant to tell him.

"The no-stress part."

"Yeah?"

"Well, he runs a retreat. It's somewhere near Fairbanks. Every couple of months he takes a few patients up there for a month to six weeks. He describes it like a health spa of sorts. He said you relax, have lots of massages, eat raw, fresh food, have laugh therapy, play games, and take lots of natural medicine."

"It actually sounds fun," Sam admitted, although the thought of her leaving for a month sent panic through him.

"I'm reluctant to leave the twins," Princess said with sadness. It pained him that she wasn't reluctant to leave him. "And to leave you that long," she added as if she had read his mind. He smiled at her and patted her cheek. They sat at their favorite spot on the big sofa near the grand piano. The babies were still asleep upstairs.

"Doctor Spenard says I would have to wean them. He says they have nursed long enough. He suggests doing it several weeks before the retreat so I'll be comfortable again. He really wants me to go and thinks he can cure me completely in that length of time." She sounded very hopeful.

Sam struggled with all this. It sounded both good and potentially bad. He didn't know Doctor Spenard any more than from one brief visit. He liked him but wasn't ready to trust his Princess on a nearly two-month trip to some isolated location.

"How many other people will be there?" Sam asked, forcing concern from his voice.

"Rob says about a dozen will be there, all female. No men at the retreat, except him of course. He'll only be there at the beginning to get it started, and the last two weeks to finish up. He may come up once in between."

"Rob?" he asked suspiciously.

"You knew his name is Dr. Robert Spenard, didn't you? He prefers being called Rob to Doctor. Most of his patients call him Dr. Rob."

"Dr. Rob," Sam said as if trying it on for size. He didn't like it. "What do you want to do?" he asked, hoping she would express doubt, or reservations.

"I want to go," she said simply. "Grandma Mahoy can handle the twins and would love it. The girls will be fine. You can manage, and when I return maybe things will be as they were before."

It was apparent to Sam that Princess had thought this all through. Even that concerned him. "Will you call, or does he keep you incommunicado?"

"That's another thing. No calls except for emergencies. He wants us to forget about the real world and just relax. He is optimistic that it will have a dramatic effect upon me. I really want to try. I need a break, and this could be the answer to my prayers. Please say it's okay. Please?"

"Princess, you don't need my permission to go. You're not my daughter. If you feel it's that important, I'll support you in it. I just want you to understand that I don't like it."

"Oh? Why?"

"I don't have a good feeling about it, that's all."

"Do you know why?"

"It has something to do with spending six weeks with a strange man in a paradise of back massages and laugh therapy. Maybe I'm just skeptical."

"Or jealous?"

"Should I be jealous?" Sam asked, unable to keep suspicion from his voice.

"Certainly not!" she replied heatedly. "Rob is my doctor, nothing more. If you think so lowly of me, maybe you're the one who needs some help. Have I ever given you reason to doubt my loyalty?"

"No," Sam replied truthfully, and humbly.

"Have I ever disappointed you?"

"No," he answered after a millisecond's delay. Even that tiny hesitation was enough to infuriate her.

"Oh!" she cried, stood, and stormed from the room. It was the first time she had blown up at him, ever. She had been angry at him before, but never over something so small. He sat on the couch in stunned silence.

Princess came home with a stack of baby bottles and formula the following day. From that moment on she was determined to go. Nothing he could have said would have deterred her.

• • •

Sam took Princess to the Airport May 12th. Doctor Spenard was there with three other patients and two nurses, all female. They were meeting others in Fairbanks, he said. Sam waited with a sinking heart until the plane was airborne. He did not like it, not at all. Princess had said good-bye happily, and kissed him on the cheek. She was far too cheerful at leaving for a six-week separation, far too cheerful for his comfort.

Time dragged by painfully. Sam spent his days busy with business, which was thriving. Every week he sent enormous amounts of money to their accounts overseas. Grandma tended the girls and was in a heaven of her own. Soon the big house became too empty for him, and he slept at his parents.

Benjamin was gone on a mission by now, and there was an extra room. Sam settled in and restlessly awaited Princess's return. He could find no joy in the waiting, and every day ground by in anguish for him. He became so grumpy that his mother told him to lighten up or go back home. Sam apologized and tried to cheer up. Whatever good humor he displayed was purely superficial. The only time he felt peace was in doing elder's quorum work. He spent many evenings out until late doing the only thing which brought him comfort.

After a whole month of waiting he received a letter in the mail. It was addressed in Princess's flowery script. He tore it open with haste. The note was written on a single sheet of paper.

> Dear Sam,
>
> How are you and the girls? I am doing much better, and have decided to continue for the full six weeks. That way I can have the benefit of working with Dr. Rob the last two weeks. The rest and treatment have been very good for me. Thank you for supporting me in this. Kiss Lisa and Bonnie for me. I'll be home soon.
>
> Love, Princess

Even though the message was upbeat, Sam read it like a funeral program. He threw it on the sofa and stormed from the house. Like a drum beating an unending cadence in his mind he kept hearing "Dr. Rob, Dr. Rob, Dr. Rob . . ."

• • •

Princess walked off the plane side by side with Dr. Rob, chatting happily. She smiled and waved at Sam as soon as she spotted him. She said something to Rob, smiled affectionately at her doctor, then turned her attention to Sam. She was cheery-faced and bright. As happy as she seemed, there was something unusual about her. Her face was deeply tanned, but that wasn't it. As he hugged her, Sam came to the startling conclusion it was that there was no light in her face. He hoped that this was just from not attending church for six weeks, and nothing more.

Princess talked enthusiastically all the way home about the retreat and her progress. She spoke in glowing, almost reverent, terms about Dr. Rob and how he had worked with her endlessly to get her going again. She kept repeating how he had pulled her through in an almost miraculous way.

She pulled open her blouse to show him her tan. "Light therapy," she said happily and laughed. They gathered up the girls, and Princess cooed and snuggled them. She seemed so happy to hold them again. Grandma Mahoy handed them back soberly. Sam already knew she was dreading giving them back, and suspected there would be some tears as soon as they left.

Once home Princess played with her babies for hours until they were exhausted. She fed them slowly, and bathed them with great care. Sam offered repeatedly to help, but Princess kindly refused. She was starved for their love, and she wanted to soak them up as much as she could. When they were finally put to bed Princess disappeared into their room. Sam fought the urge to follow her and instead sat down at the piano.

The keys felt like old friends, warm and willing. He ran his fingers across the keys until the familiar unity came, and the music poured from his soul. For a time he was lost in the joy of music, and the sadness of the burden upon his soul. The music flowed from the piano in surging waves, at times thunderous and complex, at others, longing and sad. He played with his eyes closed, thinking of nothing else. At long last the music came to its own conclusion and he lowered his hands into his lap.

"I have scarcely ever heard you play with more feeling," Princes said from nearby. He had been unaware of her presence, and opened his eyes to see her sitting on the big sofa. She had on her soft blue robe. She came and sat beside him on the piano bench and laid her head on his chest. It was something she had never done before, and though it pleased him, it also caused him to wonder.

They were still in one another's arms when the babies awoke crying at six A.M. Princess winked at him, kissed him softly, and slid from bed.

She had never winked at him before. The only person he could remember who winked at people was Dr. Rob. It made his heart sink.

• • •

Sam stayed home all that day to be with his little family. It was evening, and the babies were already sleeping when Princess came down the stairs. She joined him at their favorite spot beside the piano. Instead of snuggling up next to him as he expected, she sat with some space separating them.

"Is anything wrong?" he asked, not really believing anything could be wrong after last night.

"Yes, and no," she answered somewhat vaguely.

Sam put down the scriptures he was reading and turned to face her. "What's going on Princess? Before you leave you don't want anything to do with me, and after you return, you climb all over me like it might be our last . . ." His voice trailed off. As soon as he said it, thunder struck inside his head.

"There's something I want to talk to you about," she replied. "Something has changed inside me. I don't know why, but it has. I don't know if it is brain damage from the operation, or just the way it is. At any rate, I'm different."

Sam felt his pulse quicken, his heart pounding in his throat. "Different in what way? You seemed so happy to be home."

"I am. I'm happy because I have made some decisions which were really hard, but which I had to make. Now that I've made them, I finally feel at peace."

"That's good," he said with a smile, though he didn't feel good.

"Yes, it is. But you may not think so."

"Why? What's wrong? You're killing me with suspense here. Whatever it is, we can work through it. I love you, remember? Love can conquer any obstacle."

"Two-way love can," she replied, placing a hand on his knee. "One-way love is not healing; it's entrapping."

"Princess, you're scaring me. Get to the point."

She smiled sadly. "Sam, this is hard for me, too. What I'm trying to say is that I'm not in love with you—anymore."

"What!?" Sam stammered. He felt strangled, as if an iron hand had gripped his heart.

"I do love you, you see, but I'm not *in* love with you. I thought I was, but I've found that I'm not, and it would be unfair of me to keep you trapped in a relationship with someone who doesn't love you. Sam, I don't think I ever really loved you. I think I idealized you as a missionary, and wanted to be like you, and to have your faith and determination. I just don't think it was ever really love. I'm sorry it's just taken me this long to realize it."

"Princess, I can't believe this. I have seen such love in your eyes. I know you love me, or at least you did. How can you say this? It's not right. It's not true. It's not . . ." He couldn't think of anything else to say.

Princess averted her eyes and continued. "I know this is hard to accept. It was for me, too, but the truth is that we will be happier apart. You will still be around the girls, and they will love you just the same. It's just that I can't live with you now that I . . ." She didn't finish.

"Now that you love Dr. Rob," Sam finished for her with sarcasm in his voice.

"Even if that were true, it would be beside the point," she said. "The important thing isn't if I love someone else but that I no longer love you."

"You said you never loved me, and now you said you used to. Which is it?"

"Well, I suppose I used to, but not now."

"You said you do love me but don't love me. Which is it?" he demanded hotly.

"You're missing the point . . ."

"Why did we have such a wonderful night last night if you don't love me?"

"I felt I owed you that. I wanted you to feel the passion I felt . . ."

"With him?"

"Well, yes," she admitted. "If you want to be frank about it, yes."

"And did this passion express itself the same . . . ?"

"That's none of your business!"

"Of course it's my business! I'm your husband, for heaven's sake!"

"Not for much longer," she said hotly, but when she saw the slain look on his face, she instantly regretted it. She lowered her head and began to cry.

Sam began to cry, too, and for a long time the only sound in the house was that of sobbing.

Finally Princess lifted her head and dried her tears. "I'm sorry," she said. "I didn't want this to get ugly."

"It got ugly when you betrayed our vows," Sam said without looking up.

"I don't see it that way. I would never do that with someone I didn't love. Whether I did or not isn't the issue. The important thing is love or the absence of it," she declared.

Princess stood and left the room. When she returned she had on her jacket. "I'll be back tomorrow to get the girls. They will be living with me. If you need to talk to me, and you can be rational, I'll be at Dr. Rob's home. His number is in the Anchorage directory." She turned toward the door.

"I love you Princess," Sam said as she pulled it open.

She stopped and turned toward him. "I know you do," she said and left into the night.

Less than fifteen minutes later the phone rang. Sam let it ring a long time while he tried to compose his emotions. When it didn't stop, he picked it up.

"Sam, this is Mom. What's wrong? I have this sick feeling in my soul and it has something to do with you. Do you need me to come over?"

"Oh, Mom," Sam blurted in a sob. "She left me. She's gone to live with her doctor . . ."

"Oh, Sam! I'm sorry, Son. I was afraid when I saw her. I was afraid for her. Do you want me to come over?"

"Not now, please. I want to be alone."

"I'll come over first thing in the morning," she said, and after a long silence filled with love and support, bid him goodnight. He gave only passing thought to the fact that she had sensed his grief so far away. A mother's love is a powerful thing.

• • •

Melody arrived in Birmingham, England late in the afternoon after a slow, two-hundred mile train ride through densely populated countryside. It had rained the entire way, yet her heart sang with anticipation. Marcia and two other ladies met her at the train station. They ran into one another's arms in a tumultuous collision of joy and sorrow.

Marcia looked radiant, and notwithstanding the recent bad news of their father, happier than Melody had ever seen her. She still wore her hair long, her figure somewhat softer than before. But it all suited her very well. She spoke in glowing terms about her family, her husband, her new life, and her faith. Melody was almost motivated to accuse a new Marcia of living in the old Marcia's body.

Marcia was far too compassionate to say so, but to her eyes, Melody looked haunted and soul weary. It made Marcia's soul ache to receive her little sister in such battered condition.

They sat up until late that night as Melody rehearsed the details of the loss of their father and fortune, and her miraculous escape into Wales. Marcia wanted to know every detail, and wrung every scrap of information from her sister until she felt dry. Marcia's husband and children had long ago gone to bed. Melody's eyes were closing without her permission when her sister stood, took one step to the center of the room, and knelt down. She beckoned Melody to join her. Melody had never seen such behavior in her life and joined her there with a fuddled mind. Marcia took her hand, bowed her head and prayed.

"Heavenly Father. I just want to thank you that my sister Melody has come to be with me safely. Oh, Heavenly Father you know how much I love her, and how many times I have prayed for her safety. I was beginning to think I might be bothering you, I asked so many times. I guess I don't really believe that, but I did ask a lot. I'm so grateful you answered my prayers. Thank you, Heavenly Father.

"We are so sad about our father. He was a good man, as you already know. By now you've already had some conversations with him, and I wouldn't be surprised if he was just as abrupt with you, as he was with everyone else. But, he was that way because he had to be. And we hope you'll forgive him, and send him missionaries to teach him the Gospel. Please tell him how much I love Thy Gospel, and tell him I'll be so happy if he will listen to the missionaries you send.

"Heavenly Father, I want to end this prayer by sending my voice to your throne in gratitude once again for bringing Melody safely to me, for sending the nice old man to help her, and letting the missionaries teach her a little and give her your book. It is all truly amazing to me, but you know how I'm always a little overwhelmed by how good you are to me. I love you. In the name of Jesus Christ, Amen."

When Melody opened her eyes, Marcia's were still tightly shut. She had the distinct impression she was appending a silent P.S. to her prayer. She had never heard her sister pray. Actually, except for Sam, she had never heard anyone pray who was not a minister. She had been told that her mother prayed, but she was too young to remember. Her father certainly didn't pray, and all the prayers she had heard from ministers seemed formal and impersonal.

Her sister's prayer seemed as personal as if she were talking to a person right in the room. It was so filled with love and hope, that Melody inwardly wanted Marcia to show her how she could pray that way herself. Wanting to be able to pray suddenly caused Melody to feel peace and warmth in a way she had never known before. The feeling was very small, but so beautiful it brought tears to her eyes. Quite unexpectedly her father evolved from being dead, to simply being absent. It lightened her grief, and unburdened her soul as nothing else could. Her sister's simple prayer had brought her father back to life as surely as Jesus had raised Lazarus from the tomb. What had been an intolerable, eternal, inalterable dissolution of a man she dearly loved was now simply a separation of predictable duration. To her joy, with her father's sudden awakening in her heart, she found her Mother similarly alive, and the joy was more than her heart could hold.

When Marcia opened her eyes Melody's were closed, tears coursing softly down her cheeks.

It took months to get Melody legally admitted into the country. It was very difficult because England had no sympathy for Rhodesian refugees. It was England, after all, who had forced Ian Smith's government into economic poverty through the sanctions and orchestrated their overthrow.

Melody ultimately acquired citizenship through "alternative" means, at considerable expense. Melody paid for it all from the funds she had saved playing music in the park. She could easily earn several hundred pounds a day, approximately triple a working man's salary. She didn't like having to deal with the type of people who for a price could provide anything you desired; yet at the time it seemed she had no other choice. She was a fugitive, an illegal immigrant, political dissident, and undesirable foreigner subject to arrest and immediate deportation back to Rhodesia. It didn't take much imagination to realize what her fate would be in the hands of those who had killed her father.

After gaining citizenship, Melody simply became a young woman of modest means and considerable talent, moving through the English economic system in an unremarkable way.

During all this time Melody had been unemployed. As soon as she was legally able to do so, she scoured the area for any suitable employment. Without any formal training other than music, she could only find mind-numbing employment serving food, washing dishes, changing beds, or other menial labor. She considered going back to school to learn bookkeeping or some other trade, but her love was music and that alone. The thought of doing anything else filled her with frustration. Accordingly, she soon gravitated back to the very thing she had first discovered, playing in the park.

Melody applied for and received a business license and permit to perform on the streets, a thing she had been lacking previously, and proceeded to play at the park twice a week. She made more than sufficient for her needs with minimal effort. Besides, she loved it, was developing a devoted audience, and had plenty of time left for practicing the violin.

Her eyes first fell upon Theodore after having played a stirring collection of old English church hymns. She nearly always concluded each concert with those hymns, and it always pleased her audience, and consequently, topped off each day's tips.

Theodore appeared older, though he was not quite thirty. Melody was just barely twenty-one at the time. He had dark eyes that sparkled like sapphires, a straight jaw line and impressive dimples. His hair was parted on the top of his head, and combed down and back. Perhaps his most noticeable characteristic was his fine clothing and long, white scarf which lay loosely over his shoulders in a fashion quite uncommon.

After nearly a year of making her living as a street minstrel, Melody had encountered nearly every form of human being possible. Of necessity she had developed ready answers, quick responses, and pat comebacks for every possible situation. She had even taken the liberty of hiring the local street gang to watch out for her. Without exception, two or three longhaired boys showed up at each concert and watched after her solicitously. They hardly realized they were mostly protecting her from themselves.

When she looked up from packing away her violin Melody saw three people remaining of the rather large afternoon crowd. One neatly dressed gentleman and two scruffy teens. The gentleman was watching her intently, while the street toughs were watching him maliciously. He was totally unaware of the dangerous position he had gotten himself into.

Melody looked at the boys and shook her head with a smile. They nodded and backed away, but did not leave.

"Evenin' Miss," the gentleman said, doffing an invisible hat. His accent was British, almost aristocratic. Doffing his nonexistent hat was a quaint gesture and intended to amuse her. It had the desired effect.

She curtsied, put a hand to her cheek and said, "Why, good evening, govnah." Her words were right out of a Charles Dickens novel she had just read, and at least a century more antiquated than his. Without intending to, she struck his funny bone a glancing blow, and he laughed so heartily for several seconds that she smiled in spite of herself.

"Oh! Oh, excuse me. If it weren't for your accent, I'd have accused you of being an American," he said, forcing himself to calmness.

"Not at all," Melody admitted cheerfully. "It's from a book by an Englishman actually."

"I thought as much. I haven't actually heard someone speak like that my whole life. Where are you from?"

"From around here," she replied as she tucked her violin under her arm. She rarely carried it by the handle. She had seen handles break, and the clasps sometimes popped open letting the precious instruments fall to the pavement.

"Your accent isn't English," he replied innocently. She decided to take it innocently.

"My mother was from Australia," she explained. It was a partial truth, her mother had been born there, but had moved to England at age three. Her accent was decidedly not Australian, but only a linguist could have correctly labeled it Rhodesian.

"That would explain it," he replied cheerfully. "I have to admit that I have become a fan of yours. This is the fourth time I've come to the park to hear you play."

"I haven't seen you before," Melody said thoughtfully.

"The other times I wore my work clothes. You probably didn't notice me dressed that way. People often look the other way when I'm in my work clothes."

"That could be, I guess. I don't really pay much attention to faces," Melody responded. She started walking back toward Marcia's apartment, her two guardians tailing her at a distance. They would remain with her until she was out of their area. It felt kind of good having them back there. They had come in handy a couple of times on her walk home.

"My name is Theodore," He offered her a hand. "Theodore Lyman Tennison the Second," he said quite properly, bowing slightly at the waist. She took his hand and found it smooth, warm and gentle, much different from her father's iron-like hands.

"Melody MacUlvaney," she replied.

"Ah, a good Scottish name."

"Irish, actually. My Father's family were land barons in Ireland until some time after the turn of the century." Actually, it had been a mere twenty-five years ago.

"Yes, I believe I've read some of your family's history. Come to think of it, there are some MacUlvaneys buried in the old church cemetery where I work," he said thoughtfully.

"You work at the church?" She found it an odd employer for one dressed so well.

"Yes," Theodore replied, his mind obviously focusing on something else.

"Uhm, what do you do there? What kind of work are you in?"

"Hmm? Oh, excuse me. I was trying to remember the dates on the tombstones. I'm what one might call a caretaker."

"You take care of the building?"

"That and other things. Why don't you play with some big orchestra? You certainly have the talent," he returned in an obvious change of subject.

Melody decided not to press him. He was apparently uncomfortable telling her his job. She didn't have a particular problem with the idea that he was a janitor, or gardener, but apparently he did. Her father had been a farmer, and dirty hands seemed normal on a man. Whatever he did, he could afford at least one change of nice clothes, for he was wearing them.

"I do play with the city orchestra, and I've been invited to play with the Liverpool Philharmonic when it comes here on tour next week," Melody explained happily. It was something she was looking forward to, and for which she was dedicating many hours of preparation.

"Truly? I simply must get tickets. Will you tell me when the concert is? I should be most disappointed to miss it. I love orchestra, and I love your playing immensely. I'd love to go see you. If I don't guard myself, I'm going to fall in love with ..." This all came out in a rush. He blushed, cleared his throat and concluded " ... your music."

Melody found it quite admirable that Theodore was innocent enough to blush. It belied the sleek, confident facade that his clothing and demeanor implied.

He shuffled his feet. "Please forgive me. I didn't intend to ..."

Melody mischievously decided to reward him for his impudence in the worst possible way. She leaned toward him, kissed him softly on the cheek, straightened, flashed him her most dazzling smile, and said "Whatever for?" She walked past him without another word. She dared a glance back many minutes later, and he was still standing in that exact spot, a hand pressed to his cheek where she had anointed him with her lips.

"That'll fix him for about a week," she thought to herself playfully, fully intent on completely ignoring him the next time they crossed paths. It was a little mean, but he deserved it.

In reality, it fixed him for about the rest of his life.

• • •

Grandma Mahoy was with Sam when Princess came to get the twins. She arrived with a police car behind her. The officer stood with one hand on the butt of his pistol as Princess gathered the baby's things. The only thing she said to Sam was, "I'll be in touch." She and the officer left in a swirl of dust. Sam felt as if his whole purpose for living had just walked out the door.

The papers arrived a week later. Sam read them with deep regret. They outlined the details of their divorce. The important parts were that Princess wanted the home and all its furnishings except the piano. Sam could have the business and one car. Princess acquired sole custody of the girls, and he had visitation rights every other week on Saturday and Sunday. He would pay her a sizable sum each month until the girls reached eighteen. To him it was like reading an execution order. He tried to sign it and could not. The papers sat on the living room coffee table for weeks. Finally he wrote Princess a note explaining that he could not sign them and sent them back.

The next day he received a phone call from her attorney suggesting he contact an attorney because they were suing for divorce. With or without his signature it was going to occur.

That following evening Sam was alone in the big house. It felt like a tomb. He wanted to pack up and move out, to escape the memories. He sat at the piano and was filled with the vision of her sitting beside him, her head resting gently on his chest. He almost stood to escape it, but instead he lifted the lid, and laid his hands on the keys. He was about to play when the Holy Spirit flooded over him. There was a single message, one he had never heard before. "Record it," the sweet feeling said. He stood and found a small cassette recorder. He placed it on the piano and set it to record.

For a long moment he waited until sadness overwhelmed him, then love, then peace. Somewhere in his mind he felt the joy loving Princess had been, and how it had felt so eternal, so very forever. He said aloud "I Have Always Loved You," and the music came.

He had often felt the flow of music in his soul, but never like this. If there was a pure source of music, as there is a pure source of truth, he found it that night. Every note, every harmony, every delicate, breathlessly beautiful phrase was known to him. It was opened to his mind as clearly as if he had been taught this haunting melody in some pre-mortal childhood, and had known it all his life. He played, and as he played he spoke the words which carried the burden of his love.

The music came to him in sweet flows of perfection, and he played with deepest feeling. When it was over, it was simply over, and the feeling passed. He reached up and clicked off the recorder. He popped the tape from the machine and dropped it into his pocket. He sat for a long time in silence.

On impulse Sam stood and went into his study. He addressed an envelope to a former missionary companion whom he knew to be successfully involved in the music industry. He dropped the tape inside, and mailed it the next day.

Two weeks later to the day he received a large brown envelope. He opened it and was surprised to find a piece of sheet music inside. It wasn't until he read the title that he began to understand. "I Have Always Loved You," was in bold type across the front page. He sat at the piano and opened the music. The score was well done, and though somewhat simplified from the way he had played it on the tape, it was exactly as he remembered it. The words between the lines were his as well. He was stunned to tears. There was a hand-written phone number on the first page.

• • •

"Mike? This is Sam Mahoy. I like what you did with my song."

"Elder Mahoy!" the voice on the other end exclaimed. "I haven't heard from you since our mission, and then I get this tape with this hauntingly beautiful song on it. Hey, Sam, I knew you played, but had no idea you wrote music as well. It is a fantastic piece, and I want to produce it."

"Well, I'm flattered." Sam said. "But, it's deeply personal, and I'm not quite sure I want to throw it to the world."

"All love songs are deeply personal. All great love songs come from deep within the soul, from a place of beauty now scarred by pain," his friend observed quietly. "Anyway, this song is a masterpiece. Don't you realize that, Sam?"

"I don't know."

Mike persisted. "If you didn't want it published why did you send it to me?"

"I felt prompted by the Holy Spirit to send it to you," Sam replied candidly.

His friend cleared his throat meaningfully. "Well, let me rephrase the question then. If Heavenly Father didn't want it published, why did He prompt you to send it to me?"

"Good point," Sam replied at length, still unsure.

"Sam, if you want we can take your name off the title. You would still get the same money from it, but maybe that would help."

"I'm not concerned about money."

"Yeah, I heard you are doing really well. Listen, my friend, I'm going to publish this song one way or the other. You'll have to sue me to stop me. So what do you say?"

"I say, go ahead. I doubt it will go anywhere. It's just feelings I put to music."

"It's much more than that," Mike disagreed. "Sam, I've written and produced enough music to be able to spot inspiration. This music is timeless. If we go ahead you will become a music writing celebrity."

"I don't want to be a celebrity," Sam replied dejectedly.

"What do you want?"

"I want my wife back," Sam said with more honesty than he intended.

There was a long silence from the phone. "I'll get to work on this immediately. If I have anything to say about this, you will be hearing this tune on the radio in less than a month."

A second package arrived two weeks later with a cassette tape and a bundle of papers. Sam listened to the tape. Mike had written his song into a duet for a man and woman. As Sam listened to the hauntingly beautiful song he could scarcely believe it was his own. In fact, it was not. It was something that had come to him, not from him.

The papers were a standard publication contract. Sam didn't even read them, but signed several places and sent them back.

Mike performed the piece at his next concert, included it on his next CD, and good to his word, Sam heard it on the radio a little more than a month from their phone conversation.

The best part of it all was that no one suspected that he was *that* Samuel Mahoy. The several times someone asked if he was related, he replied; "Not at all." How can one be related to one-self? Unthinkable. Had they asked if it was he, he would have replied that it was. He was happier with anonymity.

During the intervening weeks, it seemed to Sam as if he went through definite stages with his emotions. At first he just couldn't accept that she had really left him. He kept expecting Princess to walk through the door happily returning from shopping, or something.

After that he felt angry and wanted to kill the loathsome SOB who had taken her away from him. He fantasized about throwing a firebomb through the front window of Dr. Rob's medical practice, or even better, through the window of his home right while he and Princess were there. Let them see if they can be in love while their house burns down around them, he screamed in his mind. That lasted for a couple weeks.

After that, Sam begged Heavenly Father to work a miracle and let her come home and love him again. He made promises, bargains, deals with God to get her back. Even knowing that she was with a slime ball couldn't stop him from wanting her back. The thought of her being with someone else nauseated and disgusted him, but it didn't make him stop loving her.

The most difficult stage, though, was acceptance. In time it finally dawned on him that Princess was gone for good. When acceptance finally came to him he wept for three days, grew a beard, and pouted. In time though, he began to think his heart may heal.

Sam was not surprised when his attorney delivered the final papers to his office. Sam had attended none of the divorce proceedings, preferring to never see her again. His fear was that he would start loving her again, and he was not willing to go through all that anguish. He took the papers home and flopped them on the coffee table, intending to just sign them later. As soon as he did, he would have to move out of the house, and another phase of his life would come to an end. In many ways he dreaded moving from his dream home. In others, he was anxious to get on with his life.

It was not unusual for people to come visit, especially

since word spread of Princess's absence. The ward had rallied around him, and someone came almost every evening to make sure he was all right and not suffering unduly.

When the doorbell rang its rich melody he was in the kitchen fussing with a Cajun dish he had just fixed. It was just finished. He lifted it from the oven and set it on top, then hurried to the door as it rang a third time. He switched on the porch light and pulled open the heavy oak door.

"Hello," she said quietly into the awkward silence.

"Princess?" Sam gasped. He was both pleased and appalled. He was torn between sweeping her into his arms, and strangling her there on the spot. He nearly settled the issue by slamming the door in her face, but remained paralyzed with indecision.

"May I come in, Sam?" she asked timidly, and glanced toward the big room uncertainly.

Sam realized he was blocking her way, and releasing the door, stepped aside. She smiled briefly and walked past. He caught a whiff of her perfume as she walked by, and it pierced him. Suddenly he was angry; angry that she had left him, angry that she had betrayed him, and angry that she had returned to torture him.

"Why are you here? I'll be out in a few days, and it'll all be yours. You didn't need to come and torment me," he said bitterly with the door still open.

"Sam, I didn't come to torment you. I almost didn't come at all," she replied soberly and unbuttoned her coat. It was October, and the air was frosty with the promise of winter.

Sam closed the door a little too hard. Princess winced at the sound. "I wish you hadn't come," he said honestly, not intending to be cruel.

Princess looked from the floor to his eyes, then back down again. "I had to," she replied meekly.

"Why? To gloat? To see if I have suffered enough? To survey your castle while the former occupants can still see your triumph? To let me smell your perfume one more time?" he choked out. "Why did you come here?" he demanded.

"None of that, Sam. Nothing like that."

Hearing her say his name pierced through him like an arrow. His heart tried to beat harder, and stop dead all at the same moment. It was not a pleasant sensation. He realized with a start that he still loved her, and that made him even more angry. A battle started between love and hate which tore at his soul. Tears formed in his eyes and he had to blink hard to keep them inside.

Princess walked to the piano and ran a hand softly across its rim. The lid was up, and Sam could see her face in the polished wood. He looked away.

"Is this where you wrote it?" she asked innocently.

It was an odd question. "Wrote what?"

"My song."

"*Your* song?"

"The one that plays on the radio every fifteen minutes all day long," she said and rolled her eyes into her head in mock displeasure.

"Oh, it's not your song."

"Whose then? Who did you write it for? Who have you always loved? Is there someone I don't know about?" Princess asked, looking around the room as if expecting to find someone.

"You know there isn't," he replied quietly.

"Then you did write it for me?" It was not meant to be a question, but came out unsure.

"I wrote it about you, perhaps—not for you."

"What's the difference?"

"The difference is . . . that was before."

"Before what, Sam?"

"Before you betrayed me! Before you betrayed us!" he replied with more anger than he had intended. But the anger was there, hot and insistent. It caused his skin to crawl, and his fingers ached to throttle something, to destroy something which could never be fixed again.

Princess took a tentative step toward him. "Sam, the words say 'I will spend forever loving you.' Are you telling me that you no longer love me? Has forever ended so soon?"

Sam stood in silence, rocking back and forth as if standing on a ship. He had to hold onto the piano to steady himself. He couldn't believe he was having this conversation. If she hadn't come back to torture him as she claimed, she was doing a thorough job of it just the same.

"Forever came to an end when you walked out the door and went to his bed instead of mine," he said with a steely coldness.

To his surprise a tear sprang to her eye, and rolled down her cheek. She made no attempt to wipe it away.

"Then you don't love me anymore?"

Sam almost screamed at her, if for no other reason than to hurt her, but the words would not come, and his anger was hot, not cold. Hot anger flares to hurt back as a defense; cold anger craves revenge. A long silence passed.

"Princess," her name stuck in his throat. He swallowed hard. "I do still love you, I'm afraid."

A smile brightened her face. He wasn't finished. "But, I'm afraid that I can't forgive you," he said in a small voice. "I am trying as hard as I can to not love you. I have already started to succeed. At least I thought so thirty minutes ago," he said very quietly.

"Sam, I have listened to you tell me that you love me every fifteen minutes for the past two weeks. Every time I hear that music I want to cry. I can't escape your telling me you love me. You tell me in my car, in the grocery store, in the vehicles next to me at the stop sign—everywhere! I have heard it so many times, that I realized something I didn't understand a month ago."

"What's that," he asked blandly, trying hard to convince himself he didn't want to hear her answer, and altogether failing.

"I realized that I . . ." she paused to collect herself. When she continued her voice was very small. "I realized that not only do I still love you, but I'm hopelessly *in* love with you. Very, very much. I'm sooooooo sorry . . ." She paused a long time. "I want to come home," she said. Her voice sounded very childlike, afraid and lost. It made his heart ache even more, if that was actually possible.

Sam fell into the couch as if he had been slugged. He buried his face in his hands and silently wept. For a long time he wept, until the grief was past. When he was finished he looked at her. She had been crying too, silently, painfully. She looked at him and smiled hopefully, but he could not return it.

"I wish you had not come here tonight," Sam said. "It would have been easier if you would have stayed where you belong, with *him*," he added, not intending to emphasize the last word as much as he had.

"But, Sam. I just told you that I love you. Doesn't that mean anything?"

Sam stared at her with a wounded expression. "Yes! It means you are going to be much, much harder to forget. It means that now I am going to have to hate you and despise you in order to forget you. Before, I only had to be angry and unforgiving. Now I have to be disgusted by you. I didn't want that, Princess. Don't you see? You shouldn't have come!"

Princess choked back a strangled sob. "I know you love me, Sam. Do you really want me to just walk out that door and never come back? Even though you know I do really, honestly, love you? Is that what you want?"

"No! Yes! I mean, there is no choice."

"Why, Sam? Why?" She nearly shouted between sobs.

His face contorted with pain, Sam said, "Because every time I see you, I think of you with him. Every time I think of your face, I think of him touching it. Every time I see your lips, I see him kissing them. It isn't because I don't love you, or because you don't love me! It's because I can't look at you any more! It's because I don't respect you. We have lost the glue that holds a relationship together, TRUST. It's not that I don't love you. IT'S THAT I DON'T WANT YOU!" He was shouting at her now.

Princess flinched at each of his words as if they were bullets striking her. Her shoulders trembled as she wept. She buried her hands in her face, and her soul wailed as if dying. Suddenly, she stood. She moved with determination toward the door, clutching her coat about her. Sam looked away. He heard the door open and close and she was gone from his life: hopefully, tragically, gone forever.

Sam's eyes fell on the divorce documents still lying where he had dropped them. He pulled a pen from his pocket, flipped to the last page, and signed with a flourish. He was angry again, and this time it was cold. He marched to the door and yanked it open. Princess had just started her car when saw him coming in the headlights. She opened the door and stood again, a look of strangled hope on her face.

Sam stomped up to her and jamming the papers in her face, opened his mouth to speak the last hateful words that would damn her from his life forever. Just as his voice began he felt a wash of power penetrate him, and a voice more powerful than a billion decibels blasted through his soul. Its message was unmistakable. These words thundered in his mind: "At the peril of thine own soul!"

He took a step back as if struck by lightening. He gasped, clutched his chest, and fell to the ground on his knees, divorce papers scattering on the frozen ground.

Princess was terrified by all this, and slamming the car door shut, ran to kneel beside him. She put a hand on his forehead, then on his neck to see if he was having a heart attack. She decided nothing obviously was amiss, yet something was terribly wrong.

She began to cry tears of true panic. "What's wrong, Sam? What's wrong? Please be all right. I'm leaving now, so just relax. I'm sorry I hurt you. You're right, I shouldn't have come. Can you get up? Just get up so I know you're okay, and I'll leave. I won't come back to hurt you again, I promise. Sam . . ."

She tugged on his arm. He looked up at her. Her hair had fallen onto his shoulder. It smelled that special smell that he had loved so long, so well, so perfectly.

Suddenly, unexpectedly, the anger left, the pride melted, the hurt burrowed out of sight, and he could stand it no longer. Sam looped an arm around her neck and pulled her to him so hard she literally fell into his arms. He lifted her to him, slowly, gently, and kissed her with all the love he had thought gone and forgotten.

Startled, Princess stared at him wide-eyed, then feeling his tenderness, she closed her eyes and surrendered. Sam held and kissed her for a long while, bathing her face in his tears. Finally, chilled and feeling repentant, he stood and in a single powerful move, lifted her with him. She looped an arm around his neck, her lips still pressed against his. He carried her into the house, and stood her near the piano. Wonder, fear, doubt, and hope simultaneously played on her face.

Sam studied her face, then pulled her into his arms and held her; then pushed her at arms length to study her again, then pulled her to him again. This he did many times, until they were both confused.

"Sam, please talk to me," Princess finally said as he held her fiercely against him.

"I love you," he said in simple explanation. It was exactly what she wanted to hear.

"I love you too," she sobbed back, her voice muffled against his chest. "But, can you forgive me? Can you accept me back, even knowing what I've done?"

"Princess . . . It feels so good to say your name again," he interjected. "Princess, inside me it still hurts. It hurts more fiercely than anything I have ever felt. But, I love you, and I want you, and I want to forgive you. In time, with Heavenly Father's help, I will. Until then, I'll just concentrate on what is, not what isn't."

"I'm so sorry," she sobbed, and wrapped her arms around him again very tightly. He held her for a long time. "I don't know what has come over me. I just know that I want to come home. More than anything in this whole world, I know that I love you, and I want to be with you. I want to be passionate like we used to be," she said shyly, but with certainty.

"One thing at a time," Sam responded sadly. "One thing at a time." As much as he wanted to, he knew some healing had to occur first.

"I understand. Oh!" she suddenly said, pushing away from him. "I need to get the babies. They're in the car."

"They are?" Sam demanded. "Are they all right?"

"They were fine just a minute ago. Come on, let's get them. That is, if they are spending the night here?" she asked, not entirely sure.

"Where else?" he demanded happily. "This is where they belong." Then more softly, "this is where you belong."

At that moment they were startled to hear the high-pitched whine of a jet engine and the *whup-whup-whup* of a helicopter in the yard. They exchanged puzzled looks, and Sam walked to the door while looking at this watch. It was late. He pulled open the door to a hurricane of blowing snow. The helicopter was just settling a short distance from the house, its blades blasting a hurricane of snow at them. Sam pushed the door closed against the gale. Sam knew whoever was in the chopper would wait for the swirl of snow to die down before coming to the door.

"You don't suppose that could be your father, do you?" Sam asked in amazement.

Princess's eyes grew wider. "I don't know, but I wouldn't really put it past him."

"Me either," Sam agreed with mixed feelings. "It sure is odd timing though."

"Very odd," Princess agreed.

Suspicion quickly grew stronger than curiosity. "Sam, open the door! Open it back up!" Princess cried. Sam pulled the door back open.

"Look!" she screamed. Sam's eyes followed her shaking finger. He stepped back with a gasp. The hated "22" screamed at them in large red figures from the door. Paint dripped from them like blood. At that moment they heard glass break.

Sam bolted through the door just a step ahead of Princess. A "22" had also been painted on the windshield of the car. A figure was darting toward the chopper even as it lifted into the air. Sam and Princess ignored the whipping snow and ran to the car. The passenger door window had been smashed, but the door was still locked.

Princess had snapped the electric door locks even as she ran to help Sam. The childproof rear door locks meant the door could not be opened from either side while locked. It was the only reason their babies were still in the car. A baby blanket lay outside in the snow. The tightly strapped car seats had kept the thugs from removing car seat and babies together. It was obvious they had tried. One of the harness straps holding Bonnie into her seat had been cut with a knife.

Terrified, the two carried their crying babies inside. Frightened by the noise and blowing snow, the twins quieted quickly and went back to sleep. Princess and Sam put them in their cribs in utter silence. It was too terrible to contemplate, and both he and Princess were numb. But at least they were numb together, and that mercifully softened the blow.

• • •

Theodore was at her Saturday afternoon performance in the park. He seemed impatient for the two hours to pass. He walked up to Melody straight away after the concert and held out four tickets with a huge grin as if they were winning lottery tickets.

"I've purchased tickets to all four performances!" His voice was almost squeaky with excitement.

She decided to carry through on the brush-off portion of his punishment but couldn't make herself be so rude as to completely ignore him. So she decided on a low-key response instead. "You'll surely tire of it, then. It's the same program each night."

His face fell for just an instant and then brightened. "I'll enjoy the concert the first night, and I'll just enjoy watching you the other nights," he said, in what seemed to her to be an answer he had carefully crafted and rehearsed. It was, in fact, utterly spontaneous.

"That's nice. I'll see you there, then." Melody turned and walked away. She didn't need to look back to know he was standing there befuddled. Had she looked back, she would have seen a man with a wounded heart. It's a good thing she didn't, for as tender as her heart was, she probably would have run back, begged his forgiveness, and hugged him until he was thoroughly confused.

Theodore attended all four concerts. Melody caught sight of him out of the corner of her eye. His face was plainly enraptured. She played first chair and was guest soloist for one of the Mozart pieces. She had played beyond herself each night, and the crowd was very appreciative. It was a glorious thing to be a part of such beautiful music.

Melody fully expected Theodore to come charging onto the stage after each concert to congratulate her, but he did not. After the fourth night she fully expected it, but again he evaporated with the crowd. As she rode home in the cab Melody could not help feeling a little disappointed.

Melody's enigmatic church employee did not show up for a performance in the park for almost three weeks. For the first week she felt angry that he would take her teasing so to heart. The second week she felt angry at herself for skewering him so badly. The third week she just felt deeply disappointed.

When he did return it was Melody's last outdoor performance of the year. The afternoons were beginning to be blustery with the first curtain call of fall. Soon the rains would begin and not relent until they turned to snow.

It was a brilliantly sunny afternoon, with a tease of crispness in the air. A light breeze brought the fresh smell of the ocean to the park. As if sensing this would be her last public performance until spring, and perhaps forever, loyal listeners turned out in large numbers. She no longer stood on the sidewalk, but had moved to the place of honor inside the small gazebo at the center of the park. The little building amplified sound, provided an impromptu stage, and a pleasant backdrop.

She often wore a formal-length, deep blue velvet dress with white collar, white fingerless gloves, and white high heals. To see one so attractive making such startlingly beautiful music was so unexpectedly grand that few passersby could actually pass by.

Theodore didn't arrive until late in the performance and stood far back in the crowd. When it was over he waited for the press of people to thin before coming toward her. He seemed unsure. She didn't blame him after her prank at his expense.

"Hello Melody," he said quietly. "I'm sorry I've missed so many of your performances."

"I really don't blame you," she answered.

Theodore sounded perplexed. "Oh? Why don't you blame me?" He was dressed almost as she remembered, except his white scarf was now soft wool rather than silk.

Melody blushed, which not only intrigued Theodore but also charmed him. "I owe you an apology for teasing you so shamelessly. I wouldn't have come to my concerts either."

His smile brightened. "Whatever are you talking about?" he asked, shaking his head from side to side.

"Well, when I . . . I mean because . . . Why *didn't* you come to my concerts?" she finally asked.

"I had final examinations this whole last month, plus I finished my thesis, so I just didn't have the time. I did miss your music terribly, though. I hope you don't think badly of me for not coming."

Melody looked at him incredulously, her eyebrows raised in surprise. "You're not mad at me? You just had to study?" she asked with wonder in her voice, at the same time laughing at herself. It occurred to her she had been pretty self-centered to think his whole world was in orbit around her as if she were the sun.

"Why would I be angry at you? I have thought nothing but fond thoughts about you this last month as I sat in dreary classrooms making hen scratchings on scraps of paper."

Melody gathered up her things as she tried to think of a graceful way to rescue herself from her own foolishness. "How did it go? Did you pass?" she asked in a blatant attempt to change the subject. He looked at her through narrowed eyes, then quickly smiled again.

"I did!" he finally said happily. "I'm now a full fledged Doctor of Philosophy."

"Fantastic!" she cried, hardly able to comprehend the jump from janitor to student to doctor. She blinked her eyes rapidly as if the sun were too bright.

"You never mentioned you were studying to get your Ph.D," she finally said, a note of accusation in her voice.

"You never asked," he answered cheerfully. "I have an idea. Would you help me celebrate?"

She wasn't surprised really. She had been asked out to dinner quite a few times by handsome young men, and some not so young, and many not at all handsome. She would have been disappointed had he not asked her.

"Perhaps," she replied coyly.

He smiled and took a slip of paper from his pocket and wrote on it for a moment. When she took it she was surprised to see it held the name of a church, and a date about a month away.

"What's this?" she asked suspiciously, expecting some grandiose arrangement for a date with her.

"Part of my graduation requirement is to deliver a doctoral dissertation before the faculty and the public. I have the option of having some guest speaker or performer join me. I think it would be jolly wonderful to have you play something appropriate just before my speech. What do you say? Will you do it?"

"But, I thought . . ."

"Please don't say no. It would help me relax. I'm so tense about this, you see. Every time you play you exude confidence and peace. I just know having you play for me just before will make all the difference in the world. Won't you say yes?"

"Well, with that much fanfare I don't see how I could refuse," she replied a little too soberly. She had certainly not expected this.

"Jolly good," he exclaimed. "Well, I'll see you then," he concluded, and turned to walk away.

"Jolly good," she echoed, half in jest, half in sarcasm.

He walked away briskly. He didn't need to turn back to know she was standing there trying to figure all that out. It's a good thing he didn't, for had he, he would have seen an astonishingly beautiful young woman in a blue velvet dress standing there with tears in her eyes. As tender as his heart was in regard to her, he could not have restrained himself from running back, gathering her into his arms, and confessing the depth of his true feelings for her. Then they would have both been thoroughly confused.

Except for the name of the church, Melody had no idea how to reach him. A dozen times she stopped herself from marching over there, half to inquire what type of music he desired, the other half to find out what he really did at the church, and another half to plumb the depths of her own feelings concerning him. Of course that made more than two halves, but she did feel about twice confused concerning him.

•   •   •

Sam spent all the next day talking with the police, trying to neutralize the threat of the kidnapping attempt. After a full day of probing questions and toothless promises, the police finally left. Their final suggestion was for Sam to hire a bodyguard. Their day had been so taxing that they had not had time to discuss Princess's miraculous return the night before, nor Sam's powerful change of heart just moments before the kidnapping attempt. They were just returning from putting two very sleepy little girls to bed.

"I'm exhausted," Princess said as they passed their room. "I think I'll turn in. It's been an emotionally draining day," she said with a sigh.

"I'll grab a blanket," Sam said and hurried into their room. He returned with his pillow and a blanket. He smiled at her as he passed her near the stairs. Even sleeping apart, it seemed wonderful to have her home.

"Oh, there's something else I need to tell you," Princess said as he started down the stairs. He stopped on the third tread and turned back. He was tired of surprises and being devastated by sudden revelations. His face betrayed his angst.

"What's that," he asked a little petulantly.

"You remember Dr. Rob?"

Sam's face hardened. "Oh, definitely!"

"Well, last night you asked me why I was here. The reason I came here was because he threw me out of his house," she said a little sheepishly.

"So you came here because you had no where else to go?" he asked, feeling sick inside again. He thought she had returned because she realized she truly loved him, not because she was homeless.

"Sam, he threw us out the very first evening. I never did stay at his house. We spent the whole time with my friend Heather in Anchorage."

"You never did stay at his house?" Sam asked, his voice laced with disbelief.

"That's the wrong question," she replied brightly. "You're supposed to ask me why he threw me out."

Sam was on the verge of nausea, but he complied in a small voice. "Okay, why did he throw you out?"

"Because I refused to be intimate with him," she replied, her head lowered, her eyes fixed upon him.

"He kicked you out because you stopped sleeping with him? Is this supposed to make me feel better?"

"That isn't what I said. I said, he kicked me out because I refused to be intimate with him. You have to start something before you can stop it."

"Wait a minute. Are you saying you never did . . .?"

Princess's face lit up. She merely nodded.

"But, when you came home, you were so . . . charged," he said, struggling for the right words. "How come . . .?"

Princess drew a deep breath and blew it back out as if steeling herself for a difficult explanation. "That last two weeks at the retreat Dr. Rob was very forward. He made so many advances at me. I denied him what he wanted every time. But, by the time I got home I was . . . . I, uhm, well, you were there!" She concluded, embarrassed.

"So you never . . .?" was all Sam could stammer.

"No, never," she said, a beaming smile on her face.

"You didn't . . .?"

"No." Princess shook her head emphatically. "I didn't."

"And after you went to his house? You didn't . . .?"

"Not even close. Sam, I know you had lost faith in me at that point, but think about it. I'm not promiscuous—it's not in my nature. I was confused, not sleeping around. I thought I had fallen out of love with you, but I was also very uncertain about my feelings for him. I had been sick, and he healed me. I was in love with love and hero worship, and perhaps with the idea of wild romance."

"But I accused you, and you didn't deny it. You just said you didn't see it that way, that the only thing that mattered was that you loved him and not me. You led me to believe you had—uhm, been with him," Sam complained loudly.

Princess shook her head sadly. "Sam, I'm sorry. But I think it would be more accurate to say I let you believe it, than I led you to believe it. I was surprised you came to that conclusion, and it just made me angrier. I just let you continue believing it. I was angry, and confused, and upset, and wanted you to hate me so I could feel justified in leaving you. The important point is, I never slept with him."

"Didn't he try to seduce you that first evening?"

"Oh, yes!" she replied. "Constantly. He wooed me, dined me, and promised me the sky and stars. He told me 'where have you been all my life.' It was every girl's dream of being swept off her feet by a handsome hero." She cleared her throat in an embarrassed way before continuing.

"I do have a confession to make, although not as severe a one as you previously expected." Sam sat down heavily on the top step, and Princess knelt beside him.

"That first night after I left, he tried very hard to get me to be intimate with him. He was so romantic, so persuasive and gallant. I felt so . . . so . . . female, I guess. I let him kiss me, and hold me. But, when he tried to do more, I just couldn't do it. I kept thinking about you, and I couldn't. Everything inside me cried out against it. At that point I knew I still loved you. I made him stop. It was very difficult and turned ugly. He was not a gracious loser. I almost had to fight my way out of his house. But, I did, and I left. I have slept at Heather's every night I've been gone. I haven't spoken to Dr. Rob for over a month."

"Oh," was all Sam could say. The vision of her kissing him was playing before his eyes, and he didn't like it.

"Sam, listen to me," Princess said, interrupting his dark reverie. He looked into her eyes and saw love, and deep regret. "I know I sinned. And I know I offended and hurt you horribly. But I didn't betray you. I was weak, but I was also strong. Do you have any idea how hard it is to let something go that far, and then tell them you won't go on? It was the hardest, most humiliating, devastating, embarrassing, *and stupid* thing I have ever done!" she said, tears gathering in her eyes. She composed herself and continued.

"At that point I knew I was in deep trouble, badly mistaken, and totally in error, standing in an evil man's home in jeopardy of my soul!" Princess shuddered involuntarily. In an odd way Sam could see her point. He doubted he could stop at that point, and he also imagined his chagrin at having to leave embarrassed and utterly humiliated.

"As soon as I can arrange it I'm going to go talk to the bishop, and I'll do whatever it takes to become pure again," Princess went on earnestly. "Sam, I'm so, so sorry. I know I offended you, and Heavenly Father, and the twins. But, I also know that I will never be tricked into anything like that again. And I also know that you will always be the only man I have ever loved with all my soul. I may not be sinless right now, but I am virtuous, my love."

Sam was stunned to silence. It was all more than he could assimilate and understand. His heart felt like someone had been playing crack the whip with his emotions, and he had lost grip and been flung off into a thicket of thorns.

Princess pulled the pillow from his arms, then the blanket and took him by the arm. They spent the whole night in one another's arms. They were together, apart, in love, hurting, so close, so far away. Neither of them slept.

Princess was lovingly dealt with by the Lord's appointed judges the following Sunday evening. She cried bitterly. Sam had only been invited to attend a small portion of the proceedings, and it made him weep for her to have to go through it. Yet, afterward, she was full of hope and determination. Paying a price was therapeutic, and helped her feel her way home. It was hard for her to pass the sacrament tray without partaking. It was hard for Sam to watch her do so.

Monday morning Sam contacted Crichton and Dangerfield, a nation-wide detective agency. Sam took photos, police reports, and everything he had collected regarding his tormentors. He laid $20,000 in cash on their desk and told them to use every resource to find who they were and what they wanted. Crichton and Dangerfield declined to take the case. No amount of money would change their mind—nor would they explain why.

Sam walked from their office stunned. For the first time in his life he felt truly afraid. The police were willing, but impotent. The FBI was interested but not motivated since no real crimes other than petty vandalism had been committed. Beyond all that, there were no telling clues, not even one.

As he was driving home, he prayed earnestly. For some reason, to Sam, driving was an invitation to pray. Almost every time he slid behind the wheel the Spirit would gently slide in with him. He often found solace, relief, and peace while driving. As he drove he felt the familiar stirrings of truth, and felt his soul relax and begin to soar. In a flash that warmed his soul, a memory surfaced of an account he had read in the newspaper about a year ago.

The article involved a man whose ex-wife had kidnapped his two young daughters and taken them to South Africa. The article gave a sketchy account of a daring rescue that involved international mercenaries, re-kidnapping the girls, and lots of cash. The father only acted after waiting three years for word of his children. One evening he received a brief call from his oldest daughter, then fourteen, crying and begging him to come take them home. The call lasted less than twenty seconds. The planning and eventually successful rescue took over three years.

Of course the man's name was not given in the article. Sam immediately returned to Crichton and Dangerfield, who accepted $1,000 to find the man's identity.

Scarcely a week had elapsed. Sam was grading a small shipment of diamonds at his desk. A soft knock on his open door brought him eye-to-eye with a man standing stiffly in the doorway. Sam carefully folded the gems into their packet and slipped them into his desk. He stood as the man walked across the hardwood floor, his eyes darting quickly about.

His visitor wore old denim jeans, a dark brown leather jacket and hiking boots. He wore a pony tail of dark brown hair, heavily streaked with gray. He was somewhat shorter than Sam, and walked with the ease of someone familiar with the outdoors. The man's eyes were a very light gray, and gave the impression of hidden intelligence. His face was heavily tanned beneath a leather Aussie hat whose left brim was fastened up with a gold medallion. All this gave the impression he had just returned from digging for treasure in Egypt. An air of confidence gave the added impression he had succeeded.

Sam offered his hand which the man took in a strong grip. Sam judged his age a little shy of sixty. "I understand you've been looking for me, Mr. Mahoy," the man said with a gravely voice, his eyes locked upon Sam's.

"I have no idea who you are," Sam replied as he motioned to a seat on the opposite side of the desk. Instead of sitting the man turned and swung the door closed, then took the offered seat.

"I was contacted by Crichton and Dangerfield. They said you wanted to talk to me."

"I understand now," Sam said, suddenly off guard. He struggled for a moment to know where to begin.

"What do you want?" the man asked in a steady voice.

"I need your help," Sam replied slowly.

"With . . ."

"There was a kidnapping attempt on my daughters a few days ago."

"Why contact me?"

"The police are at a standstill. There are no clues."

"Why contact me?" The stranger asked again.

"I am at a loss. I've got to do something. I read about your rescue of your daughters . . ."

"That was almost twenty years ago," the man interrupted. His voice was a little perturbed.

"The article gave no indication when it occurred. It seemed recent."

"Newspapers almost always get it wrong," he said without emotion.

"I've noticed," Sam replied, attempting to ease the tension in the room with a smile.

The man wasn't amused. "Before I walk out of here, I ask again. Why did you contact me?"

Sam leaned forward in his chair and steepled his fingers under his nose, his elbows on his desk. He did not know how to answer this question until he felt the Spirit move him. The answer was incredibly simple, because it was the truth. "I was praying urgently, seeking direction, and your name and story came into my heart. I contacted you because it was the right thing to do," Sam answered.

The man leaned back in his chair as if suddenly deflated. His slight edge of aggression seemed to evaporate. Almost a full minute elapsed in silence before he replied, "That is probably the only answer that could have stopped me from storming out of your office."

"Please explain."

"Mr. Mahoy . . ."

"Please call me Sam."

The man's demeanor, if anything, grew annoyed. "Sam, you have to understand. Rescuing my daughters sucked the life out of me. It took more courage than I actually had. It left me psychologically, emotionally and financially bankrupt. The only good thing that came from it was that I got my daughters back, and I consider it all worth it. But, I have no desire to become entangled in some new international intrigue. I don't think I could survive it."

"That isn't exactly what I was hoping you would say," Sam replied quietly.

"I know. But it is the truth. Don't get me wrong. I owe God a great deal. Our little rescue was much more a miracle than a precision rescue. We did our best, but there is no doubt in my mind that we succeeded by divine intervention. I am willing to do what I can, but I'm afraid it's precious little."

"Apparently that will be enough," Sam said, opening both palms heavenward.

"I hope so."

"Me, too."

Sam's enigmatic visitor hesitated before he spoke. "There is one tidbit of information that may help you. It's something the man from Crichton and Dangerfield told me. He mentioned that they had a client conflict with you."

"What do you suppose that means?" Sam asked.

"It means a bunch of things. First of all, it means that their firm apparently did some work for whoever is harassing you. They most probably didn't know they were assisting in a criminal act at the time. My guess is they were asked to gather and supply information about you."

"Telling you they have a client conflict couldn't have been an accident," Sam observed.

"I'm sure it wasn't."

"I'm sorry," Sam said. "I don't believe you ever said your name."

"No, I didn't. My guess is they are trying to help without getting themselves in trouble with their former client. They must realize now that their client is capable of nasty retaliation if they find out."

"They're afraid," Sam observed, forcing himself to not press further for the man's name. Sam was willing to play whatever games were necessary to save his family.

"They should be. There's something else I know that could help."

"Which is?"

"They don't necessarily want the twenty-two carat diamond."

Sam was amazed. "What do they want, then?"

"Most probably revenge."

"Why do you say that?"

The man's eyes became steely. "Because they tried to take your kids. That is an act of terrorism. They aren't after a refund. They want revenge—or they simply want your kids."

"But, I haven't done anything to them!" Sam cried.

"But you did."

Sam's shoulders slumped. "What? What did I do that would motivate them to such dark depths?"

"Apparently only they know that. But you or your wife certainly did something, or they wouldn't be after you like this. There is one other possibility."

"Which is?"

"This has little to do with you. Perhaps there's someone they wished to manipulate, who would be devastated by the loss of your daughters."

Sam was momentarily stunned that this man knew his children were daughters but chose not to act upon it. "My parents, of course, are terrified for the girls. But, they don't have any enemies I know of. Besides, they haven't been contacted in any way."

"Your wife could be the target. Does she have any enemies?"

"It is inconceivable to me."

"Can you think of anyone who could use your children to manipulate your wife into something she might not otherwise be willing to do—like leave you, perhaps?"

"Who would want such a thing?" Sam asked, stunned.

"What about your wife's parents?"

"Her father lives in South Africa. He was very upset that my wife came to America with me. If it makes any difference, he's a wealthy diamond . . ."

"Let me guess," the man interrupted loudly, "He's a diamond merchant and/or smuggler. I understand in South Africa it's often about the same thing. I'll also wager he had something to do with this 22-carat stone. My guess is he's been smuggling diamonds long before, and undoubtedly long after this incident. I'd guess the stone belongs to you, but he has it."

"Yes, yes!" Sam cried, astonished. This was, in fact, the first time Sam had realized that someone working for his father-in-law had retrieved the big diamond from the airplane, and yet Princess's father had never even mentioned the diamond, let alone returned it.

"I think you just solved the puzzle—at least in part." He sat contemplatively for a moment. "The possibilities I can see are that whoever is doing this is either after revenge against your father-in-law . . ."

When he didn't continue, Sam said, "Or?"

"Or it's your father-in-law who's behind it all."

"What?!" Sam cried.

His mysterious visitor gave him a steely look and stood. "Either way, he's the key to this mystery, and either way, the only one who can stop it." So saying, he pulled the hat from his head for the first time to reveal a shiny bald dome. It unexpectedly added ten years to his age, and made him look tired and vulnerable. He smiled and offered Sam his hand.

Before returning the handshake Sam reached into his desk and palmed a four-carat stone he had just been studying. He pressed the stone into the man's hand as they shook.

The old gentleman looked truly surprised. "I don't want anything for helping," he said, holding the stone toward Sam in the palm of his hand. It glittered like a tiny sun.

"You said you were financially bankrupt. That stone will easily reverse that."

"This stone is probably worth more than any home I've ever owned," he said in amazement.

"Then get a bigger one," Sam suggested. "Buy something nice for the girls." The man's hand slowly closed around the stone. His eyes clouded with tears, and he nodded once, turned and disappeared through the door. Sam never saw him again.

Sam immediately opened his organizer and found Grandpa Pawley's phone number. The phone rang six times before Princess's father answered, his British accent in full bloom. Sam quickly got to the point, and related everything he had just learned. His father-in-law listened quietly. "I'll take care of it," he said in a terse voice, and hung up without saying good-bye.

Chapter Eight

Harvest

Six months elapsed before Princess was restored to her former blessings. During all that time they heard nothing from the gang of 22. Sam hired a full-time bodyguard to stay near his family twenty-four hours a day. It made them all feel better, but was probably insufficient to thwart any real attempt on their safety.

That same September, Sam was called as first counselor in the bishopric. The calling both thrilled and frightened him. He knew he was willing to do anything for the Lord, and yet he was not sure he could summon enough inspiration to do it right. Old feelings from childhood, feelings of fear and inferiority plagued him. For over a week he fought random impulses to decline the offered blessing. Yet, each time he prayed, he felt increasingly like, once again, the Lord would work a miracle that would make him adequate to the calling. After all, if God was able of these stones to raise up seed unto Abraham, as John the Baptist said, then God was able of Samuel Mahoy to raise up a humble servant of the Lord.

Sam knew it would have to occur in spite of him, not because of him. His weaknesses were too great, and his capacity too small to just charge into such a thing full-speed ahead. He desperately needed the Lord to lay His hand upon his shoulder and give him strength he did not possess of his own. Perhaps the thing that worried him most was that he might just blunder ahead and do things which might prove harmful to those he was meaning to bless.

With his calling came a startling glimpse into the tumultuous affairs of the Ward. He was suddenly made aware of problems he had no previous idea were occurring. It almost seemed as if half the ward was having marital problems, and the other half was dying of some disease. Of the few who had nothing especially wrong, most were unemployed. He had to struggle to pull his heart out of a sense of despair. For the first time in his life he saw the church as a hospital, rather than a divinely appointed country club.

Of the many people with special needs was the Fowler family. Brother Fowler was a faithful brother who was nearly always away from his family driving truck. When he was at home, he seemed to have little energy for much more than long hours of watching television. Yet he responded willingly to any church assignment, and attended to his home teaching faithfully. Sister Fowler was overweight by nearly a hundred pounds. It was a strain for her to walk from one room to the other. Every ailment known to man seemed to afflict her from time to time. Her most pressing illness was multiple sclerosis which occasionally flared up and sapped her of energy and control of her limbs.

She had brought three children into the world, all with severe handicaps. Their oldest girl was blind, deformed in the face and arms, and socially inept. Their next oldest boy was physically normal, but mentally little more than half his age. Their youngest was physically perfect and unusually bright. He was also unusually active, literally bouncing off the walls and furniture. No one could control him, certainly not his mother who at times could barely move from room to room. Yet this little one was their sweetheart, and their family's only claim to any vestige of normalcy.

To make matters worse, the Fowlers were outcasts in a quiet way. The adults of the ward were friendly toward them, but none were friends. Perhaps inwardly most felt superior to the Fowlers, and silently believed this family's misfortunes were their own doings, or the results of poor diet, poor work ethic or poor genetics. Whatever the reason, they were what might be termed accepted, but not truly embraced in the ward.

The children were treated with contempt by their peers. When no adult was present they were persecuted, physically tormented and mentally harassed. If their personal problems were not sufficient to cripple them, the emotional abuse they received was more than sufficient to complete the debilitation.

Sam's first special assignment as a member of the bishopric was to fellowship the Fowlers. His assignment included special emphasis on helping the ward accept them, as well as assisting them to fit in.

Sam and Princess visited the Fowlers' home together several times. Princess became nauseated the first time they walked into their home. The halls were stacked from floor to ceiling with newspapers, books, boxes, car parts and dirty laundry. The smell of cat urine was so caustic that even Sam felt pressure rising in his throat. He could not help but wonder how anyone could be healthy in such an atmosphere.

The kitchen was piled high with dirty dishes and empty pizza boxes, while the kitchen floor was not even visible underneath the grime and litter. The living room was piled deep in trash and dirty clothing. Obvious piles of cat and dog droppings lay in the corners of the room.

The only clear spot of drab green carpet (probably not its original color), was between a new-looking leather recliner and the TV, which were also the nicest and newest pieces of furniture. Four dogs barked and danced around Sam and Princess, jumping up to put stinking paws on their chests.

The Fowlers seemed to think this cute, and made no attempt to restrain them. Numerous cats climbed and clawed everywhere one looked. Brother Fowler occupied the recliner directly in front of the TV. He alternately yelled at the kids, the cats and his wife, and spoke lovingly to the dogs as the TV blasted a dozen decibels above the threshold of pain.

Princess flatly refused to go with Sam a third time. It did seem futile, as he could not carry on a conversation with anyone while there. The only discussions were held during commercials, and usually centered on the plot of the show, movies playing at the theater, or would he like a "damn cat" to take home?

In the beginning Sam truly wanted to help them. As time went on he found them resistant to his urgings, suggestions of ways they could fit in, and easily offended by any suggestion regarding cleanliness, hygiene, or health. Slowly Sam felt his attitude being battered by what seemed impossible odds. Sadly, Sam was on the verge of concluding it was impossible to make any positive progress with the Fowlers when his heart was changed in an unexpected way.

It was just four days before Christmas that the Fowlers' home caught fire and burned to the ground. The fire could have been started by a thousand things, their home was a fire-trap. Oddly, the fire started from the electric cord going to the TV where it crossed a cat's latrine. The constant saturation of caustic urine had finally eaten through the insulation on the cord.

Sam rushed to their home in time to watch the firemen put out the last of the flames. Even the burning rubble put off a nauseating stench. Sam noticed that several of the firemen had wrapped cloths around their faces to fend off the odor of burning filth.

When Sam arrived the Fowler family was huddled in their only remaining possession, a 1964 Dodge van that no longer had an engine. They had run from their burning home in their nightclothes and had sought shelter from the blaze, and the unrelenting cold, in their van. They had been kept warm by the heat from their burning home. Sam found them in an agony of grief. Their retarded son, Anthony, had not escaped the fire and was lost. Sam had never seen such grief, such complete, unrelenting anguish. No words came to him. No comfort seemed possible in the face of such loss.

The Fowlers' plight was real and immediate. They had nothing left. In every sense they were helpless, homeless, naked in the cold night, and nearly friendless. Sam pondered the possibilities in his mind. They were few, pitiably few. There were no relatives to call on, no friends to lean on, no insurance to claim, no place to go, and little hope of finding one.

Bishop Dowling arrived while Sam was still trying to comfort them. Others came from the ward to see what had happened and to offer assistance. A team was formed to find housing for the displaced family. One brother offered a small camp trailer sitting behind his home. It was small, and it would need to have electricity and heat hooked up, but it was available. Another offered a garage with a bathroom which he and his wife had occupied while they were building their home beside it. Someone suggested renting a hotel room, another thought they should contact the Salvation Army. A thoughtful brother brought a large army tent and began pitching it on the front lawn of the burned home. Others saw his efforts and helped. Soon the tent was erected. A van arrived stuffed with clothing gathered from who knows where, and sisters began scuttling around searching for specific-sized clothes. In a short time the displaced family was clothed.

Sam watched all this with a sense of wonder and discomfort. While there were many people pitching in to help, they were working to "fix" the problem and return home. Everything he saw happening seemed somewhat less than what Sam felt this destitute family truly needed.

After a while the crowd of people began to dissipate. Vague offers of further help were often expressed just as the people walked away. Sam remained, unsatisfied, yet unable to think of anything more to do. While he was in the midst of making efforts to find them a running car, his mom and dad pulled up in their motor home. There was barely room for the big old bus amidst all the cars, but Jim found a place. Sam watch in quiet appreciation as the two people he most admired emerged from the bus, walked directly to the Fowlers, and hustled them into the bus. Before anyone fully comprehended what had occurred, Jim was backing away. With a roar of diesel fumes their problem family had disappeared into the night.

The remaining volunteers began taking down the tent with a defeated air. There seemed to be disappointment that their stopgap assistance had been upstaged in a way. Sam thought it most odd that few seemed to understand what had just happened. To Sam's thinking the Lord had sent angels to assist his children in their desperate need.

• • •

Grandpa and Grandma Mahoy rearranged their home, their lives, and their finances to make a place for the Fowlers. They wrapped their love around this lost family so completely that their only grief was for the loss of their son.

Sam visited his parents the next day and found their big home churning with orderly chaos. Grandma Mahoy immediately changed their diet to one of wholesome food. Their guests were too modest to comment about the nearly total absence of sugar from their diet, and too astounded to complain when their health and energy radically improved. Young Bobby made a radical change in a mere few days. After a week of crying himself to sleep, begging for candy, and severe temper tantrums, he accepted his new diet and quietly changed into a pleasant little boy.

Their salvation came partly in the fact that the Fowlers were economically destitute and could not buy a single item of candy for him, for they surely would have done so just to shut him up. Grandma quietly restrained him, taught him, disciplined with love, and doused him with a glass of cold water whenever he threw a tantrum. When Bobby felt the need to explode, he did it as far away from Grandma Mahoy as possible. The fits of rage invariably ended suddenly when he heard the water running in the kitchen. When the change came, it was quiet, sweet, unexpected (at least to the Fowlers), and permanent. Permanent, that is, as long as Bobby stayed completely away from sugar of any kind.

Grandma utterly, completely refused to let anyone in her kitchen, and the result was that the Fowlers had no choice but to eat wholesome food. They found themselves unavoidably, unexpectedly, and perhaps unhappily what they considered to be almost vegetarians.

Their former diet had been largely meat fried in hot grease. Their new diet, by comparison, was very little meat, usually in a thick stew or gravy. Grandma owned a big old skillet, but its only function in life was to fry eggs and zucchini. Yet when Sister Fowler unexpectedly lost fifteen pounds, and Brother Fowler found himself brimming with energy, they were very vocal in their acceptance of their new lifestyle.

Three days after their arrival, Sam's parent's TV mysteriously broke. Brother Fowler soon found himself outside the house pacing with unaccustomed energy. Before many days he was back driving trucks, but even that was too sedentary. He started looking for more energetic work and amazed himself when he found a job in a cabinet shop for a considerably higher wage. It turned out that he loved working with wood and was good at it to boot. He began a steady climb toward success in his new career.

Grandma ruled her home with the same gentle no-nonsense she had used when Sam was a child. No pets came to stay. No litter touched the floor and stayed. No one ate without also helping clean up. Bathtubs were clean before and after a bath. Spills were wiped up by the spiller, and quarrels were quickly put away with good feelings on both sides. In short, the whole family restarted their lives, and for a time, they all called her Grandma Laura.

When the example had been set to a solid gel, she let Sister Fowler into her kitchen. Flattered that Grandma Mahoy trusted her in the inner sanctum of her sparkling kitchen, Sister Fowler produced a meal largely meeting the criteria of the mistress of the castle.

To shorten a rather lengthy tale, the lost family was found, clothed, cleaned, loved, and reborn. When they emerged from their temporary home nearly a year later, they were different people. The change was startling, nearly unbelievable.

Most startling of all was that the Fowlers recognized the miracle of their metamorphoses more keenly than anyone else. As they grew they looked back on their former existence with growing revulsion and loathing. In time they knelt in prayer together and thanked God for taking away their home so they could come to know the love of Grandpa and Grandma Mahoy, and the joy of their new life.

Though this miracle was significant and life-changing, it was in reality very slow. Lessons were learned at a snail's pace, forgotten far faster, and repeated many times.

Although the change was miraculous, it was discounted by some in the ward. They attributed the squeaky cleanness, wrinkle-free clothes, and bright faces to Grandma Mahoy's tireless efforts, not to any true worth on the part of those souls wearing the new smiles.

In a way that surprised Sam, the Fowlers recognized this reaction in others as inevitable, and refused to be resentful, or to blame them. They simply changed, and waited patiently for those around them to recognize it—or not, as the case may be. In some ways they exhibited a higher level of nobility than those to whom these changes were invisible.

The Fowlers built a new, larger home on the foundation of their old one. With his new job and new energy, the Fowlers could afford something a little better. Grandpa Jim worked tire-lessly for weeks to build the new home alongside his friend. Since it was being built out of pocket, Grandpa energetically campaigned for building materials to be donated from local businesses, members, neighbors, and charities. His efforts were largely unnoticed, yet the materials arrived when needed, and the home rose from the ashes of their former plight. They moved into their new home in early December, just a little short of two years after the fire.

Sam spent many hours driving nails beside his father. It was good to have a hammer back in his hand again. He donated a few things as seemed appropriate, like a bathtub, plumbing and other small things. Even though he could have financed the entire project without any difficulty, Sam chose to give his time, and to let others benefit from giving as well. The bulk of the donations came from non-members. When it was ready to occupy, it was a sweet feeling to stand back and look at their new home—painted, carpeted, clean, and very likely to stay that way. When the Fowlers moved in—it still needed lots of work, paint, and other things; but it was warm, sound, and all theirs.

• • •

Sam was in charge of the Christmas program for sacra-ment meeting that year. He worked energetically to arrange everything just right. He wanted this Christmas to be most spe-cial, and worshipful. Yet, as perfect as every preparation seemed, there was still something missing. He troubled over what it might be right up to the Saturday before the Christmas program.

It was rather late when the phone rang and he was sur-prised to hear Sister Fowlers' voice on the line. She was cheer-ful, yet somewhat subdued, almost as if she were frightened. He had to coax out of her what was on her mind.

"Well, you see Brother Mahoy, it's my oldest daughter Catherine. She has wanted to sing a song at Christmas time for a long time. And you know, she's almost blind and all, and not real pretty," she said in a whispered voice. "She can just barely read her music by holding it very close to her face. We never felt like people would appreciate her singing. But you see, she's turning seventeen, and next year she's going away to college."

This was a revelation to Sam. He had no idea that Catherine was even in school, let alone looking toward college.

"Would you like me to put her on the program?" he heard himself ask. Even before she answered, he knew that this was the part that had been missing from the program. He felt his heart rejoice as she replied.

"Oh, would you? That would be so wonderful! Thank you. You're just like your parents. They are so special to us, you know. We just love them with all our heart. Why, they loved us like their own, and taught us how to be real people. We were like little children playing house and not even knowing how. They saved us, did you know that? Well, of course you did. We just love them, that's all."

Sam thought to himself that everyone should experience being loved so purely by a friend. But rather than commenting on that, he asked, "Who will accompany her on the piano?" He considered they might ask him to do it.

"Why, I will, of course," she asserted brightly

"I had no idea you played."

"Well, you couldn't see the piano in our first house. It was always buried under something, but it was there. I taught Catherine this song myself. She can do it pretty good. It will be good for her to finally get to sing this song. We've worked and worked on it. She's so shy, you know. She wants to go to college to study music. Did you know that?"

"No I didn't. I'm going to put her as the closing number. Is that all right?"

"Oh, gosh. I suppose so. We'll practice some more tonight." There was a moment's silence, and then she said with deep sincerity, "You're just like your Dad," and hung up.

It was the greatest compliment she could have given him.

• • •

The Christmas program was beautiful. The choir sang like a chorus of angels, and each talk was inspiring. All through the program Sam felt his suspense growing until he was nearly ready to burst. He had listed the final musical number merely as "Special musical number . . . Mary's Lullaby." He had intentionally not listed who would perform.

He did this for two reasons. One was to avoid embarrassment should Catherine decide she couldn't do it at the last
minute. The second was to forestall the inevitable prejudice that
would surround the inclusion of those names on the program.

Sam wanted the audience to have as little warning as possible, so that they might set aside their preconceptions and see
Catherine in a new, positive light.

"Mary's Lullaby" is one of the most beautiful and touching Christmas pieces ever written. It is intended to be sung by
a young, motherly woman. It describes Mary's love for her
newborn son, and talks of her sure knowledge that he is the
promised king who would die for his people. She sings a lovely,
almost sad lullaby to the Christ child, proclaiming. "One day
you will be King. But tonight you are mine."

Everyone was looking down at their programs to see who
would sing the final number as Sister Fowler led her daughter
toward the stand. Catherine tripped on the lowest step, and a
deacon snickered. Sister Fowler whispered directions, and they
climbed the steps to the stand and walked slowly toward the
pulpit. Sister Fowler turned her daughter toward the mike. It
groaned loudly as she pulled it down.

As she made her way toward the piano Catherine raised a
piece of music very close to her face and studied it with what
tiny bit of vision she possessed. Sam could see her screwing up
her face into a deformed scowl. Even he had to cringe a little,
and felt himself somewhat repulsed. The poor girl was a long
ways from pretty and very nearly painful to look at. Someone
coughed rudely, and others whispered too loudly. Sam began to
feel annoyed by their un-Christian behavior. He and the bishopric were sitting in the audience or he would have bolted to
his feet to stand by her until she could sing. As it was, she was
on her own.

Sister Fowler began to play. Her light, sure touch on the
piano pleasantly surprised Sam. He instantly recognized in her
one who loved music and for whom the touch of the keys was
a magic elixir that washed away hurt and brought peace and joy.
The music built to a crescendo, then fell to a hush. Sam waited
and prayed.

Catherine lifted her chin, twisted her face into a mask of
unpleasantness and sang. With the first crystalline note Sam felt

his heart leap. The voice that came from that face certainly could not belong to one so deformed. The music flowed as peacefully and serenely as love itself. Each note was pure, vibrant and sure. Her voice was far too mature, far too trained, far too beautiful to belong to one so young. Yet it did—with wonder and joy, it did.

The words told a story of Mary's love for her divine son, of a longing too pure to comprehend. For nearly four minutes, Catherine, the deformed, was Mary the mother of God, and it stunned and electrified everyone in the chapel. Ugly little Catherine, unsure, shy, disliked, repelled, and repelling, was for that brief moment in eternity, the most beautiful creature on God's earth. Sam listened with joy as each note filled him with love, peace, and sorrow. How sorry he was that he had ever thought of anyone with such inner beauty as ugly. How sorry he was that the song must ultimately end. How sorry he was that he had not known her beauty long before.

He opened his eyes, and Catherine was different. Her face was aglow with love. Her hands were clenched to her breast as she filled every heart with the perfect love of she who had been chosen first among women. He saw tears of sweet sorrow running down Catherine's cheeks, and his own eyes filled. He watched those short, stubby arms form a cradle as blind eyes were turned toward the baby who would be the king of all; and he knew, he felt it, he lived it, he loved as she had loved, and it filled him with tragic joy of exquisite beauty.

The music flowed to an end too soon, far too soon. Sam could not help but hear the sniffles and quiet sighs that once had been whispers of derision. Total, reverent silence waited as Sister Fowler joined her daughter, who had remained motionless where she stood, her sightless eyes still gazing at the empty cradle of her arms. Her mother took her elbow, and she smiled. It was a crooked, unbeautiful smile, but it was angelic, and it warmed every soul who beheld it. Breathless silence laid over the audience as they walked slowly down the steps. Catherine stumbled on the bottom step and four people jumped up to assist. The same deacon who had snickered earlier was the first there. He gently took Catherine by the other arm, and stayed with her until they found their seats a long moment later. The whole time he stared in wonder at the little deformed face that housed an angel of uncommon beauty.

• • •

The twins turned two the same year Connie and Fred Chapman moved next to Sam and Princess. The property already had a home on it when Sam had bought it. Sam and Princess had built their log castle a distance away. In time Sam had repaired the old home, painted it and put it up for rent. They didn't need the money but felt it a waste to leave the home sitting vacant.

Fred was not a member of the church and worked for the Alaska State Troopers. Connie was a baptized member but hadn't been inside the church since her baptism at age nine. She was a long-legged, blond-haired, blue-eyed beauty from California. Fred was large-boned with a prominent brow, square chin, blond hair, blue eyes, and a ready smile. His face was the type one expects to see snarling inside a linebacker's mask. He was energetic, happy, obviously in love with his wife, and violently disinterested in the Church. They had a three-year-old boy, Freddie.

From the start, the Chapmans were good renters and good neighbors. Sam rarely began an outdoor project without Fred coming over with an appropriate tool to help. In time they became friends. In many ways Fred was the ideal neighbor, even better than Sam himself had been to his neighbors. Yet, whenever the conversation turned to religion, Fred either quietly left for home, or simply changed the subject.

The connection Fred and Sam shared was mostly the result of being close neighbors, and Fred's gregarious nature. They had little else in common. Fred obviously took being neighbors as an obligation he faithfully honored.

Connie and Princess shared no such bond. Whatever sparks of friendship might have flared were extinguished in their first meeting which was cool and brief. Both men were surprised by their wife's reaction. Both felt powerless to change it.

With two busy two-year-olds to care for, Princess spent most of her time at home. By now Sam could handle any situation at work, and Princess simply stopped going to the office.

She loved her days at home, and pampered her girls until they thought the whole world revolved around their needs. In fact, it did.

Sam would have called the girls spoiled, but there was a definite line Princess drew in the invisible sand of their lives, which they did not cross without repercussions. They were obedient, polite and well-behaved. It was true that Princess had drawn the line in a much more lenient spot than Sam might have. Yet this was Princess's world, and he trusted her implicitly. Princess loved her twin daughters absolutely, and Sam doubted that anything in this world could go wrong with their childhood.

Even as two-year-olds, Lisa and Bonnie were strikingly beautiful and charming. Their long blond hair sparkled from repeated brushings, and their baby pink skin shone and smelled of expensive soaps. They often wore identical outfits purchased at discount stores. Though their clothes were new and cute, they were not expensive. Princess was determined to raise two normal children, not two brats from the royal family.

As the weeks and months went by, Princess saw very little of Connie, and there seemed to be no urge to change that situation. What ultimately forced a change was a love affair between Bonnie and Freddie. For reasons unfathomable, these two tykes fell hopelessly in love and would not be satisfied apart. Every other day either Freddie played at their house, or Bonnie and Lisa spent time at Freddie's house. As infant love affairs go, theirs was exceptional. They walked around holding hands, and often talked of when they would have their own house, and their own children. Princess was charmed by it all, as was Freddie's mom.

One sunny afternoon Connie's eyes were puffy as she picked up Freddie. Princess noticed immediately that she had been crying, and invited her in. Princess offered her a cup of Red Bush tea. Connie sipped silently until she finally burst open like an overfilled dam.

"Fred came home yesterday and said the troopers were going to fire him for taking a bribe!" Connie told her in a rush. "He pulled over an out-of-state driver for speeding almost a week earlier. The man explained that he was about to miss his plane at the airport, and Fred let him pay the fine to him. I didn't know that this was against department policy, but Fred did! He shouldn't have done it. But he was just being nice and was going to mail the fine that evening. No one would have known that the man hadn't mailed it himself. He was just doing him a favor. Fred's like that. He likes to help people," she said, her voice softening a bit.

Princess nodded. Fred was exceptionally accommodating. "What went wrong?"

Connie's face grew disgusted. "Oh, Fred's so disorganized," Connie said with a sad smile, "he's always misplacing things. He said he just put the envelope on his desk at work and forgot about it! It got buried and forgotten."

"Oh dear!"

"Yes, well, the man who paid the fine contacted Fred's captain to see if the fine had been paid. It hadn't. Without saying anything to Fred, they searched his desk and found the envelope with the money and the ticket. They took it as evidence, suspended him on the spot, and sent him home without pay." Tears began to flow again. Princess brought her a box of tissues.

"I just don't know what we're going to do. Fred's been with the Troopers twelve years. I know he doesn't look old enough, but he has. He has a big retirement built up, and if he gets fired for cause he'll lose it all. It's the only thing he knows how to do, and he won't be able to find a job with another police department for as long as he lives," she wailed, then broke down again and sobbed.

Princess's heart went out to Connie. She put her arms around her and held her while she cried. When the tears finally stopped, something had changed between them. Though not strong, a bond had been formed.

"What would you do if you were me?" Connie asked after she had regained her composure.

"I'd pray," Princess replied without hesitation. She realized after the fact that she had crossed the "no religion" line with her answer. Connie had wanted advice on how to solve a dilemma, not how to satiate her troubled soul.

Happily, Connie was not offended. She recognized Princess's response as sincere not pushy.

"Pray? I hadn't thought of that. I don't see how it could help, though," she replied heavily. "We need a job, not a prayer."

Princess waited until the correct answer came to her. When it came it felt right and comfortable. Even so, it took all her courage to obey. She slipped to her knees while Connie watched, a look of incomprehension on her face. "Come on. I'll show you how," she said.

Connie smiled weakly and slipped to the floor beside her. As was her custom, Princess slipped her hand into Connie's hand. Then, unseen by either of them, angels knelt with them, and for the first time in her life Connie heard someone talk to God. It unexpectedly warmed her through and through.

When Princess had finished praying, she looked at Connie and nodded, indicating that it was her turn. Connie flinched, yet nodded back and lowered her head.

"Dear God," she began as if addressing a letter. "Until a minute ago I didn't even know how to talk to you. So, you'll have to forgive me that I never tried. Now that we're having this talk, I kind of remember things my mother said about you. I remember that she said we are your children, and you love us." Connie paused here as if the idea had struck her with some force.

"God, I know what it's like to love my children, and if your love is anything like that, I know that you care about Fred and me. So, without telling you what I think the answer is, 'cause I really don't know, would you help us out? Please?" There was a long pause. "Just one more thing. Thank you for Princess and God bless her and the twins. Thank you. Uhm, Jesus Christ, Amen."

When Connie looked up at Princess she was surprised to see tears in her eyes. Princess squeezed her hand. "That was beautiful, Connie. I know He heard you."

They both stood. "I think so, too," Connie admitted. "It felt good, and I feel peaceful now. Thanks for showing me that." They walked toward the stairs to collect Freddie.

"Princess?"

"Yes, Connie?"

"How did you know I wouldn't hate you for trying to show me how to pray? I've certainly told you not to involve me in your religion often enough. Why did you do it?"

Princess concentrated on climbing the stairs. When she reached the top she stopped. "Have you ever had your conscience urge you to do something you knew was good?"

"Yeah, I guess so . . . Sure, lots of times, now that I think about it."

"It was like that," Princess explained. "I just knew it was right, and I always try to obey my conscience."

"Why? Most of the time my conscience just nags me. It's almost like having my mother around telling me what to do. Most of the time it just annoys me, and I ignore it."

"Well, the conscience we hear is the voice of the Holy Spirit. It comes from God."

Connie gasped. "No!" she exclaimed. "Are you sure?"

"That's what the scriptures say. And, that's what my experience has been. I am always the happiest when I follow the whisperings of the Holy Spirit."

"Oh my God!" Connie exclaimed, then slapped her hand to her mouth when she realized she had profaned. "Sorry," she added contritely. "It's just that, well, I had no idea. Oh my word! I'm going to have to do a lot of thinking. If what you say is true, I've been very, very naughty. If I was my mother, I'd spank me!"

They both laughed at that, and the bond between them deepened.

Princess asked, "What would your mother have done if you were naughty?"

Connie chuckled. "She'd probably have done something to try to teach me to behave and to listen to what she told me. She was an inactive church member, you know. But she really believed it, even if she didn't go to church." It was obvious her memories of her mother were fond ones.

By this time they had arrived at the girls' room, and found them happily playing together with Freddie. They watched for a moment before collecting Freddie. Princess felt the sweet stirrings again, and asked: "Why wouldn't a loving Heavenly Father do just the same—teach us in some loving way to listen to Him, so that we could be happy?"

"I suppose He would. Do you think that's what this is with Fred's work, a teaching thing from Heavenly Father?"

"I'm sure of it," Princess replied.

"Then will it go away after we learn the lesson?"

"I don't know, Connie. It may, or it may not. What I do know is that whatever it costs you to learn this lesson, your lives will be much happier afterward. I believe we came to this life to be happy. I believe the only way to be truly happy is to learn the lessons Heavenly Father teaches us, and then our earthly happiness will eventually become eternal happiness."

"That's a beautiful perspective on life, I think," Connie replied softly. "I'll think about all this. Thanks Princess. You're a good friend. And a good Christian," she added hastily.

Nearly a week passed with little more conversation passing between them than what was needed to shuffle the kids back and forth. Princess felt content to wait for Connie to broach the subject again. When she did, it was with a sense of wonder. They were once again sitting by the big piano, sipping Red Bush tea.

"Princess, this past week I've thought and thought about what you told me. And, each time I ponder what you said, I feel a glowing feeling right here," she said laying her hand upon her breast. "I've been anxious to talk some more to you about it but wasn't sure how to bring it up."

"I think you just did," Princess said happily.

"Right," Connie said with a smile. "Well, what I did in the meantime was to try out what you said. I've been listening very carefully to my conscience. And, guess what! It works! I couldn't believe it. Even Fred noticed the difference."

She paused here to sip her tea. Her face fell a little. "It's demanding isn't it," Connie observed.

"What do you mean?"

"Well, my house has never been cleaner. All my laundry is done. I've been reading the bible every evening. I've been extra loving with Fred . . . and I'm exhausted!" she said emphatically.

"But, you're happy," Princess appended.

"Absolutely. I've never been so filled with peace in my life. I can't remember a time when my life was so fulfilling, so together. Fred's convinced that I'm pregnant. I got like this when I was first pregnant with Freddie." They laughed again.

Connie grew sober and set her cup aside. "Something else happened, something I don't understand."

"What was that, Connie?" Princess asked with concern.

"Well, I have a cousin who lives in Talkeetna. She's the family rebel. She's single and has two kids by two different men she never married. She lives on welfare and is a drug addict. She pays for her addiction by selling herself to men. She lives in a filthy little apartment."

"Wow, I feel sorry for her," Princess said unhappily.

Connie shrugged. "I never have. She chose her life, and did it against her own common sense and a lot of free advice. I barely know her, and I certainly don't like her. Anyway, she stopped at the house yesterday."

Princess's eyes widened. "I saw a little beat-up white car pull up yesterday."

"That was her. She knocked on the door and asked me point blank if she could borrow a typewriter. She didn't even say hello, just 'Do you have a typewriter I can borrow.'"

"Did you loan her one?"

"I was going to tell her no. I knew she was going to go directly from my home to the pawnshop. She's done it before. My mouth was already open to say no when my conscience kicked me in the back of the head."

"I've had that happen," Princess said sympathetically.

"I had made myself a promise that I was going to give this conscience thing an honest try. I really meant it, and knew it had brought me happiness so far, so I yielded to it."

"So, what did you do?" Princess asked eagerly.

"What I said was that I did have one. I invited her in, and went to get it. I have two typewriters, and I got the better of the two. I actually carried it out to the car for her. I was about to ask when she would bring it back when out of my mouth comes, 'It's an extra machine. You can just have it.' Both she and I were amazed. She thanked me and actually smiled before she left. I just stood there in shock watching my typewriter drive away."

"You did the right thing," Princess replied with certainty.

"I know. I was so shocked. And Fred? Fred was furious. He blazed around the house. Here we are, out of work, and I'm giving away valuable things. He was right, and I knew it. It was hard to explain to him why I had done it."

"Oh, Connie, I'm so proud of you! You are truly amazing. It must have been very hard, and very hard to explain to Fred."

Connie snorted. "You have no idea!"

"Perhaps I do," Princess chuckled

"But you know what the odd thing is, Princess? I was about to make up a good excuse to Fred when my conscience butted in again and wanted me to tell him the truth, all of it."

"Really!" Princess replied. "What happened?"

"Fred believed me. He listened to my explanation, and he accepted it. I was stunned . . . I think he was stunned."

"You can include me in that list," Princess assured her, then more seriously. "Would you mind if I shared something very precious with you?"

Connie nodded happily. "I'd be honored," she said.

Princess stood, crossed the room and returned with a leather-bound copy of the Book of Mormon. She didn't immediately hand it to Connie.

"I feel like we are good enough friends that I can give you this. I'm not doing this to try to force you to read it. That's not the point really. The point is, this book has brought me lasting joy. This is where the things I've been sharing with you largely come from. I don't feel like I would be a real friend if I didn't give you your own copy. Will you accept it in the same spirit I'm offering it?"

Connie slowly took the book and turned it so she could read the title. Her face was expressionless. She lifted the front cover and read the handwritten inscription inside. In Princess's flowery script it said:

To my dear friend Connie.
May joy always be the measure of your days.
Princess Mahoy

Connie was slow to look up. When she did her eyes were bright with happiness. "I will treasure this book as long as I live, if for no other reason than for what you have written inside the cover. Thank you."

Princess beamed. "You are most welcome."

"And," Connie continued a trifle uncertainly, "if my conscience tells me to read it, I will. I vowed at one time I would never touch this book again, but I'm learning so many wonderful things from you, I don't want to place any stupid limitations upon any of it."

"I can't imagine you doing anything stupid."

"You haven't known me that long," Connie asserted, then laughed heartily.

• • •

No sooner had Connie left the house than the phone rang. It was Sam.

"I have bad news," he said without preamble.

"Oh dear, what is it?"

"We were broken into last night."

"Oh no! By whom? What did they take? Have they been caught?" Princess asked in one breath.

"I don't know, almost everything. They got away," he replied soberly, answering every question.

"How did they get past the alarms? Did the alarms even work?"

"They knew how to bypass them, I guess. It looks like a professional job, the police say."

"Did they get into the safe?" Princess asked breathlessly.

"Yes, but I had taken everything down to the bank vault that evening. They didn't know that of course. They ruined the safe trying to open it. They used a cutting torch. Can you believe that? They almost burned down the building. The carpet was on fire at one point, and they used our fire extinguisher to put it out. The place is covered in a yellow powder. It's awful."

"Scum-sucking bottom feeders!" Princess hissed. It made Sam chuckle with dark humor.

"They also took the sampler from my desk."

"Low-lifes!" she exclaimed.

"I agree. The Sampler alone had about $10,000 our cost, but that's only a fraction of what could have been in the safe had I not taken it to the bank."

"Sam, we've got to do something. They'll be back. The next time, we may lose even more."

"Princess, there's something else. They cut a big '22' in the door of the safe."

"Oh!" Princess gasped. Then in a subdued voice she added, "I wish they had gotten the contents of the safe now. Maybe they'd leave us alone if they did."

"I know. I had the same thought. Somehow I still don't think it would be over. Just the same, we have to take strong precautions. How do they handle security in South Africa?"

"They have twenty-four-hour-a-day guards. Not just alarms, but live, armed guards."

"I do think we need an armed guard at least at night," Sam agreed.

"I think I know where we can find one," she said with sudden cheerfulness.

"I do too," Sam agreed. He had had the same idea before he dialed the phone. It pleased him that they were in sync again.

• • •

Fred resigned from the Alaska State Troopers just as the snow began to fall that year. He resigned before they had completed their investigation. By doing so they were forced to accept his resignation and leave his retirement intact, since no formal charges had been filed. They chose to simply drop the matter. It was an unexpectedly happy conclusion to a nasty affair.

Fred accepted Sam's offer of a job that same day. The pay was lots better, the benefits not quite as generous, and the hours abysmal, but Fred was overjoyed. He strode through their offices making numerous suggestions. They did everything he suggested.

He was on guard that next night.

• • •

When the bank heard that Sam had hired a night guard, they offered to extend Fred's pay, improve his benefits, and add an elaborate lock box system if he would also patrol the bank below them. He readily agreed. In a short time he started his own security firm, and launched himself into a career which provided handsomely for his family from that day on. It wasn't too long before Sam and Princess subdivided the second house from their property and sold it to Fred and Connie. In addition to being great neighbors and business associates, they became dear friends.

• • •

Shortly after Fred went to work, Connie knocked on their door. Princess was taking cupcakes from the oven and was slow getting to the door. When she opened it Connie stood there with a slip of paper in her hand, her face aglow with a childlike look of expectation. Without saying a word she handed Princess the paper.

"You're pregnant!" Princess cried.

"I am," she replied happily. "I think listening to the Spirit is to blame for this," she added. They laughed then hugged.

"Congratulations!"

"Thanks. There's something else I want to tell you. Something almost as wonderful."

"Come in. Sit. I'll get some Red Bush tea."

"Hear me out first."

"Okay. Is it that important?"

"It's that wonderful is all."

"I'm anxious to hear it," Princess said as she settled in beside her. "You remember Angelica, my cousin?"

"The drug addict with your typewriter."

"Right. Well, this is all your fault, you know."

Princess laughed. "Tell me what I did."

"You taught me how to listen to the Holy Spirit, and nothing's been the same since. Well, we have two cars, as you know. Fred's Suburban and my Subaru. I kept having this feeling that I should give my Subaru to Angelica."

"Give it to her? That's your only transportation while Fred's at work. And she's got that little white car. I saw it."

"Those were my thoughts, too. Anyway, I kept getting this weird impression that I needed to give her my car. This was before you guys hired Fred, and money was a big problem. So for a time I ignored it, but it kept getting more insistent. Finally, I recognized that I was disobeying, and I reminded myself that every time I obey I receive wonderful blessings. So I loaded up Freddie and we drove the Subaru to Talkeetna."

"That's a long drive."

"Yeah, it took several hours. When we arrived at her apartment there was no white car outside. She had totaled it weeks earlier. I found her sitting in her filthy little apartment crying."

"That's so sad." Princess shook her head.

"It gets worse," Connie assured her. "I just walked up to her and held out the keys to the Subaru."

"'What's this?' she asked me. There were tears dried on her face where she hadn't even bothered to wipe them away. Her two kids were crying in the bedroom.

"I told her, 'I've brought you my Subaru. I don't need it any longer.' She just stared at me with big wide eyes. She looked at me like that for the longest time, then just broke down and cried uncontrollably. I held her and held her. It was so pathetic. My heart melted, and I cried with her." Connie stopped here to brush tears from her cheeks.

"Anyway, after she was done crying I asked her what was wrong. It was a stupid question, because everything in that child's life is wrong. She smiled sadly and told me the most incredible story, Princess. Is it all right if I try to tell what she said in her own words?"

Princess nodded for her to go on.

Connie nodded. "Angelica said—You know my life is messed up, Connie. You know I'm a bad person. I do drugs, I neglect my kids, I steal things to pay for my habit, and I sleep around for money. What you couldn't have known is that I hate myself, and hate what I've become, and hate where I'm going with my life. Two weeks ago I crashed my car. It was my fault. I was high, and I just plowed into someone. I didn't hurt his truck much. I slept with him, and he didn't file a police report, but it ruined my car.

"My car was my only security in life. It gave me freedom and mobility. I have been cooped up here in this stinky hellhole now for two weeks. My kids are hungry, I'm broke and too beat up to even sell my body for money. In short, I'm at the end of my rope. I have nothing left physically, emotionally, monetarily, or morally. I have been sitting here wishing I could die, and lacking the courage to kill myself."

Princess gasped. "Oh, no!"

Connie nodded grimly. "It was awful to hear. Then she told me—I didn't get out of bed this morning until almost noon. The only reason I did get up was because the kids were crying 'cause they was hungry. I fed them half a bowl of sugar puffs in water. It's all I had. I went back to bed and cried and cried. I cried until I was so depressed that I actually knelt down beside my bed and talked to God. You know me. I'm hard, and I'm defiant, and I'm bad. I ain't prayed to God since my mother last made me when I was six years old. But I prayed. I says, 'God, I know you're up there, and I ain't never doubted that. But I can't imagine you even know I'm alive. God, everyone in my life has walked away from me except you. And, I suppose in that case I was the one who did the walkin'. God, I don't want nothin' from you, and I'm not worthy to ask for nothing. But I would like to know something. I would like to know if you are aware I even exist.'"

"Oh, Connie, this is depressing," Princess said sadly.

"Yes, but listen to the rest. Angelica said—That was this morning. I have sat here all afternoon contemplating ways to end my life. If I had a phone I would have already called the Child Welfare people to come take my kids from me. I do love them, I really do, but I'm not good for them. Everyone knows that, even them. So when you walked up to me holding out those car keys, even before you said a word, this flood of warmth and love came over me."

Connie paused to wipe away a tear. "Then, Princess, she stopped, crossed her arms over her chest, and hugged herself, a sad smile on her grimy little face. Angelica's voice was strangled as she said—I've never felt anything like it, and I knew . . . I just knew in some way deep inside me that this was my answer. God really does know me, and He really does care. What I felt at that moment was pure love. I've never felt that before from anyone, not even from God."

Connie's eyes refocused on Princess. "I stayed there long enough to pack her and the kids up. I brought them home with me. I may be nuts, but I couldn't leave them there. I bought them food, and they ate like little piglets. You should see those poor babies. They're skin and bones. Mikey is six and looks three. Thomas is four and looks two. As soon as I got them home I gave them more food, and put Angelica in the bathtub. She just sat there in a daze until the water turned cold. I warmed it up again and bathed her just like a baby."

Connie paused as if reliving the experience. "I've never bathed a grown woman, Princess." Connie choked on her words and had to pause. When she continued, her voice was heavy with emotion.

"Her body was covered with scabs, bruises, and sores. She's been beat up so many times, Princess. Her body is absolutely devastated from disease and abuse. Her breasts are bruised, her arms are black and blue, she's almost skin and bones, and there are needle tracks on her arms and legs."

A look of horror, then compassion crossed Princess's face.

Connie's eyes focused far away. "She just stood there like a child and let me care for her. She has absolutely no pride left, Princess. Something happened there in that bathroom. I felt love inside me as if I were her mother, and she my desperately ill daughter. I suppose I felt the way that father did in the scriptures when he placed the robe and gold ring upon his returning prodigal son. I know Connie felt it, too. She just stood there and smiled sadly as I attended to her. I was as gentle as I could possibly be, and yet everything I did was painful to her. I believe she is in constant pain and just says nothing because no one cares."

"Oh, that poor child!" Princess exclaimed.

"I cried the whole time. As I washed her body, I think something was cleansed on the inside, too. I dressed her in my best gown and tucked her in my bed. I even kissed her on the forehead and told her I loved her. When I left she was still sleeping. It was all more tragic and more beautiful than anything I have ever experienced before."

Connie was quiet for a long time, then added. "I've made arrangements to enroll her in a drug addiction clinic. She's agreed to go and really give it a try. Oh, Princess, it's just the most pathetic thing I've ever seen in my life. Believe it or not, she's actually a member of the Church, and I've made arrangements for her to meet with Bishop Dowling."

She laughed an ironic-sounding laugh. "I haven't told you this, but I've been reading the Book of Mormon you gave me. I have a zillion questions, and now I'm going to be teaching Angelica. She needs the gospel desperately. I know the Church is true, Princess. I think I've known it all along, but was too proud to live it, or too lazy, or something. I don't know, but I do know Angelica needs me to be solid, which I'm not. I need a crash course on religion, Princess, and I need to know what times we meet on Sunday. I really need your help. I'm in way over my head!"

"And, you feel happy inside," Princess appended.

"Oh, oh yes," Connie replied softly.

• • •

Sam and Princess invited the missionaries to their home to teach Angelica. Fred and Connie came and listened intently. Because of their deep concern for Angelica's spiritual welfare, they turned their whole attention to acquiring truth, not filtering it through their own prejudices. They were so cooperative with the missionaries that Angelica probably never realized Fred was not a member, and Connie hadn't been inside a church in over twenty years.

During the fifth discussion the missionaries asked Angelica if she would like to be baptized after she was able to get her life in order. Angelica answered that she was already a member. An awkward moment of silence followed while the missionary who had asked the question turned red. His companion poked him in the ribs with an elbow, and the room erupted into laughter. When solemnity returned Sam realized that Fred had not laughed.

"Fred," Sam asked. "Is something troubling you?"

"Yes," he answered frankly. "I'm grateful that Angelica is taking the missionary lessons and is finding the truth for herself. But I'm the non-member here, and nobody has bothered to ask me a single question."

There was a moment of silence while everyone, including Fred, pondered the meaning of his complaint. One of the missionaries started to apologize, and to promise to ask Fred more questions. But Sam politely interrupted him.

"Fred, would you like to be baptized?"

"Well, yes!" he almost shouted. Connie turned to him with an expression of total amazement.

"Fred!" she exclaimed. "I had no idea you knew it was true, too!"

Fred fumbled with his hands, then looked directly at his wife. "I watched a miracle take place in your life and now with

Angelica because of the gospel. I'm stubborn, Connie, but I'm not stupid. I know something good when I see it, and I want to be a part of it. I want to have these miracles a part of my life from now on. Yes, I know it's true." He smiled happily. "Don't look so amazed!"

"I'm sorry, Honey. It's just that I, well, you, I mean, we never . . ."

"When would you like to be baptized?" Sam asked, interrupting Connie's stammering.

"As soon as it can be arranged," Fred replied forcefully.

"That would be tomorrow night," the senior of the two missionaries replied. Fred merely nodded and smiled broadly.

• • •

Melody's life took on a pattern of quietude and security she had never known in her whole life. She filled her days practicing, playing in the park, and thinking of Theodore, whom she found a charming enigma. She decided to do a little quiet research and found that his last name was Tennison, descended from the wealthy Tennison family so prominent in English and American history. His family proudly wore the status, the title and the old money which their name endowed upon them.

Melody was sitting in her sister's apartment rehearsing a complex passage in a Rimsky Korsakov work of sweeping minors and intricate rhythms when a firm knock at the door interrupted her concentration. She laid her violin aside and opened the door with some curiosity.

Two men in business suits stood officiously before her. "Miss Melody MacUlvaney?" the shorter of the two asked without introduction.

"Yes?"

He nodded and pulled an official-looking envelope from his jacket. "You are hereby served to appear before the Magistrate to answer charges regarding illegal immigration and living in this country with forged papers. We suggest you hire a solicitor, Miss MacUlvaney. He can advise you of your rights."

Melody was thunderstruck. "What? I'm just . . ."

"Do you intend to appear?" the man asked, sparing her the need to reply.

Her mind spun in a thousand directions. Only one idea emerged with any clarity: deny everything! She opened her mouth with those words on her lips when a quiet urging literally lifted the words from her tongue even as she forced air through her lips to speak them.

"Of course," she said quietly.

Both men nodded as if satisfied. They had turned to leave when the taller of them turned back as if on impulse. His face was impassive, his voice apologetic. "Miss, it's good you said what you did, miss. We'd have had to arrest you otherwise. Sorry to frighten you, but the department has received a tip from someone very respectable with some very damning evidence. There's an accusation that you may be a spy for the outlawed Rhodesian colony. These are very serious charges, mum. I again suggest you get a very good solicitor, mum," he said. His voice lost all hint of apology. "And don't attempt to flee the country. You are under close surveillance." So saying, he touched the rim of his small hat, nodded once, and walked briskly away.

• • •

Melody consulted the best solicitor she could find in their little town. The old barrister listened to her plight with interest as she explained through tears what had brought her to Wales, and then England, and of her struggle to obtain papers, then of her decision to "purchase" legality.

"I understand your decision, and the plight that motivated it," he concluded after listening carefully. "However, I am sorry to inform you that under English law, the truth of what has occurred is the controlling factor. That a law was broken, not why it was broken, is the rule of law. The magistrate will attempt to determine whether the charges are true, and if they are—since they are—there can be no defense. You *will* be found guilty of those charges and punished accordingly."

He leaned back in his chair and pondered for a moment. "Even though your motivation for doing what you did has no bearing upon your guilt, it may soften the ultimate punishment. I suspect in the least you will be fined and deported."

Melody fell back in her chair, crushed and terrified. Her voice was frightened. "How much fine?"

"More than you possess, I'm sure. The purpose of the fine is to strip you of all your assets plus enough to prohibit your return to England."

"That's the best case? What's the worst case?"

"In the extreme the court could find you guilty of all charges, including espionage, and sentence you to a very large fine, and as much as twenty-five years in prison."

"Twenty-five years! But I haven't committed espionage!"

"Then all you have to do is prove you are innocent."

"How can I prove I am innocent? Is there no presumption of innocence?"

He raised his chin as if the idea were repugnant to his thinking. "The assumption is that you are guilty or you would not be accused. You yourself told me you are guilty of the lesser crimes."

"God help me," Melody whispered to nobody present.

"Indeed. God may be your best hope," the old gentleman replied pensively.

• • •

Sweet peace hovered over Sam and Princess as they prepared for bed. The missionary meeting with Fred and Connie had been sweet and spiritual. Both he and Princess rejoiced deeply in Fred's desire to be baptized and in the blossoming of Angelica's soul.

"I'm going to go look in on the twins," Princess said as she slipped a light robe over her nightgown.

Sam had just opened his mouth to say he was sure they were fine when they distinctly heard a door bang downstairs. Sam looked at Princess and bolted from their room out onto the landing. The door to their room was directly at the top of the large stair. Below them the big front door was wide open, still moving ominously.

Princess stifled a scream. Sam ran down the hallway barely ahead of Princess. The twins' door was open. Sam flipped on the light, his heart paralyzed by fear.

Both beds were empty! On Bonnie's bed a dozen stuffed animals had been arranged into a large "22." Princess screamed and ran from the room.

Sam spun to follow and was slammed by a sound that seemed to shake the organs within his body. It took his mind a few seconds to realize it was the report of a gun from inside his home.

To be continued

in

Angels Forged in Fire

Volume 3 in the Millennial Quest Series

Excerpts from

Angels Forged in Fire

The hardest thing Sam ever did in his life, before or after, was to get out of bed the next morning and go to church. He had to force himself to take every footstep toward church. He turned back a thousand times, and waged a running battle inside his soul. By the time he was walking out to the car holding Lisa's hand he was sick to his stomach from conflict. Yet he was determined to do what was right, no matter the cost. This cost him more than he had inside and tore things apart which should be immune to such damage.

• • •

Theodore's uncle was dressed in a silk smoking jacket with a wide black collar and gold embroidered body. He was in his late seventies, and still hale, though somewhat stooped. He commanded a sprawling empire that stretched across most of Europe. His name was universally honored and feared. His hair was full and perfectly white, which he wore full, to his shoulders.

Uncle's voice was booming with welcome. "Come into my study! What brings you out into the country? It must be urgent."

"Uncle, you know I love you," Theodore began in a warning voice.

His uncle smiled, and holding up both hands, sat in a plush red chair. "I better sit down for this one."

Theodore sat opposite him. "I just pieced together several statements I remembered your making last weekend."

His uncle smiled. "About the spy from Rhodesia?"

"Uncle, I met the person in question, and she's no spy."

"Of course not! But she is a person of unsavory background and hardly fit for association with one of noble birth," he said forcefully, though still amiably.

Theodore wagged his finger at his uncle. "Are you playing matchmaker again? I thought you were going to stay out of my love life."

"I do stay out of it!" he cried. Then his voice grew conspiratorial. "That is, unless you start gravitating toward gutter tripe and street musicians."

Theodore bridled. "Melody is a marvelous woman of great talent and depth."

"Melody. What an appropriate name for a street musician."

"Uncle, you're being haughty. She plays in the park for the love of music . . ."

"And to make money!"

"She makes money because she is a world-class musician, and because our government denied her a visa and passport, and, with that, any possibility of making a living. A lesser woman would have turned to something menial or prostitution. I tell you she is a noble woman."

"Posh! She's a street musician."

"Uncle, if you met her you'd be charmed, too, and probably ask her to marry you yourself."

His uncle laughed heartily. "You know I can never deny you. You charm me even when you defy me. What do you want me to do?"

"I want you to stop her prosecution. It was you who started it. Don't deny it."

"I do what I must to protect my kingdom," he said airily. "What's in it for me?"

"There's nothing you don't have, including my undying fealty," Theodore avowed with a regal wave of his hand from chin to knee.

Uncle grew serious. "I want you to marry in your class. I want you to possess all this," he said with an expansive wave of both arms. "After I am gone, or even before. I don't want you to sully my name by marrying beneath yourself."

"Then, I will give you a challenge," Theodore said upon a sudden inspiration.

"You? Challenging me? You grow bold in your cleric's collar," he said jovially, but with an obvious nip of warning.

"A challenge even you can't resist."

"Intriguing, go on."

"Elevate whomever I choose to accompany me on life's journey, to whatever status you feel appropriate. Or perhaps you haven't the power to raise, only to tear down," he said, his words tonal with jest, his eyes flashing with gravity.

"I can turn a potato into a princess if I desire!"

"Then I challenge you to do whatever you must to satisfy your lusts, and still leave my happiness to my discretion. I'm afraid if you destroy this fragile flower, I shall be forever moody and sullen when I'm around you," he pouted only partly in jest.

"Happiness has nothing to do with women, love, or discretion. It has to do with power."

Theodore stood slowly. "Then I offer you the happiness of using your power to restore my street musician to her station. She needn't know anything of it, and I prefer she does not. I only ask that you cease to persecute her."

"It is an intriguing challenge," his uncle said as he took his chin in both fingers.

"You will do it then?"

"You know I can't say no to you," Uncle affirmed, once again amiable. Still, there was a steely look in his eyes that conveyed strict warning.

Theodore smiled slyly. "A fact I was counting on. Still, Uncle, I thank you with all my heart."

"Posh. You just want my money."

"That, too," Theodore laughed.

"Get out of my house!"

"Yes, Uncle," Theodore smiled broadly and hurried to the door.

Uncle Tennison watched him until the butler began to open the door. "Theodore," he called across the large room.

"Yes, Uncle?"

"Well played," he said softly.

• • •

"Excuse me Sister Wadsworth," a man's voice said. Sister Wadsworth was standing in the row directly behind Sam and

Princess. She turned to see who had spoken to her. Sam was pleased to see the older gentleman from his quorum meeting the previous week. The old gentleman extended his hand with a warm smile.

"Sister Wadsworth, I just wanted to tell you how sweet your testimony was to my soul today. You made me remember my own mother, and I can tell you, at my age, that is no small affair." He chuckled to himself. "It was long, long ago." He smiled meaningfully. "You bore a sweet testimony. I shall remember your words a long time."

Sister Wadsworth smiled. "Well, thank you. I don't believe I've met you before. You already know who I am. May I ask your name?"

"Oh," he said as he leaned forward slightly. "I don't have a name. I'm just one of the three Nephites going around visiting the Saints." With this he released her hand, glanced pointedly at Sam, and turned away.

"What do you suppose he meant by that?" Sister Wadsworth asked Sam with a puzzled expression.

As she spoke Sam was watching his old gray head move slowly down the crowded row, greeting people as he went. Reluctantly, he turned his attention to Sister Wadsworth.

"I think he's telling the truth," Sam replied emphatically. "I want to talk to him some more." Having so said they both turned to where the old gentleman had been but seconds before.

He was gone.

• • •

Six years had passed: six long, soul-stripping, desolate, debilitating years. For the first time in many years Sam knew he would survive, and his survival would be rich and rewarding, not as a refugee shivering in the cold blizzards of reality. With equal intensity he realized that his torment these last six years had also flowed from another untimely farewell. His soul had languished dreadfully from the absence of the Holy Spirit. Now that healing had begun, he felt as if an unjust sentence of death had been commuted.

• • •

She had sought out Sam at his sister's home to apologize, and to say good-bye, or so she told herself. In reality, she had gone to feed her aching heart, to hear his voice one last time, and to finally close a chapter of her life that had been too long open to the ravages of the cold winds of unanswerable love. Somewhere inside, unseen, and unrecognized, she was also desperately hoping to unplug the storm drain in her soul that she might not utterly drown in the torrential downpour of a shattered dream.

Had his sister's home been another half-block away, she would have never made it. A dozen times she had turned back, and a dozen and one times, she had turned again and pressed forward. Walking with him in the cool evening, feeling his warmth beside her had not healed, had not saved her from drowning, but had in fact increased her pain. In a way only those who have faced imminent death can understand, the only reason she had not run from him was that to do so was to close the coffin lid on an already dead dream. She remained, without hope, without reason, in fact beyond all reason, simply because there was no other option.

She had asked foolish, intimate questions of Sam about love, and had run from him at last in embarrassment. He had kissed her then; beyond wonder, beyond hope, beyond dreams, he had kissed her. She had been too stunned to do anything but stand there. She couldn't even form her lips into a kiss, or close her eyes, but he kissed her, and love flowed into her until a huge steel door slammed shut in her soul, and the cold winds of despair ceased to ravage the landscape of her heart.

Then she had kissed him back, at first carefully, with breathless disbelief, then with wonder, and finally with passion fired by a desperation whose thunder voice had but a magic moment ago been rendered mute.

●   ●   ●

The opening through the veil grew smaller until it closed entirely, and Sam was left alone . . . . He slowly reached out and ran his fingers across the deep pile of the carpet which still held the precious imprint of two bare feet.

About the Author

John M. Pontius was born in Idaho and raised in Utah. He is a life-long member of The Church of Jesus Christ of Latter-day Saints. His mission to South Africa and Rhodesia provides much of the background for this and the prior book in this series. His first church "job" was playing organ and piano for Primary when he was nine years old. He has since served and taught in many church capacities. He presently delights in teaching sixteen and seventeen-year-olds in Sunday School.

Brother Pontius lives in Alaska amid the very splendor he describes in the series. His love of Alaska and its wild beauty often surfaces in his writing. Many of the experiences in this book, such as getting stranded in snowdrifts during hundred mile-an-hour windstorms and almost becoming lunch for a snow blower, have their origin in his life experience.

His sweet wife is the inspiration for the romance and spiritual depth in the females in his books. She truly is an angel, the prototype of all righteous women. It is their joy that their children are all faithful, active in the Church and temple-worthy people.

As far as Babylon is concerned, John is a business owner, oil industry consultant, principle electrical designer and author.

His personal pursuits include teaching, writing, piano, singing, studying the gospel, oil painting, photography, woodworking, politics and many other pursuits. He has never met a hobby he didn't like.

Brother Pontius began writing books in 1977 during a bizarre period of his life when he didn't have a TV. In an attempt to entertain his younger siblings during that long, dark Alaska winter, he began writing a short story which later blossomed, by popular demand, into a novel. With the enthusiastic support of family and friends he has written nearly a dozen additional novels, most of them science fiction of questionable value.

Brother Pontius wrote his first doctrinal work, *Following the Light of Christ into His Presence,* in 1993. Writing this book was a lifetime high. During that time he often had to push back from the computer to keep tears from falling into the keyboard. Daybreak Books initially published this book. Cedar Fort eventually brought it to nationwide circulation.

The Millennial Quest Series was written in an attempt to graphically illustrate the principles in *Following the Light of Christ into His Presence.* It is, after all, the light and love and benevolence of our dear Savior which brings all other aspects of life into focus, which fires our souls, gives us the will to breathe in and out, and gives the greatness to contemplate a place for ourselves in yonder eternities.

It is the author's hope that all who read these books will be tempted to dream the mighty dreams.